DATE DUE

SEP 0 6 2006		
OCT 2 6 2006		
APRIL 3,2012		
AUG - 3 2013		
JAN 2 0 2015		
		JUN / / 2006

07

West Lights

by

Rose Daniel

writers@HiddenBrookPress.com
www.HiddenBrookPress.com

West Lights

Author – Rose Craigie Daniel
Editor – Jennifer Footman
Layout and Design – Richard M. Grove
Cover Design – Christopher R. Grove

Printed and bound in Canada

Library and Archives Canada Cataloguing in Publication

Daniel, Rose Craigie, 1931-

West Lights / Rose Craigie Daniel.

ISBN 1-894553-65-9

1. Tay Bridge Disaster, Dundee, Scotland, 1879–Fiction.

I. Title.

PR6104.A64W48 2005   823'.92
C2005-904395-4

First Edition

Dedicated
to my children
Ian,
Derek,
Scott
and
Graeme Mooney,
and
Roselyn Young

Acknowledgements:

I wish to thank my husband David, my children Ian, Derek, Scott, and Graeme Mooney, Roselyn Young, Ken Daniel and Cathy Szczepanski, my brothers Tom, Andrew and Jimmy Craigie and my sisters Pat Ferrier and Margaret Waddington, my grandchildren, nieces and nephews, without whose patience and support this book may not have been written.

I also wish to thank Catherine Huhn, Angela Valente and Vicki Wright for their ongoing encouragement and many happy hours spent helping me achieve my goal. And finally, Fr. Gerry Legge for helping me choose the etching used on the cover.

Images courtesy of:
Eduardo Alessandre, Studios Dundee.
Cover and pages X, 227, 296 and 297

THE ILLUSTRATED LONDON NEWS.

REGISTERED AT THE GENERAL POST-OFFICE FOR TRANSMISSION ABROAD.

No. 2119.—VOL. LXXVI.   SATURDAY, JANUARY 10, 1880.   WITH TWO SUPPLEMENTS | SIXPENCE. By Post, 6½d.

Chapter Headings

West Lights

CHAPTER

1

Journey Home

Feet, clattering like horses' hooves, echoed along the grey marble corridor, as a group of nurses, who had just finished night duty, hurried home. Their long crisp dresses, adorned with white starched collars and cuffs, rustled as they moved. Slung casually over shoulders, their cloaks revealed a blaze of bright red flannel lining. Dangling, cowl-like at the nape of each girl's neck, sat a bonnet, tied loosely underneath the chin; a black bag was clenched firmly in hand.

Chattering eagerly they made their way to the duty office to sign out. Long hours and lack of sleep had taken their toll. They were all pale-faced and drawn. As they approached the kitchen, there was the unmistakable slamming of oven doors, the clatter of hot pans and, a moment later, a waft of freshly baked bread. How wonderful it smelled. How hungry the nurses were.

When Gus, the porter, entered the duty office that morning, the clock on the wall above the desk began to strike the hour. "Phew!" He hung his coat on a hook behind the door. "Thank God I made it on time. Nasty weather this morning, Peter," he commented to the night porter and wiped his wet face with a handkerchief.

"So I believe," answered Peter, puffing away on his pipe. "See you tomorrow, Gus," he said pulling the flaps of his bonnet over his ears as he left. He had to smile at Gus' comment about making it on time, Gus always just made it on time.

Gus slipped on his overall and sat in the swivel chair at the desk. He used the time waiting for the nurses to arrive by catching up with his paperwork. A register lay open on the desk. The heading on the open page was "Friday, January 28, 1879, A. M."

A happy-go-lucky fellow, Gus laughs readily and honestly with a kind word for everyone. His ruddy complexion and dazzling hazel eyes reflect his jovial personality. Horn-rimmed spectacles straddle the lower part of his nose, allowing him to look out without raising his head.

"Good morning, nurse," spluttered a scraggy voice as I approached the office window. With a radiant smile, Gus put the register down on the window ledge and handed me a quill.

I took the quill from him and signed the register, 'Roselyn Carey'. I glanced at the clock on the wall across from him and noted the time beside my name.

"I suppose you've already heard all about the terrible assault, Gus!" I returned the quill to him.

"Assault! What assault? Where? When?"

"In the Cowgate. Last night."

"In the Cowgate? What in the world happened?"

"Well, I don't know the gory details. I overheard two nurses talking about it in the dining hall. Apparently a woman was rushed into casualty on the stroke of midnight, bleeding from multiple stab wounds. Evidently the constabulary are treating the incident as attempted murder!".

"Murder! In Dundee?" he choked, "you're no saying that?"

"I didn't say 'murder', Gus. I said, 'attempted murder'!"

"Well ..." he shrugged. He leant forward, propped his elbows on the window ledge and cupped his face in his hands "Right. So who was the woman?"

"I've no idea."

"God help the poor soul, whoever she is," He rolled his eyes and looked me straight in the eye. "It's a wicked, wicked world, nurse."

"It most certainly is, there's no doubt about that!"

I tied the ribbons of my bonnet securely and walked to the exit. I turned to Gus and asked what the weather was like.

"Ooh," he puckered up his lips and pulled a dour face at the same time. "It's dreich. Better make sure you're well wrapped up. That wind would go right through you. And be careful on the brae! It's no half slippery. I'd hate to see you fall."

"Don't worry. I'll be careful," I smiled and waved my gloved hand.

"Cheerio nurse! God bless!" I caught the tail end of the sentence, as the immense oak door slammed shut behind me.

I hugged my cloak around the slender frame that housed my spirit and stepped out to a bitter morning. The wind threw icy drizzle on my face, reminding me of the season. I crossed the dark courtyard. The tall iron gates at the entrance rattled incessantly. A pale blue flame flickering in one of the street lamps cast intermittent shadows on the wet cobbles. The foul smell of gas, escaping from another lamp, compelled me to put my handkerchief to my nose.

A wave of grief for a young patient flowed over me. Connie, a Yorkshire woman, had slipped peacefully away in her sleep just after midnight. I had grown so very fond of her all the time I'd been nursing her. Profound optimism was one of her many fine qualities. She had convinced herself that a miracle would take place and restore her good health. But of course, that hadn't happened. I had not been able to take my eyes off her empty bed and now ...

Two burly constables came marching into the courtyard breaking into my thoughts, their thick rubber capes making a loud swishing sound with their movements. The clanging on the pavement, caused by their heavy tackety boots, was exaggerated by the stillness of the early hour.

"Good morning, Nurse," their gruff voices said and I replied with the same words.

Rainwater dripped off the rims of their helmets. They crossed the courtyard and disappeared through the casualty entrance.

"What the devil are they doing here? Why, of course. How stupid of me. It'll have something to do with the assault in the Cowgate." I shuddered at the thought. Drawing my cloak even more tightly around me, I proceeded down the brae. The rain turned to snow and I could barely make out the lights that usually twinkled and sparkled so vividly on the opposite side of the river. I chose each step carefully and convinced myself that the wind was trying desperately to rip the cloak off my back.

The disadvantages of living in Tayport and working in Dundee are twofold. Firstly there's the inconvenience of having to travel back and forth by train or ferry. Oh, that train trip is something I have got used to, but every time my spine tingles at the thought of crossing such a mass of water on a slender structure. Secondly there's the effect on my emotions of the all too-visible poverty and disease, existing in the town. Tall chimneys of the mills reach up to the sky, continuously filling the air with thick smoke. The foul smell of raw jute about the town is vile. Drab four-storey tenements have filthy middens in their back courts. There, the tenants dump their domestic and human waste, providing a breeding ground for rats and disease.

My heart bleeds for the barefoot, scantily dressed children. Their undernourished bodies are so vulnerable to every disease known to man. Many of the children reek of carbolic soap and the thick, gooey ointment spread thickly on their skin after they've been scrubbed until they bleed. The latter is the agonising treatment they receive to combat the scabies mites. Shaved heads are commonplace, exposing large, weeping sores.

The route to the railway station passes by the west wall of the Howff. The Howff, a meeting place and one of the oldest graveyards in the district, dates back to 1564. Mary Queen of Scots gifted the land to the people of Dundee to be used as a new cemetery. During her visit to the town in 1564, she had been told of the inadequacy of the existing burial land in Dundee. It's one of Dundee's most visible links with the past and contains the bones of medieval citizens, both great and common.

My heart was racing as I approached the Howff. My imagination began to run wild. Large oak and willows fringe the gloomy graveyard. Their wispy branches slouch relentlessly over the tall tombstones. Howling through the trees, the wind moves the branches, making them resemble long spindly arms. I swear to God, they're reaching out to grab me. Quickening my step, I turned and took a quick look in the direction whence I'd heard a loud screeching noise. A cat, bolting out of the shadows, ran blindly across the road, cleverly scaling the cemetery wall and disappearing into the darkness. Convinced that I was being followed, I glanced back over my shoulder several times expecting to see someone there. The snap of a twig, the wail of the wind and the echo of my lonely footsteps all added to my apprehension.

Gathering my cloak around me, I lifted my skirt above my ankles and took to my heels, running as fast as I could, not stopping until I had reached the busy High Street. I used to laugh at my brother Tom when he spoke of 'ghosts in the grave yard'. Perhaps he was right.

The lively hustle and bustle as I emerged from the eerie darkness of Barrack Street was comforting. At the corner of the Nethergate and Union Street, a one-legged man was sitting on the pavement selling the morning newspaper. His only protection from the cruel weather was the overhang of the building and a worn-out cape draped over his scrawny shoulders. Straggly hair clung to his egg-shaped head, emphasising a large hooked nose protruding from a gaunt, expressionless face. A grubby checked cap lay on the ground in front of him and, to his left side, propped up against the wall, a homemade crutch. Compassion fills my heart whenever I lay eyes upon him. He is the most pathetic sight I've ever seen.

"Dundee woman stabbed!" he shouted out at the top of his voice, repeating himself continuously. A crowd of people swarmed about him anxious to buy a newspaper. Stooping down I tossed a penny into his cap. He pulled a paper from underneath his cape and, with a clever flick of his fingers, he folded the paper, handing it to me without stopping his shouting.

I tried to read the report but a gust of wind blew my bonnet to the back of my head, whipping my hair across my eyes and almost wrenching the paper out of my hands. Holding my hair back with my gloved hand, I swiftly crossed the road, the wet snow stinging my face, my cloak ballooning in the wind. In the doorway of the Royal Hotel at the top of Union Street, I took refuge to read the report. It read: Mistress Mary Ann McKinley of 25 Cowgate was brutally attacked in her home last evening. She suffered multiple stab wounds as well as bruising to her face, neck and arms. She is currently fighting for her life in the Dundee Royal Infirmary.

"Good Lord!" I gulped with an uncontrollable surge of emotion, covering my mouth with my fingertips, "I can't believe it. I just cannot believe it." Mary Ann's Gus' sister. My mind in a whirl, I folded the paper nervously slipping it into my bag. Straightening my bonnet, I tied the ribbons more securely and hurried to the station. Pausing momentarily at the top of the stairs leading to the platforms, I took a quick glance at the West Station clock. It was ten minutes to eight. "Ah! There's still plenty of time to catch the train."

The scene at Tay Bridge Station was typical of the hour. People were huddled in small groups awaiting the arrival of the seven fifty-five express from London to Aberdeen. Two elderly gentlemen, thick woollen scarves wrapped around their throats and deerstalker hats pulled down over their ears, stomped feet vigorously as they swung their arms to and fro across their chests. Their red noses were dripping. Water from their eyes trickled down the crevices of their wizened faces.

Six brightly painted coaches waited on the southbound line while the engine was having its boiler filled. Many passengers had already boarded the train. Ladies, dressed to the hilt, were peering aimlessly out the windows. Some wore sober poky bonnets. Others wore pretty, wide-brimmed hats tied in huge chiffon bows underneath the chin. Gentlemen were all occupied either reading their newspapers or puffing away on their pipes. A small boy's face, round, with bright rosy cheeks, his nose pressed hard against the window, caught my eye. He smiled shyly at me, his large blue eyes filled with wonder. I waved my handkerchief to him and he responded enthusiastically, waving a tiny gloved hand.

I noticed the Tayport train was ready to leave from platform three. Holding my bonnet in place with my free hand, I ran. The cold dampness penetrated my bones. My eyes were watering with the wind. When I reached the train, I lifted my skirt above my ankles and clambered, harassed and out of breath, into the compartment immediately ahead of the brake van. When the guard was satisfied that all the doors were shut he gave a blast on his whistle, waved a bright green flag and climbed into the guard's van. Moving away from the platform slowly at first, the train gathered momentum as it passed the marshalling yard, hurtling out of the station and leaving the dismal greyness of Dundee behind.

I sank into the seat by the window, removed my bonnet, shook my head and ran my fingers through my hair. It felt wet and grimy. Tired and weary, I rested my head against the soft upholstery and allowed my eyes to close. The huffing and puffing of the engine, rumbling slowly across the bridge, lulled me to sleep.

"Waken up, lassie! Waken up!" A lively porter, arousing me with a shake, startled me. "Been working you too hard have they?" bellowed his piercing voice.

"My goodness," I gasped, hand on heart, yawning simultaneously, "what a fleg you gave me. I feel as if I just closed my eyes and here we've arrived."

"We have that, lass, we have that." He held the carriage door open, for me to disembark. Staggering to my feet, I retrieved my bag from the luggage rack, placed my bonnet on the top of my head and buttoned up my cloak. As I went to alight, I stumbled.

The porter surged forward, grabbing my arm to steady me. "Oh take it easy, lass, take it easy." With a quick word of gratitude to him, I braced myself and followed a handful of people through the exit gate.

It had stopped snowing but the aftermath of dampness was everywhere. Slush filled the gutters, melted and gurgled into the drains.

Dawn had replaced darkness and the razzle-dazzle in the street was evident. A dapple grey horse harnessed to Pragit's Dairy wagon waited in front of the Ship Inn, while the master delivered his daily orders. The horse continually pawed the road with its metal-shod hoof. Sparks were flying. Timorous of such a mighty animal, I gave it a wide berth.

Graeme Henderson, the baker's boy, bonnet tilted to the side of his head, whistled 'Bonny Lassie' as he followed close on the milkman's heels. The aroma of freshly baked rolls escaping from his basket caused my tummy to rumble. I reached into the pocket within the lining of my cape to retrieved an apple, which Jessie Hampton, a nursing friend, had given me. The juice trickled down my chin when I bit into the fresh crisp fruit. I was starving.

Jock Morris, a local worthy, who walks his dog at the same time every morning, came marching across the road the moment he spied me. "Nurse Carey! Nurse Carey!" he shouted at the top of his voice. "Ad say the weather's gonna settle doon. Look! Look! Up there!" He was pointing his cane to where the clouds parted and a glimmer of pale wintry sun peeped through.

"Well! How about that? It's not before time we had a change of weather." His wind-burned face beamed at my positive reaction. Promptly he folded his hands over the handle of his cane, as if he'd settled down to a morning of yapping. Meantime, Megan, his collie was licking my gloved hand.

"Megan doesn't mind this nasty weather, Mister Morris,"

"Heavens no, she's happy as the day's lang when oot for a wak. Rain, hail, or shine maks nae difference tae her."

An untimely gust of wind blew his moth-eaten kilt up over his face compelling him to drop the cane. Well, I couldn't help but laugh. Quick as a flash, I retrieved the cane and handed it to him. Out of sheer embarrassment, I focused on Megan. "Ah, Megan," I fussed, running my fingers through her silky coat. "You're a bonny wee doggie, so you are. I've noticed how friendly she is with children, Mister Morris."

"Aye, she is that! Why, she'd befriend Auld Nick himsel!" With his grey, wiry hair poking down from underneath a Harris-tweed-hat and his crooked nose cocked in the air, he reminded me of a leprechaun.

"I've had a terrible pain in this leg of mine a' winter," he whined, rubbing the leg in question with the palm of his hand. "Is there anything you could recommend that would ease it, you being a nurse?"

"Heavens no, I wouldn't jeopardise my job. Your doctor will prescribe something to help." He hummed and hawed and would've prattled on forever, so I tactfully bid him good day.

CHAPTER

2

Reminiscing

I was overjoyed to be in my beloved Tayport. This is where I was born, where I grew up. And every street holds special memories for me. I looked about with pride in my heart, filling my lungs with the cold damp air and feasting my eyes on the beauty that surrounded me. The narrow cobbled streets are bordered with quaint little houses. Their windows are tastefully clad in stark white lace, tied back with broad satin bows. Doors boast bold brass knockers, and nameplates shine to perfection. On the rooftops, chimney pots stand to attention like little toy soldiers, puffing swirls of smoke into the air, evidence of coals burning in the grates.

As I approached the humpbacked bridge straddling the railway tracks, Allan, dressed in a green capecoat and a woollen scarf flung loosely around his neck, hurried to greet me. "Good morning, my beautiful one!" He welcomed me with outstretched arms, taking my hands in his, cheeks glowing, eyes watering from the wind. His voice was soft but masculine. A merry twinkle about his bright hazel eyes told me he was delighted to see me.

"Good morning, Allan," I beamed, squeezing his hands. Crisp, auburn hair curling away from his forehead and a smile that stretched from ear to ear sent excitement through me. We paused for a moment gazing into each other's eyes. Then taking me in his arms, he kissed me softly. In a voice that vibrated with love he whispered, "Oh God, Roselyn, I love you."

"I love you too, Allan," I responded spontaneously.

"I was beginning to think you'd missed the train. What took you so long?" he teased, rubbing my nose gently with his.

"Day dreaming, I suppose," I smiled, raising my brows. "I'm always so content when I'm home." My voice rang out with pride. "Oh, I almost forgot, I stopped to pass the time of day with 'Old Poochie'."

"Aha! That explains the delay. I'm surprised you were able to tear yourself away from him." He laughed out loud and we continued hand in hand, along the narrow path skirting the shoreline to West Lights.

"It's wonderful to see you, sweetheart." His voice churned with joy. "Seems forever since you were home, I miss you terribly. Of course you already know that, don't you?" He poked me in the ribs. "I hope you weren't overdoing things at the hospital," he added firmly. "You look exhausted."

"Oh, Allan, Allan, what a worrywart you are. Of course I wasn't."

"Well! You really don't expect me to believe that rubbish, do you? You've always done more than your fair share. I hardly think you're about to change now," his eyes were full of admiration. "What's new at the hospital these days anyway?" he asked, as an afterthought.

"The victim of a brutal stabbing."

"You're joking."

"I wish I were. What a shock I got when I read the report in the paper. The victim's Gus's sister."

"Gus, the porter's, sister?"

"That's right."

"What happened?"

"Your guess is as good as mine. Of course, gossip has it her husband tried to kill her and, according to the report, he's nowhere to be found. Run away. Because he's run away, they think he did it. Here, read it yourself." I fumbled in my bag and retrieved the newspaper and handed it to him.

He glanced at the newspaper. "Well! Well! I'd say Mary Ann McKinley's a lucky woman. According to this report, she'd have bled to death if her neighbour hadn't got her to the hospital so promptly." He folded the paper neatly and returned it to me.

"Oh, Allan!" I burst out, changing the subject. "I hate passing the Howff in the dark. It's so scary, I've been toying with the idea of applying for a position in one of the hospitals on this side of the river. Not until I've finished my training, of course. St. Andrews General would be my first choice." I looked to him for approval.

"Fiddlesticks, Roselyn! The dead can't harm you, you know that. I'd be more concerned about that bridge. I hate the idea of you going over that bridge. The dead are harmless."

"Ah ha," I pointed my finger, "that's no consolation to me when I'm alone in the dark. Besides, I want to spend more time with my parents. And you, too, of course," I added quickly.

"Oh, come here, scaredy cat." His eyes were full of devilment as he slipped his arm around my waist. "What am I going to do with you?"

West Lights is a hamlet on the east coast of Scotland, nestled on the south shore of the River Tay a short distance from Tayport. It boasts several family dwellings and a lighthouse. The latter, a well-known landmark, has long been a distinctive aid to navigation, clearly visible to mariners making their way upstream to the Dundee harbour. When haar rolls in from the German Sea, it lies on the river like a shroud. Fog horns sound every six seconds, making a haunting wail, like lost souls crying out in the wilderness in search of a final resting place. The muffled thundering sound of the tide is like a herd of horses galloping in a sea of dense fog.

Summer presents an incredibly different panorama. On the opposite side of the river, the Sidlaws display umpteen shades of green. Rising in natural splendour, like the soft curves of a woman's body, they blend with the bright blue sky and powder-puff clouds. Hosts of wild flowers, interlaced with vivid blades of grass, flutter in the breeze. The heavenly fragrance from honeysuckle and wild roses fills the air.

I heard the town clock in the distance striking the hour, as we approached my home. Allan and I had prattled on and off, catching up on the latest gossip since I'd last been home. And we wondered if the constabulary were making any progress ferreting out Alex McKinley.

"I hate to think how Gus will react to this, Allan. I've heard he has the most uncontrollable temper, especially when he's riled."

"You don't suppose he'll do anything foolish do you?"

"Anything foolish? Like what?"

"Well! If he has such a violent temper, he might take it upon himself to find the culprit. And who knows? He might kill him."

"Nah! Gus wouldn't go that far. At least, I don't

think so." A fragment of doubt crept into my mind.

My thoughts began to wander to our past. How vividly I remembered the day I met Allan. It was my first day at school. At last I was all grown up. Or so I thought, until playtime when, much to my horror I was so self-conscious, I didn't know what to do. Here I was in a world full of strangers, abandoned by my best friend, my beloved mother. Brokenhearted, I slouched against the vine-covered wall surrounding the playground, head bowed, hands folded in front of me. A shadow was cast over me and when I raised my head, standing before me was a stocky freckle-faced boy whom I had never laid eyes on before.

"Hello there," he smiled happily, "I know how you're feeling." A high pitched, squeaky voice poured from his lips. "I felt exactly as you do on my first day at school. My name's Allan, Allan Robertson. What's your name?"

My mouth dried up, my face flushed and, in a timid little voice, I stuttered, "Roselyn Carey."

"Roselyn Carey? What a pretty name. Roselyn Carey," he repeated as if to memorise it. I lowered my head and blushed to the core.

"I'd like to be your friend, Roselyn. Well, what say you?" he persisted.

I bit my lip and after a moment stammered out, "Okay, whatever you wish." I was scared to death to say anything to the contrary, for I knew not this stranger who overshadowed me.

"Good! Then let's seal that with a handshake." His face beamed as he took my hand in his and shook it with zeal. "Would you care for one of these, Roselyn?" he asked, delving into the pocket of his breeks and retrieving a brown paper poke. A smile like that of the cat that caught the canary came over his face. His eyes widened, as he opened the poke and offered me a sweetie.

"Dolly mixtures! Why Allan, these are my favourites!"

"They are? Then you may take as many as you wish." With a twinkle in his eye, he confessed they were his favourites too. The sincerity in his voice, and the profound honesty reflecting from his eyes, convinced me to trust this stranger. I was deeply relieved to have someone with whom I could talk. After all we did have something in common - dolly mixtures.

Allan Robertson was a freelance journalist, which allowed him the 'privilege', as he put it, of walking me home whenever the occasion arose. He had celebrated his twenty-first birthday on the first of December. What a day to remember. His parents had flung a surprise birthday party for him, in the Tayside Hotel in Newport. I'll long remember the look of astonishment on his face when we entered the dining room and all the guests stood up and applauded his arrival. He blushed and he trembled. Plainly he was very embarrassed. After all, we'd planned a romantic evening, having previously reserved a table for two by the window, overlooking the river.

A five-piece orchestra, partially obscured by a huge aspidistra, played sweet music in the background, while relatives and friends joined the Robertson family in their happy celebration. Local venison was the main course, followed by birthday cake, for dessert.

After dinner, Mister Robertson called attention as he stood tall and proud, raising his glass in honour of his son. Champagne flowed, and the moment formalities were over, Mister Robertson turned to the maestro and, in an enthusiastic, happy tone, said, "Now, let's have some good old-fashioned waltzes." He then took his wife by the hand and escorted her to the dance floor.

Exquisite dresses, in delicate hues of yellow, turquoise, blue and green, swirled and swished about as the ladies waltzed the evening away with their partners. What a wonderful party.

All these memories flashed through my mind, as we continued along the path from the station. We sat on the park bench a few yards short of my home. "Now, Kitten." Allan whispered gathering me in his arms, "promise you'll have a good rest today. You look exhausted."

"Cross my heart and hope to die! As soon as I've eaten, I'll go straight to bed." I laughed mockingly, crossing my heart with my forefinger.

"Good! Now don't forget we're meeting tonight. I'll call for you at six. Please be ready." He tapped my nose with his forefinger and kissed my brow. A wave of embarrassment engulfed me.

"Oh no, Allan, I completely forgot all about the concert! What am I going to wear?"

"Why, that pretty yellow dress you made last autumn! You look lovely in it! It reminds me of daffodils in springtime. It's by far my favourite."

"Is it really?"

"Certainly!" He smiled flirtatiously and again kissed my brow. Reluctantly he tore away, walking briskly in the opposite direction.

My heart was bursting with joy as I ran the remaining few yards, my cloak billowing, my happy voice filling the air with lines from songs I knew. When I reached the house, I found the garden gate ajar. My father insists upon it being kept shut, no matter what. "Och well!" I shrugged and closed the gate, making sure the latch was secure. I paused briefly when I entered the house, inhaling the delicious waft of sizzling bacon. How mouth-watering.

"Is that you, Cuddle?" Mother's sweet voice came fluttering through the half-open kitchen door.

"Yes, Mother. It's me!"

"What a treacherous night we've had here, Roselyn! Terrible winds all night long and torrential rain, turning to snow early this morning." She prattled away while I hung my cloak in the press. Standing on a stool I put my hat and bag up on the shelf.

"Bob Wilkie, the lighthouse keeper, thought he spotted something on the sand banks upstream. He thinks it might be a dredging boat run aground. Your father and a couple of the neighbours have gone out in the coble to investigate. What was the weather like in Dundee?" she asked, the moment I stepped into the kitchen.

"Much the same as it was here, by the sound of things."

"Oh Roselyn," Mother sighed as I crossed the room. "I worry myself sick about your having to travel across that bridge. Especially when it's windy as it was earlier. Rumours have it the structure's far too weak. People say it'll never withstand the winds that come thundering down the firth. And the old woman who lives in Burkie, the same one that people call 'the seer', claims she's had many a vision of a mangled bridge. A premonition, one might say, that the bridge is doomed; doomed to destruction." Her eyes were bulging as she spoke.

Stepping forward, I put my hands on her shoulders and kissed the worried frown that creased her brow. "Mother, Mother! I wish you'd stop worrying yourself over what people say. What authority are they on engineering? 'That bridge', as you put it, was designed and built by one of the most prominent engineers in the country. He has designed and built many bridges in his day. Besides, do you think the railway company would allow an unsafe structure to be built? Well, do you?"

"No! No! I don't suppose they would." Her voice bore a hint of doubt.

"As for the Seer of Burkie's premonitions, I'd take that with a pinch of salt if I were you. Heavens Mother, it's not so long ago that you worried yourself sick about me having to cross the river on the ferry. You were convinced the boat was going to sink. You even pictured the mysterious waters swallowing me up and carrying me out to the German Sea. Well!" I grinned spreading my arms, "Here I am!" A look of embarrassment came over her and she pouted. "Anyway, your worries will soon be over. I'm going to apply for a job in Fife, when I finish my training. Will that make you happy?" I joshed with her, tickling her in the ribs.

"Oh Roselyn!" she gasped and giggled and sighed, all at the same time. "You know perfectly well it will." Her face beamed and her eyes danced with delight at the very idea. Mother was happy. "The weather's supposed to clear up by noon, according to your father. She moved deliberately over to the window and pulled the curtains back. She glanced up at the grey clouds scurrying swiftly across the sky. "Let's hope he's right, but it doesn't look too promising out there to me."

I moved over and joined her at the window. "At what time did the men leave?"

"A little before eight," she answered casually, taking a quick look at the clock. "You needn't bother looking for them yet," she added. "They won't be back for ages. It's a long tough row on those rough waters."

The H.M.S. Ambassador, one of the naval training ships, was battling against the fierce wind and high swells as she made her way out to sea. She was being tossed about furiously which added to my concern for my father's safety. "Bob Wilkie infuriates me," I blasted, wringing my hands as I paced the floor. "He's forever spotting something on the river. And does he go out there? Oh no! Not our Bob! It's other people who put their lives in jeopardy investigating his fantasies. He could've called out the lifeboat, if he was so concerned, as would any other lighthouse keeper. Just look at it, Mother. What chance does our wee coble have when it's taking the Ambassador all her time to hold a steady course?"

"For heaven's sake calm down, ranting and raving isn't going to help. You know perfectly well that Bob can't call out the lifeboat. That is, unless he's absolutely sure of his facts. He's cried wolf far too often. Besides, your father and the others offered to go. It's not as if Bob twisted their arms. So please, Roselyn, give the man the benefit of the doubt. In the name of goodness lass, you look as if you're freezing." Her voice was warm as she reached out to touch my hands. "Go sit by the fire and I'll bring your breakfast on a tray." She fussed about, chattering away nineteen to the dozen, dishes tinkling and cutlery clattering, as she set the tray.

I moved over to the hearth and, sinking into a chair, rested my feet on the shiny brass fender. Leaning forward I held my hands in front of the crackling coals and all at once the flames flared up, flickering through the grill and casting coloured shadows on the ceiling. I watched the flames as they continued to dance around the coal and gradually the chill that had penetrated my bones began to leave my body.

Mother brought the breakfast tray and placed it on my lap. "Now! For heaven's sake stop worrying about the men. They'll be all right. Enjoy your breakfast while it's nice and hot." Smiling sweetly, she asked if I had remembered to bring the newspaper.

"Of course, it's in my bag." I gestured to the back hall and went to rise.

"Sit still, sit still!" she insisted raising her hand, "I'll get it." And before I could say any more, she was gone. Upon returning she sat in the armchair on the opposite side of the hearth. She crossed her legs and rested her left foot on the fender stool. She unfolded the paper and began to read.

"Goodness me!" she declared in disbelief when she read the headlines. "What in the name of heaven is this world coming to? God help that poor woman."

"Isn't that a dreadful thing to have happen, Mother? You'll never guess who the woman is."

"Who?" She peered over the top of her spectacles.

"Gus's sister."

"Gus's sister," she gasped, her eyes immediately swung back to the paper and she continued to read on.

Snuggling deeper into the chair, I sipped slowly, enjoying the fresh brew. "This is what I call a good cup of tea Mother. Not at all like the dregs we're served at the hospital."

"I'm glad you're enjoying it, Cuddle," she grunted without lifting her head.

"Incidentally, the garden gate was open when I arrived home. Did you have a visitor this morning?"

"A visitor at this time in the morning? Heavens no! Who in their right mind would visit at this early hour?"

"There's no need to be hoity. I only asked. After all, the gate was open and you know as well as I do that Father insists upon it being kept closed."

"Well! He was in a dreadful hurry when he left. You'd have thought all the devils in hell were chasing him. He'll be the culprit."

"Father, the culprit? Never! He wouldn't leave the gate open, even if he was in a hurry."

"I pray to God that man's still in Dundee and not over here."

"What man?" I snipped, forgetting she was reading about the assault.

"Alex McKinley, the murderer. That's what man." She glowered at me while waiting for my reaction.

"Now what in the world would he be doing over here?"

"Hiding from the constabulary, what else?"

"Don't be silly Mother! Besides he isn't a murderer. His wife isn't dead." I ate my breakfast in silence while Mother continued to read the newspaper. When I had finished, I wiped my mouth with my hankie and moved over to the table to set the tray down. "I'm off to bed now, Mother." I said with a yawn, stretching my arms above my head at the same time. Pausing briefly in the doorway, I reminded her about the concert and asked if she'd waken me at four o'clock. "Allan's calling for me at six. I want to look my very best."

"Oh, Roselyn, Roselyn," she sighed shaking her head, "your looks'll be the death of you. Be off with you now." She motioned with the back of her hand. "I put your piggy in your bed more than an hour ago, so it'll be nice and cosy. And don't fret. I'll rouse you in plenty of time. Would you like me to iron your dress?" She stood up quickly.

"Yes please, I'd appreciate that very much. Allan likes my yellow taffeta one, so the yellow taffeta it'll have to be." I closed the door quietly behind me and went straight to my bedroom.

My lovely little room. The papered walls are a faded shade of rose with delicate sprays of apple blossom. Crisp lace curtains frame the small leaded glass window. A signed lithograph of The Beggar's Opera, which was bequeathed to me by my late grandfather, holds pride of place. In the corner of the room by the fireside, a rocking chair is piled with assorted cushions. I keep my necklaces and trinkets in an ornamental box, inlaid with mother-of-pearl, brought by my father from India. Carved bookends support my favourite books on the chest of drawers. And an oval picture frame on the dressing table holds a studio photograph of my parents, my brother, and me. This is my happy place.

Quick as a flash I undressed, slipped into my nightgown and snuggled into bed. As my head sank into the soft pillow, my thoughts were of Allan.

CHAPTER
3

The Spirit

The unmistakable sound of the front door closing woke me up. Pulling myself up to a half-sitting position, I rubbed my eyes, and peered sleepily at my watch. "Only quarter past two." I was annoyed at being disturbed so early.

My thoughts immediately turned to my father and I wondered if he had yet returned. Perhaps that was Father coming in? No, it couldn't be him. He'd have used the back door. I tossed and turned and, try as I might, I couldn't get back to sleep. Pushing the covers aside, I swung my legs out of bed, slipped my feet into my baffies and went to the kitchen with the idea of a cup of tea in mind. To my surprise there was no one there.

"That's strange! I could've sworn I heard someone come in." Perhaps I was dreaming. "Mother, Mother!" I called, running up stairs two steps at a time, expecting to find her in her bedroom. But, to my dismay she wasn't there. A bone-chilling cold doused the house and I began to shiver. It felt as if ice cold water was being poured down my spine. My arms were covered with goose bumps. Standing at the top of the narrow staircase for what seemed an eternity, I finally plucked up enough courage to return to the ground floor. My hand was trembling as I gripped the banister and, with great apprehension, I slowly descended the stairs.

Overwhelmed by an uncanny feeling that someone's eyes were following me, I went directly to the kitchen. My throat was dry and I heard my voice speaking words that my quivering lips formed. "Whoever you are, please go away." I nervously scanned the room with frightened eyes. Then in a firm tone, I added, "Ask God for help." Even in this moment of great fear something within me whispered, "God will protect you, Roselyn!" I began to pray from the depths of my soul. "Dear Lord, help me! Please, please be with me." All at once, a warm composure came over me and I knew the eerie presence had gone.

I sat on the fireside rug and drew my knees up to my chin. I gazed at the door. I began to consider the number of times I'd had similar experiences. Curiously enough and without exception, the incidents had always taken place when I'd been home alone and they had followed an identical pattern. The front door always opens and bangs shut. Footsteps, frequently accompanied by the tapping of a cane, go straight to the kitchen and, on the odd occasion, to other parts of the house. Doors within the house open and close and objects, such as photographs and trinkets, are moved from place to place. It's as if a spirit is desperately searching for something. Of course, my parents flatly refuse to listen to my story. They prefer to think that I allow my imagination to run riot.

A noise in the back garden unnerved me even more and my heart began to beat rapidly all over again. I tiptoed over to the window, nervously pushed the curtains aside, and peeked out. "Och, it's only Nicky," I gasped somewhat relieved. Nicky is our neighbour's dog and she was having a wonderful time frolicking on the lawn with a piece of driftwood.

"Where can Mother be?" I paced the floor, wringing my hands. "You're being ridiculous, Roselyn. You'll have to pull yourself together." And, little by little, I forced the current incident to the back of my mind – for the time being anyway.

The kitchen table was laid for the evening meal. A fine muslin cloth, embroidered in a pretty lazy daisy pattern, covered the setting. Blazing coals crackled in the grate and a gleaming copper kettle, sitting upon the hob, was slowly coming to a boil. I peeked in the oven and a meat and potato casserole simmered gently. From a giant cast-iron pot, the heavenly aroma of mixed spices escaping with the steam filled the air. I lifted the lid. "Ah! I might have guessed, a clootie dumpling!"

I moved to the living-room and, glancing out the window, noticed our coble lying on the shore. Its bowline was tied to a mooring ring and the oars were propped up against the hull.

Footprints in the sand continued along the footpath to the back door. Undoubtedly they were my father's. "Thanks be to God!" I sighed. For a brief moment, I stood at the window watching two bold seagulls fighting frantically over a paltry scrap of fish. Highpitched squeals filled the air. Feathers were flying everywhere.

Feeling a little more at ease in the knowledge that my father was safe, or so it would seem, I returned to the kitchen to make a pot of tea. When the tea was brewed, I poured a cup. With cup and saucer in hand, I backtracked to the living room, hooking the door shut with my foot. I sat on the rocking chair in front of a blazing fire, sipping slowly on the piping hot liquid. Tea, it seems, is the magical cure for everything. While I rocked in the rocking chair, I enjoyed the warmth that was radiating from the coals. Where could my parents be? Mother couldn't have gone far, otherwise she wouldn't have left all that food cooking on the hob. She must have gone to Bob's with Father. Yes, that's it, they'll be over at Bob's.

I lifted the poker and poked casually at the coals, more for something to do than anything else. As I did so, a splatter of rain hit the window and trickled down the pane. I hoped it didn't foretell the beginning of another storm. Stepping over to the window, I looked up at the sky. A pale sun blinked through the tattered clouds. It was hard to tell whether or not a storm was imminent.

My attention was drawn to a three-masted sailing ship being tossed about furiously as it entered the main channel. When it came into clearer view, I realised it was an incoming ship from India, bringing raw jute to Dundee. How fortunate we are to have such a splendid view. I stood watching the Pride of India passing by, her flags flapping violently in the wind.

Our cottage is long and low, ivy grows thickly on the gable facing the German Sea. It climbs courageously up the chimney and trails down on the roof. White window frames contrast with the grey granite stonework. A low stone wall surrounds the garden. In summer, hollyhocks stand thickly massed against the west wall. Their pretty faces smile happily to the noonday sun. There are borders that blaze with wallflowers, marigolds and pansies, and quieter ones of forget-me-nots and love-in-a-mist. Soft pink ramblers climb graciously over the arched trellis, framing the front door. Dense clusters of raspberries and brambles line the walk that leads down the side of the house to the river.

I moved over to the bookshelves and tried to choose a book. My finger ran along the top row and I picked "A Tale of Two Cities" – an unread Christmas gift from Allan's parents. I sat in the window-seat and made myself comfortable by tucking my legs under me. A quick foot on the path startled me just as I had opened the book. I snapped the book shut and with book in hand, rushed to the back door. My mother was at the door, dressed in her navy blue winter coat and hat. A soft, blue scarf hung, knotted loosely around her throat and a rolled umbrella in her hand. Her cheeks were glowing from the wind. An expression of shock came over her at the sight of me. "My goodness, Roselyn, what a fleg you gave me! I didn't expect you to be up and about yet."

Her question wasn't worth a reply. "Where's Father? Is he all right?"

"Of course he's all right. Why wouldn't he be? He's just nipped over to deliver a newspaper to Bob. For heaven's sake, take a grip on yourself. Just look at you, you're a bag of nerves." She scurried across the hall and went directly upstairs to hang her coat and hat in the wardrobe. When she returned, she flopped down on a chair by the fireside, removed her shoes and slipped her feet into her baffies. "Ah! That feels better," she sighed. "Now tell me. What are you doing up so early?"

I coughed, clearing my throat. "Well, whoever came into the house half an hour ago disturbed me. I thought it might be Father ..."

"Oh no," she butted in, "it wasn't your father. He was with me. We just went out for a breath of fresh air and to pick up a newspaper for Bob. I said that already. Listen, will you. Now, who the devil could it be?" Her face took on a puzzled expression and she quietly stroked her chin with her fingertips. "Och, you must have been dreaming, Cuddle," she said at last, cleverly brushing what I had to say under the carpet. "By the by, I've some interesting news for you." She gave a little shiver and lifting her shawl off the back of her chair draped it loosely over her shoulders, snuggling down. "I was talking to Margaret Haxton in the greengrocer's. She had an appointment with the ear, nose and throat consultant at the Infirmary this morning. While in the waiting room, she overheard a conversation between two nurses. Apparently, when Gus saw the condition his sister was in, he ran blindly out of the building. He was yelling at the top of his voice, "I'll kill the scoundrel. I'll kill him! So help me God, I'll kill him!"

"Ah, poor Gus, sounds as if he's convinced that Alex's guilty. Well, all I can say is, the constabulary had better hurry up and find whoever did it, otherwise they really will have a murder on their hands."

I moved over and sat on the arm of her chair and taking her hand in mine looked her in the eye. "Incidentally, Mother, someone did enter the house. But ..."

"But what?" She stiffened, pulling her hand away.

"I think - I think it was a spirit."

"A spirit!" she exploded. An expression of disbelief came over her face. "Spirit, be damned!" she said, giving me a long penetrating look. "Now listen here, Roselyn, I've had enough of your nonsense. I've told you till I'm blue in the face, it's all in your mind. In the name of heaven, you're forever hearing something. Don't you think it's strange no one else in the family does?"

I reached over and brushed her arm. "It's not all in my mind, Mother, please, please believe me." She jerked her arm back, as if I had the plague. She sprang to her feet, went over and knelt in front of the hearth and shovelled some coals onto the fire. I clenched my hands in an effort to control myself. "It's not all in my mind."

Father bounced into the room, full of life, and interrupted this tense conversation. I wasn't sure if I was happy to see him or sad to have the conversation interrupted. "Brrr." He shivered, rubbing his hands, eyes watering from the wind. "It's not half cold out there, it wouldn't surprise me one bit if we get more snow."

I rushed forward and flung my arms about his neck. "Oh Father! Father!" I sniffled, tears of happiness filled my eyes, "I'm so relieved that you're safe. I've been worried sick about you."

"Worried about me? You'd no need to worry about me, lass." Mother helped him out of his coat. She shuffled into the back hall and hung it up in the press.

"You two, go sit by the fire in the living room. I'll fetch a nice cup of tea. I just brewed a fresh pot. You certainly look as if you could use one, Father."

He smiled and slipped his arm around Mother's waist. "Come along then, Liz," he said and off they went, happy as larks.

I was livid at Mother's attitude but decided not to pursue the matter. It would only make things worse. The only time she and I have words is when I mention the supernatural. Quick as a flash, I set a tray and arranged sultana cake on a cake stand. "Here we are!" I said joyfully, pushing the living room door open with my elbow. Putting the tray down on the tea trolley, I wheeled the trolley over to the fireside and served my parents tea.

"Ah! This is a grand cup of tea, Roselyn," Father smiled coyly, smacking his lips, "as a matter of fact it's the best cup of tea I've tasted in a long time"

"Well fancy that! You've never complimented me on my tea making before. Just goes to show."

"Goes to show what?" he arose from the chair with cup and saucer in hand. Stepping over to the trolley he added a little more sugar and milk to his tea.

"That wonders will never cease," I replied haughtily.

"Now, now, Roselyn, sarcasm doesn't become you," he said as he resumed his seat.

I stopped dead in my tracks as I was leaving the room and asked Father if there was a wreck on the sandbanks.

"Heavens no!" he laughed cynically. "It was only some debris washed up with the tide. Bob was disappointed as usual."

"Then it was just as well he didn't call out the lifeboat. You were right after all, Mother."

"What did I tell you?" She beamed.

"Indeed you did, Mother, indeed you did!" I left them toasting their toes, one parent on each side of the hearth, Mother in her easy chair, Father in his rocker. They prattled away like a couple of turtle doves enjoying each other's company.

CHAPTER

4

Titivating

I returned to the kitchen, filled the basin with warm water and gave my hair a good shampoo. I rinsed it thoroughly with a jug of cold water. Yes, that felt good. A huge towel wrapped round my head, I went directly to my bedroom to dress. My hair's always a major project. Mother maintains, "The more you brush, the shinier it'll be." Whether that's true or not is irrelevant. I sat poised at the dressing table and practised her theory, brushing with stiff strokes and setting my scalp tingling. The result was most satisfactory. I combed the sides high on the crown and tied them with a satin ribbon to match my dress and let the soft natural curl fall in ringlets.

Mother popped in and out of my room, bubbling with excitement. Evidently, she had forgotten all about our recent disagreement. Smiling admiringly, she put a stray hair that straggled over my forehead into place. Her eagle eyes scanned my happy face. Sauntering over to the bed, she fingered the clothes lying on it, as if reminiscing. Promptly she left the room, only to return moments later with my boots. "I polished these earlier to save you time," she said, laying them on the sheepskin rug in front of the fireplace. She was so excited I couldn't believe it. One would've thought she was going to the concert. She is so impatient for me to get married, to settle down, to have grandchildren for her.

"Let me help you with these." she eagerly surged forward, taking my petticoats from me and carefully slipping them over my head. "You mustn't untidy your hair. It looks so pretty the way you have it! Now, slip your dressing gown on and come for tea. You can finish dressing later!" There was lightness in her step and a twinkle in her eye. She waltzed across the room.

"I'll be there in a trice, Mother. I want to make sure I've not forgotten anything." "Good idea! But don't be long." She did a little pirouette before leaving the room and quietly closed the door.

The gold brocade slippers, made for me by my brother Tom, were in a dolly bag hanging on the hanger with my cloak. A fine lacy shawl was strewn over the back of a chair, and on the bed lay a white fur muff.

I'm fair lucky to have a brother who's a shoemaker. Tom, with his wee business in Cupar. I'm sure that there's not another nurse with a pair of Tom's shoes. Important people from all walks of life commission him to make their shoes and boots. Someday my big brother will have a manufacturing company. That's his dream and Tom makes dreams come true. He will, I know he will. All the country will be able to afford his beautiful shoes, not just the wealthy. And who knows? Perhaps one day, the world.

I sat at the dressing table and reached up to fasten my gold chain around my neck. My heart was fluttering and butterflies leaped in chaos in my tummy. Suddenly I sprang to my feet as I realised I hadn't yet practised the music I'd planned to play at the concert. I dashed through to the living room and, sitting on the music stool, began to play the pianoforte. My hand slipped and I hit a wrong key. I was furious at myself for being so careless.

"Tea's ready, Roselyn, tea's ready." Mother's impatient voice called from the kitchen. I quickly ran through the pieces once more, greatly encouraged by my parents' applauding and their jolly, "Bravo! Bravo!" as I entered the kitchen. Mother was fussing about as usual. She filled the milk jug with fresh milk, topped up the sugar bowl and poured boiling water into the teapot.

"There now," she sighed and served me a portion of meat and potato casserole. "There's lots left over if you want more." I was so excited I could hardly eat.

A thud in the back garden had startled us. "What was that?" we burst out simultaneously, looking from one to the other.

"Someone just passed by the window," I shouted jumping to my feet and looked out of the window. Father dropped his fork and knife as he leaped out of his chair, and bolted out the back door. Mother, in the midst of pouring the tea, dropped the teapot on the floor when she dashed to the window.

"There's nobody out there," Father bellowed, shaking his head as he re-entered the room. "It's your imagination again, Roselyn!"

"Oh, really! I suppose we all imagined the noise?"

"An animal must've knocked the rake over. That's all it was," he came back quickly. Mother was furious; I could tell by her aloofness. She totally ignored the conversation as she and I mopped up the spilled tea. Instead of rejoining us at the table, she chose to sit on the fender stool. Resting her elbows on her knees, she circled her face in her hands and stared at the blazing coals. Abruptly she turned to father and, in a worried tone, said, "What are we going to do with her, Larry? The girl needs help!"

I almost choked. I couldn't believe what I was hearing. "Would you please elaborate further on that statement, Mother?" I demanded. "What exactly did you mean? Did you forget that you and Father heard the noise too?"

"I was just thinking out loud, that's all."

"Oh Mother! How could you say such a thing?"

"For the love of God, would you two stop it!" Father quipped and, rising out of his chair, lifted the newspaper off the dresser and escaped to the living room.

My face burned and my lips tightened into a thin line. My mouth was dry as a starched cloth. Try as I might I couldn't comprehend my mother's reasoning. How dare she insinuate that I was wrong in the mind. I stormed out of the kitchen and went straight to my bedroom. I sat on my bed and wanted to die. I wept. It wasn't fair. I hadn't asked for this gift. I hadn't wanted it. The way she went on, anyone would think I was making it all up. No, nothing was fair. Right. That's it. From now on, whatever happens in the future I'll never admit to hearing or seeing anything, ever again. From now on, I'll be a liar. See nothing. Hear nothing. Let them think I'm seeing things. I'll play their game. Now, get ready. Can't go out with red eyes and in this mood.

I concentrated on breathing deeply until I was composed. I splashed water on my face. Looking in the mirror, I didn't look that bad. One more deep breath and return to the kitchen.

Mother bent over the table, singing away merrily while she cut the dumpling into finger-sized pieces, the glow of the fire flickering warmly on her face. She had promised earlier to prepare some food for our concert and had almost finished the task. All the while she completely ignored me. It was as if I wasn't even there. I went over to the sink, filled the basin with warm water and began to wash the dishes, gazing aimlessly out the window. Perhaps Mother's right. Maybe I do let my imagination run riot. No, I know exactly what I saw and exactly what I heard and no one will convince me otherwise. I am not mad.

I watched the fishing boats leave Broughty Ferry harbour. Now was this a vision too? Come on. I know what's real and what isn't. The vivid colours of red, green, and gold from their running lights danced on the clear water as the boats wobbled out to the main channel. I continued to watch them until I could no longer see the lights. It was an unusually calm evening and I have no doubt the fishermen were hoping to take advantage of the clear weather for a good catch.

"Let's get you into your dress," Mother suggested, the moment she'd finished what she was doing. "Time's getting on." She rolled up her sleeves and glanced at the wall clock at the same time. "Allan will be here soon." She was calm and collected and behaved as if nothing had happened. I knew she was humouring me, pretending that everything was normal. No, don't give into her. I bit my lip and said nothing. She followed me into my bedroom and with her help, I slipped into my dress.

She stood back from me, her eyes glittering. "There now, you look lovely."

I looked in the mirror and saw a pale ghost looking back at me. Far too pale and white. I pinched my cheeks until they were bright and glowing. I took my little perfume bottle from the dresser and dabbed my neck with rose water. I dabbed a little cream on my lips. Twirling around in front of the mirror, I inspected myself once more. "That's better," I declared with a smile. But Mother frowned. She eyed me up and down with that certain look, the look she has when something isn't quite right.

"What's the matter? Is there something wrong with my dress?" I pulled at my skirt, twisting this way and that, to get a better view of the back.

"Heavens, no! There's not a thing wrong with your dress, but there is something missing. Just wait a wee minute." She hurried from the room and returned moments later, a blue velvet box in hand. "These should be just perfect to finish your dress. These will be just right." She grinned and handed me the box.

"What in the world is this?" I had no idea what she was up to. One minute I am so angry with her and the next I love her more than any daughter had ever loved a mother.

She sat on the edge of the bed with her arms folded over her bosom.

"Come on, lass, open the thing. Get on with it." She watched intently as I did as I was told.

The moment I saw the contents, my heart almost stopped. So beautiful. "Oh Mother!" I gasped, tears of happiness in my eyes. "My Granny's earrings!" I removed the earrings and fastened them to my ears. I looked in the mirror and turned my head this way and that way. The earrings were examined from every angle. I didn't have the right words to thank her and mumbled, "You're absolutely right, Mother, now my outfit's complete."

A combination of nerves and excitement triggered butterflies in my tummy all over again. There's no doubt about it, I was on cloud nine and was as excited as could be. Be calm. Be normal. Don't show how excited you are. Make polite conversation and act like an adult. "Thank goodness it's not raining tonight, Mother," I commented as I entered the living room. "In fact, it's a beautiful evening."

"It certainly is." she said pushing the curtains back to look out the window. "And the moon couldn't be brighter. Look, I think I see a light approaching." She pressed her nose hard against the windowpane to get a clearer view. "Yes! Yes, I do! Listen!" she said, circling her ear with her hand. "I hear horses' hooves. The cab's approaching." Her eyes were dancing, her face beaming as she continued to prattle on. I stepped over beside her and took a look outside. She was right, the cab was coming, its lights erratic with the movement.

"Come on then, Lass, you'd better get your cloak on!" Mother put her arm around my shoulder, ushering me to the front hall. Father came to join us. He gasped when he saw us. I knew that his heart was filled with pride.

"Well, look at my little Princess." He took my cloak off the coat rack and draped it over my shoulders. "Now, I want you to have a wonderful evening, Roselyn, but we'll expect you home no later than eleven o'clock." I had to smile to myself at the way my parents fuss over me whenever I'm going anywhere special.

A rap-a-tap-tap on the knocker prompted Father to open the door. He opened it to Allan, who stood there as handsome as could be all dressed up in his formal wear. Everything, from the top hat on his head to the shining shoes on his feet, was perfect. A white silk scarf, casually draped around his neck, highlighted the whole outfit.

"Good evening, Mister Carey - sir," he stuttered out, doffing his hat and offering Father his hand at the same time.

"Good evening to you, Mister Robertson," replied Father calmly shaking Allan's hand. "It looks as if it's a fine evening."

"It is, sir! It's a glorious evening. Yes, glorious. Wonderful, sir, just ..." He is intimidated by my father and I could tell he was eager to get away from him and to have me to himself, but, of course, formalities ruled the roost.

."Now Mister Robertson, I'm entrusting you with my daughter. See to it that you have her home by eleven o'clock sharp."

"Don't concern yourself about Roselyn, Mister Carey. She's in good hands. And you have my word of honour I'll have her home by eleven." Allan's face radiated love as he reached over and took my hand. "Well, just look at you. My beautiful girl. A picture, so you are."

Mother, who had scurried off to the kitchen to fetch the food, entered the hall just in time to hear Allan's comments.

"For goodness sake, Allan," she smiled. "Surely you can tell her all that on the way." She handed him the basket. "You take charge of the food, Allan, and make sure you keep the basket upright."

"I certainly will, Mistress Carey. Thank you for the donation. We really appreciate it!"

"For heaven's sake, lad, think nothing of it. It's the least I can do. Now, please take care of Roselyn, and remember, she's a good girl. Treat her with right respect. Think of her reputation."

Allan flushed, "You have no need to concern yourself, Mistress Carey. I wouldn't dream of discrediting her." Mother ignored Allan's comments and reaching over, lifted the hood of my cloak, arranging it on my head.

"Do try to keep warm, Lass, I don't want you to catch a cold." She kissed my brow and gave me a hug tight enough to crack a rib. We said our goodbyes and left at once.

"Phew! So much for that!" I breathed, the minute we were out of earshot, running my hand across my brow. "I apologise for my parents' behaviour, Allan. You'd think I was a five-year-old, the way they carry on."

"Don't be too hard on them, Roselyn. You're the apple of their eye and they love you dearly. Just as I do," he added.

CHAPTER

5

The Concert

I was totally happy. Allan tucked a tartan rug over my lap the moment we settled into the cab. We snuggled, holding hands and enjoying every minute of the bumpy, hoof-clopping journey to Tayport.

Towards the mouth of the river, the running lights of the fishing boats twinkled like little glow-worms in the moonlight. I pictured the rugged fishermen on board, thick turtleneck jerseys underneath their macintoshes. Sou'westers were pulled down over their ears leaving only a tiny fragment of their faces exposed to the harshness of the cruel sea air. "How brave they are to trust the German Sea with their lives," I thought. For a few moments I sat in silence, with the glow of the moonlight shining on my face.

"A penny for your thoughts?" Allan's voice jolted me back.

"My thoughts aren't worth a penny, I can assure you. I was only day dreaming. But I must admit I'm nervous about playing the pianoforte tonight."

"Nonsense! You've no need to be nervous. You

play beautifully. Just pretend you are playing for me alone and you'll be all right." He smiled softly giving my hand a squeeze.

"But supposing I miss a beat? Or play a wrong note? What if my mind draws a blank! I would die!"

"Come on now, Kitten, settle down. If, by chance, you do make a mistake no one will even notice. They'll be thinking how lucky I am to have such a pretty, talented lass, so please don't worry. As soon as you start to play, the tension will leave."

When we arrived at the town hall, people had already started to queue. Everyone seemed to be in good spirits, despite the cold blustery weather. "Whoa! Whoa," commanded the cabby, pulling back on the horse's reins as our cab swung into Ogilvy Street. The obedient animal gave a loud spluttering snort, shook its head and came to a complete standstill.

"Mind your step, Roselyn," Allan cautioned me, offering me his hand to help me alight. His arm around my shoulder, he led me to the side entrance.

The anteroom was buzzing with activity. Members of the women's group were dashing about every which way. Kettles were being filled with water, to make tea. Cups and saucers tinkled and rattled as they were brought out to be wiped clean. Dainty sandwiches were arranged on silver serving trays. Cake stands were filled with fancy cakes and chocolate biscuits.

An exciting programme was planned to commence promptly at seven o'clock, following a word of welcome from Andrew Henderson, the local accountant.

First on the list was Jim Smith, the celebrated Scottish accordionist. He sat tall on a high stool towards the front of the stage, caressing his instrument with great enthusiasm, tapping his feet while his nimble fingers moved swiftly over the ivory keys. He squeezed out a delightful selection of Scottish folk songs, with the occasional distant look in his eyes. Perhaps he was thinking of bygone days. His dynamic playing was generously rewarded by tremendous applause from the audience.

The Tayside dancers, in full Highland dress, followed closely on Jim's heels. Brilliant colours of red, blue, green and yellow blazed on the stage. Kilts swirled and swished about in every direction, as the girls danced Highland Flings and Scottish Reels. Razor-edged swords glistened and flashed as they were laid on the floor. The dancers took up their positions to commence a war dance. As the dance intensified, it had a hypnotic affect on the audience, working them up to frenzy. By the time the climax was reached everyone was hysterical and shouting, "Bravo, bravo! More, more!"

Without warning, a violent brawl broke out at the back of the hall, distracting the attention of the audience. Two drunks had begun by shouting and cursing at each other and had ended up at each other's throats. There was a terrible rumpus as a burly constable and a young cadet threw the drunkards out.

The crystal clear voice of the renowned Morag Meldrum soon brought the crowd to order. She poured out the 'Eriskay Love Lilt', 'Afton Water' and 'My Love Is Like A Red, Red Rose'. Silent tears trickled from the eyes of many, white handkerchiefs held to their noses to muffle the odd sniffle.

I filled the air with the 'Ode to Joy' and 'Fuer Elise', two of my favourite Beethoven pieces. My supple fingers rippled over the keyboard of the pianoforte, echoing memories of yet another time. The audience listened intently while I played. And to my surprise, as well as to my delight, I made no mistakes.

Feet tapped and hands clapped time to the music

as Allan and his musician friends played a delightful selection of Scottish country-dance music. Everyone was rocking in his seat. A group of young people stood up and began whistling and shouting, "More, more, more!"

Jim Smith, after a few drams too many, returned to the stage for the finale. His face was flushed and his eyes were as large as saucers, as he bellowed out a selection of old-time waltzes. Everyone applauded enthusiastically and at the final curtain there was a standing ovation. What a marvellous concert.

Those who had stayed for the refreshments, helped clear away the rows of chairs. Folding tables were quickly set up and covered with white linen tablecloths. The setting was most appealing when the women put the fancy trays and dishes on the tables.

Small groups congregated about the hall as they waited for the food to be served. I overheard numerous comments such as, "What a delightful concert," and "My, wasn't that marvellous." It was evident the concert had been a success.

Throughout the evening, Allan and I shared secret glances, speaking to each other with our eyes. Standing proudly in the wings, I had been completely enthralled by his performance. "How handsome he is, in his formal wear," I'd whispered under my breath. I had noticed several young women giving him the glad eye. But Allan was oblivious to their glances. My eyes alone held his.

I had to smile to myself as memories of our childhood flashed before me. In my mind's eye, I pictured him as a boy, dressed in light-coloured shorts, his lanky legs climbing trees with unyielding determination. Of course, climbing trees, especially oak and chestnut, was our favourite pastime. The taller the tree, the more it appealed to us. We also enjoyed fishing off the jetty at the harbour. Rods made from a narrow branch, a piece of string, and a safety pin hook. We were big gamblers, always laying bets as to who would catch the first fish, the biggest fish or the most fish. But alas, with such primitive tackle, neither of us ever caught any fish. Well, maybe a tiddler or two.

Over the years, Allan and I had developed a deep insight and understanding of each other's feelings. We shared the same love of music and art. We both had deep compassion for the sick and needy.

By the time everyone had satisfied his appetites, it was almost half past nine. Allan had booked a cab for a quarter to ten, so after bidding friends goodnight, we left immediately. "How time flies when we're enjoying ourselves!" I commented as Allan draped my cloak over my shoulders.

"It certainly does, Kitten," he agreed, ushering me to the exit and out to the street. Clouds of vapour puffed out of the horse's vibrating nostrils. Shining brass bridle irons gleamed in the lamplight and a clump of bright green and red plumes decorated its forehead.

The cabby was huddled up in a thick woollen blanket, a heavy scarf wrapped around his throat and a hat pulled down about his ears. He gave us a nod and a grunt as Allan opened the door of the cab to let me in. Lifting my dress above my ankles, I carefully climbed aboard, sliding over to make room for Allan.

"Take us to West Lights via the common," Allan politely requested as he himself climbed aboard.

"Consider it done, sir," answered the cabby. Jerking the reins to the right he gave a loud crack of the whip and with a firm. "Giddy up, giddy up," he steered the horse with great skill down Ogilvy Street and past the bobbin factory to the common.

Allan and I sat in silence with a soft tartan rug tucked about our legs, the glow of the gaslight flickering on our faces.

"You were terrific, Roselyn," he whispered softly, kissing my neck. "I was so proud of you; you had perfect timing and not one mistake. You certainly held your audience tonight."

"Huh! What a fluke that was."

"Oh Roselyn, Roselyn! I wish you'd stop making yourself less than you are. You must stop that. It's not right for you to do that. You're as good as anyone. And, if I might add, a lot better than most."

"Go on with you Allan, you're forever saying nice things like that." I looked into his eyes and smiled. It is lovely being complimented and told how wonderful I am. "I thought you were wonderful too", I giggled, teasing him and poking him in the ribs. "I enjoyed the waltzes best of all. I closed my eyes and pretended we were dancing while they were being played."

"Oh you did, did you?" He gave my hand a squeeze.

"Yes! I certainly did."

When we reached the common, Allan tapped on the skylight and beckoned the cabby to stop. We stepped out to the most dazzling evening of the winter. "Give us ten minutes," Allan requested and the cabby courteously moved the cab a few yards ahead.

"Why did we stop, Allan?" I asked in surprise.

"So we can waltz in the moonlight," he answered. He stood up straight and held out his hand for mine. I placed my hand in his and let his strong hand circle mine. The brilliance of the moon displayed every star in the universe. The calm water of the river glimmered and shimmered with silver and gold, as if it had been sprinkled with star-dust. Holding me in his arms we took up our position to dance. He began to hum. *Tales from the Vienna Woods*. I moved with him, gliding, hardly touching the ground. We moved over the crisp, frosted grass. Whirling and twirling, our cloaks swaying and swishing, we danced the waltz to perfection. I was in heaven. Nothing could be better than this. Nothing.

The remainder of the journey flew by so quickly, we'd hardly caught our breath when the cab jerked to a halt. I was in a dream. Dazed. We strolled up the garden path to the front door.

"Well Roselyn, my dearest, thank you for a most memorable evening. I'll remember it as long as I live. Incidentally, sweetheart, you were by far the loveliest girl at the concert."

"Go on with you, Allan!" I stroked his face. "I saw dozens of pretty girls there."

"Perhaps you did, but I only saw one." He put his arms around me and kissed my lips softly "I love you with all my heart, Roselyn," he whispered gazing into my eyes. The sincerity in his voice and the love in his eyes made my heart beat even faster than before.

"I love you too, Allan, forever!" A ray of moonlight made his face plainly visible as he kissed me once more, and a feeling of ecstasy ran through me. It seemed that time stood still, allowing us to capture that precious moment.

"It's time to go, Roselyn," his husky voice, brought me back. "I promised your father I'd have you home by eleven."

CHAPTER

6

The Constables

A shaft of light, filtering through my bedroom curtains, awakened me the next morning. I sat up in bed, only half awake and piled the pillows high behind my head. My body still tingled with delight. I could feel his lips on mine. His hand on mine. Every detail of the night was clear. Each precious moment was imprinted in my mind forever. The heat of his body beat against mine under the star filled night. I could feel him right here beside me. We waltzed over the icy grass.

The forceful pounding of a heavy fist on the front door abruptly interrupted my thoughts. I heard my father running downstairs to answer it and moments later the drone of unfamiliar voices in the hall.

"Are you awake, Roselyn?" Father tapped softly, poking his head around my bedroom door. "You'd better get up," he whispered. "Two constables are here to questions us." He closed the door quietly behind him and I heard him ushering the unexpected visitors to the living room.

I threw the covers aside and leaped out of bed. It was as if my heart was jumping inside my ribs. "What on earth do the constables want to question us for?" I mumbled, as I slipped into my baffies. For a brief moment I felt I was a criminal.

Wrapping my dressing gown around me, I tied the cord tightly around my waist and moved over to the dressing table, quickly running a comb through my tousled hair. I braced myself and went directly to the living room.

"Good morning, Miss Carey!" bellowed the elder of the two constables. "Allow me to introduce myself," he offered me his hand, as he came to greet me. "My name is Mitchell, Sergeant Mitchell, to be precise," he announced in the most arrogant manner. I shook his hand limply and quickly crossed the room. I sat on the music stool with my back straight as a poker and folded my hands in my lap. I looked straight ahead and told myself that I would not be upset by this horrible man.

"Please don't be alarmed, Miss Carey," he said firmly. "We only want to clear up a few things." Without warning, he sneezed and, fumbling in his trouser pocket retrieved a huge red handkerchief and wiped his nose. "I do beg your pardon, Miss," he mumbled, wiping his brow with the handkerchief before putting it back in his pocket. "Now, let's get back to business. We have reason to believe that Alex McKinley, the suspect in a brutal assault which occurred in Dundee last night, may have taken refuge in this area. Your parents have told us that you had several unusual experiences yesterday. Is that correct?"

"Yes, that's correct."

"In your own words please tell us exactly what they were."

"Well! When I arrived home at nine o'clock in the morning, our garden gate was ajar. I was puzzled because my father insists upon the gate being kept shut. Then during my nap, I was awakened in the early afternoon by the sound of someone entering the house. When I went to investigate, there was no one there. My mother insists I was dreaming, but I know I wasn't! Later in the afternoon, just as we were about to have out dinner, there was an almighty clatter in the back garden and a moment later someone passed by the kitchen window."

The young constable stood, tall and silent, with his back to the fireplace, recording every word I said in a little black notebook. He was a clean-shaven lad and had the most expressive blue eyes I have ever seen. A wisp of strawberry blond hair straggled loosely over his forehead and a thin moustache outlined his burgundy lips. The sergeant, on the other hand, was a solemn-faced man, full of his own importance. He strutted back and forth in the centre of the room like a bantam cock, with hands clasped firmly behind his back, commanding every one's attention. He sported a bushy moustache. Sideburns reaching down to his chin softened his high cheek-boned face. Some people may have considered him handsome, but I did not think him at all good looking.

Bursting with curiosity, I couldn't contain myself a moment longer. "Do you think Alex McKinley is hiding here at West Lights, Sergeant Mitchell?"

"Miss Carey!" he bellowed in a stern tone, peering at me over the top of his spectacles. "I'm questioning you! Now, will you please describe the person whom you claim to have seen."

"Of course! Tall and gave the impression that he was stooped over."

"When you say, 'tall', Miss Carey, what exactly do

you mean? Was the person as tall as your father, taller, shorter, what?"

Eyeing my father up and down for a moment, I replied in a positive tone, "A little shorter than my father."

"Was it a man or a woman?"

"Why, Sergeant Mitchell," I teased, "I haven't the slightest idea. It was dark outside."

"Humph," he grunted moving over to where Father was standing barefoot, with untidy hair and robe haphazardly tied at the waist.

"Mister Carey, when your daughter shouted, 'Someone passed by the window' what did you do?"

"I ran outside to investigate, but there was no one there."

"In your opinion, Mister Carey, if someone had been out there, would you have seen him?"

"Yes, definitely! It only took a few seconds for me to run outside."

"Did you check all around the outside of the house while you were there?"

"Of course."

He then turned to Mother who was huddled up in an easy chair. She was dressed in a soft blue dressing gown, her feet tucked up under her, her braided hair hanging loosely over one shoulder. The expression on her face was like that of a frightened child; she was white as a sheet.

"Mistress Carey," his voice changed to a softer tone, "did you see or hear anything?" He towered over her and no doubt she felt intimidated by him. She looked first at Father, then at me, then back to Father.

"I heard the noise, but I saw nothing." She spoke in the faintest tone.

"Speak up, Mistress Carey," he demanded. "I can hardly hear a word you are saying." I wondered why

51

he had to be just so nasty. There was no need for it.

"I said, 'I heard the noise, but I saw nothing'."

He didn't question us further but turned to Father and asked permission to check outside.

There are not too many hiding-places in our back garden. We watched intently from the living-room window as they looked inside the shed, behind the berry bushes and over the sea wall at the bottom of the garden. They returned to report there was no evidence of anyone having been outside the house the night before.

"Time is of the essence, Mister Carey," declared the sergeant. "We must find this McKinley fellow." He handed Father a sheet of paper on which there was a sketch. "This is his likeness. If you or any member of your family does see him, please notify Inspector Key of the Dundee Constabulary at once. I strongly advise you to keep all your doors and windows bolted. Perchance he's on the prowl." They left. We were totally bewildered.

"Huh! So much for your vision of someone passing by the window," Mother spoke calmly. Springing to her feet the minute the constables left, and whirling about, she gave me a piercing look. "I'm going to start breakfast!" she said marching off to the kitchen.

"I did see someone! I did!" I shouted after her with tear-filled eyes. How could she be so stupid?

My feelings were shattered. Like a rat, I scurried across the room and sat at the window and gazed out to sea. The anger inside me simmered and simmered and eventually boiled. I was ready to explode. At the same time I was sorry for Father. He was betwixt and between. It was plain he didn't know what to do. He put his arm around my shoulder and said, "Come now, Roselyn. Don't let all this nonsense spoil your weekend."

I forced a smile. It wasn't his fault he couldn't deal with my mother and me. It wasn't his fault he didn't have the strength to support me. I slipped from his embrace and ran to my bedroom and threw myself onto the bed. It was as if my heart was breaking. So much sobbing. Yes, let the fury recede. Let it go out like the ebb tide. I must release it and free myself from it.

CHPTER
7

Jim's News

Once composed, I sat at the dressing table. Elbows propped on the dresser, I cupped my face in my hands and stared into the mirror. It seemed only yesterday that Mother and I had spent most of our time together. She taught me so many things. And yes, I was keen to learn. Both of us have always been fascinated by the tide thundering in, crashing its powerful waves in upward sprays against the granite rocks, receding slowly, softly, gently, only to return again and again more forcefully. As the snake is charmed by the sound of the flute, Mother and I were charmed by the sound of the tide. Happy days full of love and safety. We would go beach-combing and gathering wulks off the rocks. I can still see us wobbling home, barefoot, tired and hungry, our buckets overflowing with wulks. The sweet smell of the seaweed filled the air. Our spirited voices sang out old sea shanties.

What had happened to that beautiful relationship Mother and I once had? She has always been extremely upset when I mentioned the supernatural. But the incident last night had nothing to do with that. It was real.

It was as real as my elbow on the dresser. The answer to this will be found.

When I returned to the kitchen I did feel a bit more relaxed, but at the same time wouldn't have been surprised at more of Mother's criticism. Not a word was said. She was standing bent over the hob stirring the porridge, her face long as a fiddle.

"Let me do that for you, Mother," I offered as I moved across the room. She didn't fly off the handle as I'd expected from the look on her face; on the contrary, she was as sweet as could be.

"Don't stop stirring or the porridge'll stick to the pot," she said, handing me the spirtle. "When the porridge is ready, put the eggs on. I'll make the toast." Her attitude had turned around, and the friction that had existed between us before had vanished.

No sooner had we settled down to breakfast, when there came a loud, persistent knocking on the back door. "Now, who the devil can that be?" Father sighed, heaving himself from his chair and stomping off to answer it. "Good Lord, Jim!" he declared the moment he swung the door open. "What in the world brings you here so early in the morning?" He ushered Jim to the kitchen and helped him remove his overcoat, slinging it over the back of a chair. He turned to Mother. "Set a place for Jim, Liz!" But she was a step ahead of him and was already doing that.

Jim Carey is my father's cousin, but could quite easily pass for his twin. He's six feet tall and broad-shouldered. His most beautiful deep blue eyes light up his whole face. His black wavy hair, turning grey at the temples, gives him a look of distinction. He's worked for the City of Edinburgh Constabulary for as long as I can remember. Deeply religious, he gives freely of himself to others and spreads the word of God as a lay preacher for the Church of Scotland.

Jim's usually bright face was tight and white. Something had to be drastically wrong. The minute he sat at the table, he burst out crying. "It's Annie," he sobbed, "she's dying!"

"What?" we burst out simultaneously.

"The doctor has given her six weeks to live. That's if she's lucky. Oh dear, Oh dear! What will I do without her? I knew there was something terribly wrong when she couldn't get rid of that ghastly cough. Cough, cough, cough, from morning till night. I begged her, time and again, to go to the doctor. But would she? Oh no! Not her! Too damned stubborn, she is. Takes after her late mother, she does. Lord, have mercy on her soul. Oh God, Larry, what am I to do? I can't bear the thought of losing my bonny wee bairn. I'd give my life gladly if hers could be spared."

Father fetched a bottle of whisky from the sideboard and poured a nip for Jim. "Drink this down. It'll settle your nerves." He handed Jim the glass and Jim swallowed the whisky in one gulp.

"And what did the doctor say was ailing the lassie?" Mother urged him on.

"He said it's consumption and as we all well know there's no cure for that." Tears trickled down the crevices of his face as he went on sobbing, not even stopping to wipe the tears away.

Jim's wife had died in childbirth more than two decades ago, when Annie, their only child, was born. Annie had given birth to an illegitimate daughter when she was sixteen and had named the child Catherine Rose, after her late mother. Jim was brokenhearted at the time. He had huge plans for Annie's future. Ever since she was a little girl, he had brain-washed her with the idea of going to the university. However, being Jim, he had made the best of the situation and had always taken good care of Annie and Catherine. In return, Annie kept house for him.

We were devastated at the heartbreaking news Jim had just given us. Mother brought a freshly laundered handkerchief from the sideboard drawer and gave it to him. "The doctor isn't always right, you know, Jim. There is always hope."

"Aye, but his partner has confirmed that she's got the consumption." He buried his face in his hands and cried like a baby. When he lifted his tear-drenched face, the depth of sorrow in his eyes saddened our hearts.

In silence, we sat looking from one to the other, not knowing what to say. Slowly, as if he were saying a prayer, Jim continued, "I'm here to ask a favour on Annie's behalf. No need to make a hasty decision. But Annie would like to know as soon as possible what you decide." He hesitated as if trying to find courage to carry on. "I don't know what ... I don't ..."

"For the love of heaven," Mother butted in, "don't carry on. You know we'd do anything for Annie. What is it she wants?"

"Well, needless to say, she's extremely concerned about Catherine's future and she said she'd go to her grave a happy woman if you and Larry would adopt her."

"What?" Mother choked and her eyes flashed straight to Father's and his to hers. "I'm flabbergasted, Jim! Why does Annie want us to take Catherine? You're the child's grandfather, why not you?"

He tried desperately to curb the tears, and in a broken voice stuttered out, "Well, as you can imagine, Annie has given the matter a considerable amount of thought. When she discussed it with me, she told me that although I have done my utmost to give her the best there is she's been desperately lonely all her life. She doesn't want that for Catherine. She often wished she'd been born Roselyn Carey. Not that she was ever jealous of you, Roselyn. Oh no! For heaven's sake, don't ever think that," he raised a trembling hand. "But you see, in her eyes your life has always been full of variety; so many people around you and no time for loneliness." Turning to Mother and Father, he continued, "She told me that if you adopt Catherine she knows she'll have the best of care and will never be lonely." Covering his face with his hands, he cried his heart out again.

An awkward silence followed. It was Father who eventually spoke up. "I understand how torn apart you are, Jim, and God knows, we sympathise with you profoundly. Liz and I will have to give Annie's request a great deal of consideration. It's a big responsibility. Neither of us is getting any younger. We'll let the lassie know, one way or the other, by the end of next week. What do you say, Liz?" Mother nodded approval.

Father got up and stood behind Jim's chair. He put his hands on Jim's shoulders. "You look exhausted. Have a wee sleep before making the return journey." As he patted him on the back, he added kindly, "Well, what do you say?"

Jim stood up slowly wiping the wetness from his eyes. "I'd say that's a good idea. I'm very tired. I haven't had a decent sleep since we received the bad news."

Mother sprang to her feet and went to Jim and put her arms round him. "Come on then, lad, let's go!" She held him by the elbow and led him to the spare room.

"Ah, what a terrible shame," Mother gasped as she re-entered the room. "His heart's breaking, Larry. I'm so sorrowful for him." She sniffled, and wiped a tear from her eye with the corner of her apron. "He's certainly had his fair share of grief. He could've done without this! He asked to be roused at half eleven. I told him I'd ..."

"Don't you concern yourself about it, Liz. I'll take care of it," Father said, glancing at the clock. "Good heavens, look at the time! Almost ten o'clock already and I promised Bob I'd help him clean the lamps. I must be away." Mother accompanied him to the back hall, prattling nervously as she helped him into his overcoat. "See you later, Roselyn!" Father called, as Mother was about to close the door.

I felt that I had to suggest something to take our minds off the terrible news. "Let's sew this morning, Mother. That's if you feel up to it, of course."

"Yes I do, I do, I think that's a very good idea. It'll occupy my mind and keep me out of mischief," she gave a little grin. "Perhaps we should try to finish the garments we've been working on for the orphanage," she said, as she went to leave the room. Hesitating momentarily she took a quick glance at the clock, "My goodness how time flies! We'd better get cracking if we want to achieve anything this morning." She went straight to the cubbyhole underneath the stairs and brought out the work basket.

It was nearly eleven o'clock before we were prepared to sew. Mother placed the basket on the rug in front of the fireplace and sat in her favourite chair, her feet propped on the fender stool. I retrieved the dress I'd been working on, and sat on the footstool by Mother's side, unfolded the dress and started to sew. This was almost like the times before we had started to drift apart. I was enjoying her company. We prattled back and forth about nothing much. Trivial news about such things as what had happened at work since the New Year.

"I'd like to go to the market in Dundee soon, Roselyn! We're fast running out of just about everything. I need some cotton prints. Time flies you know, and summer will be upon us before we know it. The little orphan lassies will need pretty dresses for the warm summer days. Let's go on your next Saturday off?"

"Absolutely, Mother, absolutely," I agreed without lifting my head, nimble fingers moving swiftly along the seam.

Mother was deliberately avoiding the current issue. Of course Annie's illness, and the effect it would have on little Catherine, was foremost on our minds. Finally, I raised the subject. "You know, Mother, when you and Father consider Annie's proposal, perhaps you should ask yourselves what your decision would be if God made the request."

She folded her work and placed it on her lap. She took off her spectacles and looked me square in the eye. "I understand exactly what you're saying, Roselyn, but don't forget I've already raised two children and to start all over again with a five-year-old? Well, I just don't know! Honestly, I don't think I could cope. Besides I have my hands full taking care of you." She rolled her eyes.

"But let's face it, Mother, you may not always have me. Catherine would be wonderful company for you. She'd certainly keep you on your toes. There's no doubt about that."

"What are you talking about? 'I may not always have you'? Are you planning on leaving?"

"Heavens no, Mother, I'm not leaving. Not yet anyway. But let's face reality. I'll probably get married one day, whether it's to Allan or someone else." For a split second the strangest feeling came over me, a feeling I just couldn't put into words but which filled me with an overwhelming sadness. I quickly released the feeling. "Forget it, Mother, I had no reason to say such a thing. Let's change the subject."

Mother started to fidget and move around in her chair. She got up and went to the window and stood gazing out to sea. "My, it's a glorious day!" she commented. While her words were cheerful, the tone of her voice was sad. She scanned the cloudless sky with a faraway look in her eyes, as if she were pondering our conversation. She was absolutely right about the weather, though. It was beautiful. A pale yellow sun reflected gold shimmers on the water.

"How was the concert last night, Roselyn? Did you enjoy yourself?" she asked and crossed the room to resume sitting in her chair.

"I had a marvellous time; the hall was choked with people and more than half stayed for refreshments. I bet there'll be a huge profit. By the by, I've been meaning to tell you about the decision made at the church committee meeting, last month. We're going to treat the elderly members of the parish to a day's excursion to Edinburgh. That's if we can raise enough money, of course."

"What a great idea, let me know if there's anything I can do to help."

"Well, we're planning a sale in the church hall, in early April. Perhaps you can help there?"

"I certainly will. There are lots of odds and ends in the attic. I'm sure I can find something suitable up there to donate. And what if I organise a baking day with some friends? That would be fun."

"Great! I knew I could count on you, Mother."

"Did you notice any of my friends at the concert?" she asked.

"As a matter of fact, I did. The lady who sometimes comes for tea with you was there. What the devil is her name, again?"

"May Fraser?" she suggested.

"No, no, not May, the other one, the woman whose husband died last year. Och! You know who I mean." I said, tapping my forehead with my fingertips.

"Agnes Ambrose?"

"Yes, that's the one! Agnes Ambrose!"

"For heaven's sake! What do you know? And how is she keeping?"

"I don't know. I wasn't speaking to her. I only caught a glimpse of her from a distance. But I was talking to your dear friend Lydia. She sends you and Father her love and said to tell you to expect her for afternoon tea, a week on Tuesday."

"Oh that's marvellous!" she sighed in a joyous tone. "I'll look forward to that. Lydia is my oldest and dearest friend, you know."

She had told me this many times before. She and Lydia had been friends for countless years. They had gone to school together.

"I really enjoy her company," she went on to say. "She has the most wonderful knack of turning any situation into a pantomime." She pondered a while, gazing into the fire, then added. "I'll have to make some short-bread for that occasion. Lydia loves shortbread. I'm surprised she came all the way from Dundee to attend a concert over here, though. Was Jim not with her?"

"Of course, there's no show without Punch! They were with Frank and Jean. Lydia and Jim are spending the weekend at the farm with them."

"Aha! That explains it. I couldn't imagine her returning to Dundee on the late night train. She's nervous enough travelling across that bridge in daylight!"

"What do you think of this Mother?" I asked,

showing her the dress that I had just finished.

"Why, Roselyn, it's beautiful, absolutely beautiful." She reached over, took the dress from me and examined it in detail. "What a beautiful job you've made of the smocking. And the colour combination - well, what can I say? I've always wanted to learn the craft of smocking, but I don't think I have the patience for such intricate work."

"Nonsense, Mother. If anyone has the patience, it's you."

"Then perhaps you'll teach me, one day." She gave a little smile, returning the dress to me.

"Your Father offered to make the dinner today." I suspected that she was up to something. She smiled. "He thought it would give us the chance to spend some time together. He's going to give Jim a bite before he leaves, then he'll call us."

"That's considerate of him. What's he making?"

"Fried herring, dipped in oatmeal, your favourite dish."

I glanced at the grandfather clock standing tall and proud against the west wall loudly ticking the minutes away. It was about to strike the hour.

"We've accomplished a great deal today, Roselyn. That's only one o'clock," Mother commented at the first gong, removing her spectacles. She covered her mouth with the palm of her hand and yawned.

"We keep each other going, don't you think?" I remarked.

"We certainly do. What do you think of this?" she asked, spreading the green velvet cloak she was working on over her lap.

"That's pretty! The white fur trim around the hood gives it an added touch of class. You should be proud of yourself."

"I am. But you know what makes it all worthwhile? That it'll brighten up some poor wee lassie's day. And look, Roselyn," she burst out excitedly, as she rummaged in the basket pulling out a hunk of white rabbit fur, "there's enough of this fur left to make a matching muff."

"Wonderful!" I started to tidy things away, while Mother, bent on one knee, stoked the fire.

"Well, lass," she smiled staggering to her feet, "let's go and see how the cook's doing."

"I thought you said he was going to call us?"

"I did, but I can't wait any longer, I'm starving. I'm surprised you're not." She quirked. "What time is Allan calling for you?" she asked, casually glancing at the clock.

"He's not, I'm going to meet him halfway. His mother invited me for tea this afternoon, and what with all the commotion we've had around here this morning, I completely forgot to mention it to you. I'm very much looking forward to my visit."

Jim was putting his coat on when Mother and I entered the kitchen. "I'll be out of your hair in a jiffy, ladies," he blurted out. Looking directly at Mother he said, "I just had a grand plate of your ham and pea soup, Liz, and goodness me, it was good. Warmed the cockles of my heart, it did." He reached over and gave Mother a hug. Then turning about, he gave me a hug too, and left at once.

Father put the fish into the frying pan as soon as Jim had gone. It sizzled the moment it touched the hot fat, sending out a mouth-watering aroma. "Everything's ready," he said with a smile, pointing at the table with the fish slice. "Sit down! The fish only takes a minute to cook."

It was a rare occasion for Mother to have dinner

made for her. She sat gracefully poised in her chair, acting as if she was the Queen of Sheba, watching Father's every move with loving eyes.

Our cook did himself proud. The fish was excellent and generous helpings were enjoyed by all.

"Do I smell what I think I do?" I smiled wide-eyed and wiping the grease off my chin with my serviette.

"You certainly do," Mother piped up. "Baked rice with raisins."

"I knew it; I knew it!"

Father was delighted that Mother and I had such healthy appetites, an appropriate reward for his efforts. "If we tell you you're a fabulous cook, Father, it'll go to your head, so we are not going to, are we Mother? However, I must say I enjoyed every mouth-watering morsel."

"As long as my girls enjoyed it, that's all that matters," his voice rang out with pride.

I excused myself and went to my room to get ready for my visit to Allan's parents. I chose a pale blue wool dress with a white lace colour. I donned my royal blue coat and hat, white muff, and a white angora scarf knotted loosely around my throat.

CHAPTER
8

Cragiebank

A cold breeze tingled my cheeks as I hurried along the shore to meet Allan. As I walked, I thought about my parents. How devoted they were to each other. They enjoyed every minute of every day as if to make up for lost time. Oh, that terrible time when Father was in India during that five-year term as a major in the Armoured Corps. I had often overheard Mother crying in the privacy of her bedroom before turning in for the night. She had prayed to God, to "send her Larry home safely". She'd never complained, nor had she ever displayed emotions of loneliness to Tom or me. That would have gone against the grain. On the contrary, she had filled our home with joyous laughter. As she went about her daily chores, her sweet voice filled the air with old Scottish folk songs, passed down from her grandmother to my Gran, to her. Her long black tresses glistened in the sunlight and her jade-coloured eyes sparkled when she smiled, illuminating a face of transparent loveliness and making Elizabeth Carey look like a delicate, porcelain doll. How fortunate Father was to have such a beautiful wife.

High-pitched voices, filling the air with gales of joyous laughter, jolted me back to the present. Several families were out enjoying the pale winter sunshine. The cold breeze blowing up the firth polished their cheeks, making them look like glossy red apples. Little children chased each other. Older boys kicked a football about on the grass, their happy voices ringing out in shrill shrieks. Most of the parents were aloof, pretending not to pay attention to their offspring and yet all the while watching over them with eagle eyes.

A pretty little girl, with the most gorgeous brown eyes and long auburn ringlets hanging from beneath her bonnet, tripped over a boulder on the beach. Her nose began to bleed as she ran screaming into the arms of her mother. The mother seemed to panic at the sight of the blood. It was obvious she had no idea what to do. Dashing forward, I offered my assistance, which the mother readily accepted. "Now, now, my child." I spoke in a calm, but firm voice, as I sat her down on a bench. "Sit quite still and be a good little girl." She stopped crying. I wiped the blood away with my handkerchief and applied pressure to the bridge of her nose. In a trice, the bleeding stopped. "Now, since you were such a good patient, I have something for you." I reached into my coat pocket, brought out a treacle toffee and gave it to her. Her eyes danced with delight as she gave me a lovely smile. The grateful mother thanked me profoundly and together they left hand in hand, happy as could be.

"Roselyn! Roselyn!" Allan's voice carried on the wind as he hurried across the humpbacked bridge. The moment we saw each other, we ran the remaining few yards that separated us. He grabbed me around the waist, swept me off my feet and twirled me around several times before he let me down. A chime of joyous laughter rang out, filling the air just as it had when we were children.

"Oh, Roselyn!" he gasped excitedly. "I missed you."

"And I, you," I replied lovingly.

"I can hardly wait until we're together again, whenever we're apart." He whispered.

"Do you suppose it will always be this way, Allan?"

"Of course!" he answered in a positive tone. "My mother asked that we arrive no later than four o'clock," he said, changing the subject. "She wants to have a good old chin wag with you before tea."

"That's all right, isn't it?"

"Oh I suppose so, but I could think of a dozen things I'd rather do. Incidentally, my granny has been on heckle pins, all morning, because you're coming to visit. She's going to ask you to play her favourite songs for her."

"But surely you could do that Allan?"

"Of course I could. But you know what she's like," he teased poking me in the ribs. "She wants you to play them."

"Oh isn't that sweet? It's a bit awkward, though, when both you and your mother play."

"I'm quite sure you'll have no problem dealing with it," he smirked.

"I've always liked your granny. She's kindness itself. Remember the time we fell into the harbour and were soaked to the skin? She had a fit in case our parents would find out. Made us strip to the skin and wrapped us up in warm blankets until our clothes were dry."

"Ah yes, how well I remember! And she insisted on giving us a beaker of hot milk. Oh how I detest hot milk. But I loved the thick toast she made, melted butter running down our chins. Those were the days, those were."

With fingers linked together, we strolled along the cobbled streets and inevitably ended up on the common. Last night this had been our Eden. Today we shared it with a multitude of people out for a Sunday afternoon stroll. Everyone was appropriately dressed in warm winter coats, thick wool scarves wrapped around their necks and hats pulled down over ears against the bitter cold.

Over the years, Allan and I had spent many happy hours on the Common. It's where lovers stroll in the twilight and where families enjoy outings, as they were doing now.

We were intercepted several times by friends, anxious to get some inside information about the stabbing incident in Dundee. It was obvious from their faces that my inability to elaborate further disappointed them.

The breeze blowing up the firth turned into a stormy wind. White caps rode triumphantly on the surface of the water surging in upward sprays against the granite rocks. Black clouds hurried across an angry sky and the pale lemon sun, responsible for bringing people outdoors, had vanished. Gulls that had ridden proudly on the crest of the waves moments ago, had fled for safety, taking refuge underneath the wide beams of the jetty in the harbour.

"We'd better make tracks, Kitten," Allan suggested, putting his arm around my shoulder. "It looks as if a storm's brewing and we don't want to get caught in it, do we?"   The force of the wind on our backs helped us to our destination with little or no effort on our part. By the time we reached the brow of the hill, the wind was so strong we could hardly keep our feet. Huge ice pellets fell from the sky and splattered on the pavement, sparsely at first, and then it was as if the heavens had opened up and poured tears of sorrow on the world.

When we arrived at Craigie Bank, Allan had to lean all his weight against the gate to force it open. The Robertsons' house is one of the most impressive family dwellings in Tayport. It stands high on a hill, commanding a breathtaking view of the Tay Valley.

Allan's father, David, is a solicitor. His comprehensive legal knowledge, combined with his sincere personality, contribute to his success, allowing the Robertson family to enjoy an affluent life style.

As we entered the garden, Mitzy, the family dog, came bounding over to greet us, barking and yelping as she came. Her legs were going every which way to keep her balance. Her bushy tail was being blown to one side as she gave us a heart-warming welcome.

Mistress Robertson, huddled in a tartan shawl, was standing in the vestibule waiting to greet us. Mitzy's barking had undoubtedly alerted her of our arrival. "Hello, Roselyn!" She welcomed me with a warm smile as I approached. "Come in quickly out of the rain. Goodness me, you're soaked! Let's get you out of that wet coat." She turned and handed the coat to Allan, "Be a pet, son. Hang the coats on the pulley. I'll take care of Roselyn." He obeyed her without question.

"It's lovely and warm in here, Roselyn," she smiled softly, as she tucked my arm in hers and led me to the living room.

"Ethel has been on edge all morning waiting for you to arrive. She loses all track of time you know, and becomes extremely impatient. Look who I found on the doorstep, Ethel," she teased the moment we entered the room.

I was shocked at how frail Granny had become since I had last seen her. She was huddled up in an easy chair, with a light beige lacy shawl draped over her narrow shoulders. Wispy white hair framed her aged face.

What a tear-jerking sight. But her bright hazel eyes, which could have been Allan's, sparkled with delight the moment she set eyes on me.

"Hello, Granny!" I burst out with a happy smile, crossing the room to where she was seated by the fireside. "How are you doing?" I asked, giving her a big hug and kissing her on the forehead.

"Why, Roselyn," she gasped, taking my hand in hers, "I was beginning to think you'd got lost. What in the world took you so long to get here? And Allan, where is Allan?" She asked, looking beyond me to the door. "Didn't he come with you?"

"He certainly did," I assured her, "he's just gone to hang up our coats."

"Good." she beamed and immediately began to fumble in the pocket of her dress to retrieve a silver snuffbox.

"Here, let me help you with that," I offered, taking the snuffbox from her. I removed the lid and gave the box back to her. She acknowledged my gesture silently with a grin, as she sprinkled a pinch of snuff on the back of her hand and sniffed a little up each nostril. There was a little more animation in her voice after she'd taken a good sniff.

"Ah! That's much better." She replaced the lid and slipped the snuffbox back into her pocket. "Now, where was I? Oh yes, you were asking how I was doing. Well, if the truth be known, I haven't been too well of late." Her voice was weak and her head shook spasmodically as she spoke.

"I'm sorry to hear that, Granny!" I said, taking her hand in mine and stroking the back of it.

"Pull over a chair, lass, and sit here by my side," she gestured, patting the arm of the chair with the palm of her scrawny hand. "You have no idea how much I've been looking forward to your visit," she gasped breath-lessly. "My, you're looking well." She leaned back in her chair folding her hands on her lap. "Allan tells me you've been working too hard and he's forever at you to take things easy. But he said he might as well be talking to the wall. Is that true?"

"Well, yes and no. I..." She continued to prattle on, not waiting for an answer. Every now and then she would chuckle away at thoughts only she could hear. "Fancy that! He has little room to speak. He won't listen either." She smiled proudly. "He's an awful laddie, you know! Now tell me. How are your parents keeping? I couldn't tell you when last I saw them. Must be at least two years. No, come to think of it, it's longer than that. I haven't seen them since before I had my stroke, and that was more than three years ago now."

"They're both in the best of health, thank you, Granny. They're going to be taking a charabanc tour to Pitlochry this summer. They'll enjoy that. They have such love for the Highlands."

Allan's mother couldn't get a word in edgewise. She sat quietly on the opposite side of the hearth with her feet tucked up under her, elbows resting on the arm of the chair and chin cupped in her hands. Her eyes radi-ated love as she listened intently to Granny's idle chitchat.

Esther Robertson, Allan's mother, was an extremely compassionate woman with a heart of gold. She had been nursing her mother-in-law ever since she'd suffered a minor stroke, three and a half years before. And it seemed she enjoyed every minute.

Allan came bouncing into the room, full of beans and carrying a tray of drinks in stemmed glasses. "I've taken the liberty of pouring a sherry for everyone. That is, with the exception of you, Granny. I poured you a glass of your favourite brandy. Now, don't be letting it go to your head," he teased as he handed her the glass.

"Oh Allan," she laughed. "You're a good wee laddie for taking care of your old granny. What in the world would I do without you?"

We all settled down to a pleasant afternoon of chatter, sipping our sherry and enjoying the lovely warmth radiating from the coals. We laughed helplessly as we recalled funny situations that Allan and I had got ourselves into when we were children. We even revealed some of our darkest secrets.

Out of the blue, Granny turned to Allan, and with a twinkle in her eye asked, "Is it not about time you two were getting married?" Her eyebrows arched in enquiry as she spoke and there was a look of determination about her. "You have certainly known each other long enough, and if you don't hurry up and do it, I'll not be here to see it." She chuckled to herself before continuing, "I'd really hate to miss all the excitement. What do you say Allan?"

"Now, Granny," he blushed, "don't be so nosy. You'll be the first to know if and when Roselyn and I set a date. I promise."

I was taken aback at her comment and felt a little embarrassed. I quickly changed the subject by telling them about the constables coming to West Lights in search of Alex McKinley.

"And what do you think, Roselyn? Is Alex guilty, or is the constabulary just having to pin the blame on anyone?" Mistress Robertson asked, genuinely interested. She was brimming with curiosity.

"I really don't know. Sergeant Mitchell certainly seems to think so. He has Alex slated as the attacker and would have him carted off to the gallows, as quick as a flash, if he had his way. Don't quote me; that is only my opinion."

"I was hoping you'd play the pianoforte for me, Roselyn." Granny interrupted. "Not until after tea, of course," she added quickly and continued to sip on the brandy. "I simply loved that tune you played last Hogmanay. It was a bonny wee song! Now what the devil was it called?" She pondered momentarily. Then with a wide smile she said, "Remember, the one about Bonny Prince Charlie? Dear me, my memory's not serving me too well lately."

"I know the one you're thinking of, it was '*The Skye Boat Song*'. You must have really enjoyed it."

"Oh I did, I did! It had the most haunting melody I've ever heard. Captivated my heart, it did." Her voice was warm and soft as she spoke, and with a faraway look in her eyes, she sighed, "Perhaps you'll also play my Geordie's song?"

"Of course! It'll be my pleasure, Granny!"

Our conversation was interrupted when Mistress Robertson sprang to her feet the moment she heard the back door open. "That'll be David and Patricia now," she said, smiling happily. "I'll put the pie in, now that everyone's here."

Both Mister Robertson and Patricia were in high spirits despite the dreich weather. The moment they entered the room, Allan dutifully went into the kitchen to pour a nip of whisky and a pint of beer for his father. He brought lemonade for Patricia who complained. Everyone else had a 'real' drink.

"Please accept my humble apologies for not being here when you arrived, Roselyn." Mister Robertson beamed as he greeted me with a hug.

"My, you do look pretty in that dress. The colour matches your eyes perfectly," he commented. There was a genuine ring of admiration in his voice as he moved over to the fireplace to re-stoke the fire. "I think we're in for snow, it's certainly cold enough for it" he added with a shiver. "Allan! Allan!" he called. "Your granny's glass is empty, bring her a refill please." He took the empty glass from Granny and handed it to Patricia saying, "Be a pet and give this to Allan." Putting his arm around Granny he said, "I've got to take good care of my wee mother! Haven't I?" He grinned and gave her a hug, kissing her on the brow. Granny's eyes lit up as she looked adoringly into his.

"I think there's a conspiracy here to get my granny drunk." Allan joked merrily, returning with the drinks.

Patricia settled herself nicely on the hearth rug in front of the fire, knees bent up to her chin and both hands wrapped around her glass. She seemed totally enthralled with the conversation and put the odd two pennies' worth in, here and there.

Allan has his younger brother Ian, and of course his 'little' sister, Patricia. Ian was a student at St. Andrews University. His ambition was to become a dental surgeon but whether or not that would ever happen remained to be seen. He was a philanderer and all too often neglected his studies. His face bore a strong resemblance to Allan's, but he was lean, with a shock of jet-black curly hair.

Patricia, on the other hand, was short and plump. Her pretty auburn hair fell in ringlets to her waist. It was usually braided and tied up with big bows at the sides, making her look like a rag doll. All this was complemented by her light blue eyes. Her mother kept saying that her plumpness was all just due to her being young and that she'd lose it when she got older. She had convinced Patricia that it would all disappear when she reached twenty-one. Patricia was a trainee cook, at a private school for girls in Edinburgh. She took violin lessons at the Royal Conservatory of Music, in Dundee. Her secret ambition was to play with the Scottish Fiddlers.

"Tea's served!" Mistress Robertson announced, crossing the room to help Granny out of her chair. With the assistance of her husband, they escorted Granny to the dining room.

The moment everyone was seated at the table, Mister Robertson stood up and, with praying hands and bowed head, said grace.

Plainly Mistress Robertson had gone to a great deal of trouble in preparation for my visit. The dining-room table was beautifully set, with an arrangement of dried flowers making a centrepiece. Fine crystal glasses sparkled in the candlelight, casting a multitude of colourful shadows about the room.

She served each of us a hearty portion of cheese and onion pie together with home baked crusty bread. A sponge cake with chocolate icing and a selection of cheese followed.

Over tea in the living-room, Granny let it be known she was tired. She suggested I play her requests before she retired for the night. Allan, with his accordion, and Patricia, with her violin, accompanied me on the pianoforte. The rest of the family members joined in singing. Mister Robertson's vibrant tenor voice filled the room. He stood with thumbs tucked in the armholes of his waistcoat, blasting out 'Silver Threads among the Gold', Granny's Geordie's song.

Granny thanked everyone for making her happy. Turning to me, she said. "If I wasn't so tired, I could sit here and listen to you playing all night long, Roselyn, but unfortunately I am. But haste ye back, lass, haste ye back. Good night all!" Her voice trailed away, as Allan led her out of the living room and down the hallway to her bedroom.

When he returned, he suggested that we should leave. I thanked his parents for having me and they in return made me promise to visit again soon.

There had been surly gusts of wind all afternoon following the rainstorm. Now that the storm had passed, and the night air was cold and crisp with a fresh sweetness in it, the odd snow flurry swirled in the wind. Our noses shone brightly like little red lanterns glowing in the moonlight, as we hurried along the Cupar Road and down the narrow cow-path to West Lights.

CHAPTER

9

In Church

O n Sunday morning the Tay valley was alive with the sound of pealing church bells ringing out in all their glory calling the faithful to the house of the Lord. Far in the distance, on the opposite side of the river, a cracked bell croaked, sounding as if it was mocking the others. But without the discord of that cracked bell, I wouldn't have felt at home.

It was a glorious morning, bright and crisp with a fresh sweetness in the air. A pale winter sun splashed the snow-covered cobbles making them sparkle like diamonds. A blustery breeze blowing up the firth compelled me to cover my ears with my gloved hands. My parents and I braced ourselves and hurried along the single lane footpath like sheep to our church.

Majestically poised on a hillock, at the east end of town, St Giles was surrounded by grand old oaks and chestnuts. The magnificent Gothic architecture of the building is a visible link with Medieval times. In summer, the fragrance from the rose garden drifted into the building, filling the small basilica with a heavenly bouquet. Ivy grew on the gable facing the river, embracing the building with its long clinging vines, as if to protect it from intruders. It was by far the prettiest church in the district, with its red tiled roof and beautiful stained glass windows.

Reverend Ralph Valente, the vicar, stood tall in the pulpit, like a shepherd towering watchfully over his flock. His smoothly shaven face was sombre as he delivered the sermon, anger in his resonant voice. The topic he chose to discuss, "Violence resulting from overindulgence in alcohol", held the attention of all.

"The outrageous tragedy which occurred in Dundee last Friday is typical of what happens when a mind is pickled with the 'evil spirit'. Let it be a lesson to all of us," he bellowed out, crashing down on the pulpit with a clenched fist. "May God have mercy on the guilty soul." He lowered his voice and scanned the pews with piercing eyes, as if he expected the guilty one to jump up, like a jack-in-the-box. In an even tone he added, "And may He wash away the sins of this wicked, wicked world." This was so unlike the minister, He is usually so soft spoken.

There was many a guilty looking face in the pews. Had he hit on some home truths? God alone knew. With bowed heads, we prayed that God, in His loving mercy, would ease the pain and suffering of Mary Ann McKinley. And of course, we prayed for forgiveness of our own sins.

Sarah Craig, the headmistress at Tayport primary school had played the church organ for as long as I could remember. She sat tall and prim, a red squirrel fur draped around her scrawny neck, face screwed up like a sour grape.

I was distracted by the white feather in her hat, fluttering in time to the music as she bellowed out, 'The Lord is my Shepherd'.

The sweet voices of the congregation rang out so loudly the church seemed to vibrate. At the closing prayer, a shaft of sunshine burst through the stained glass windows, reflecting a dazzling array of colour throughout the whole house of the Lord.

When in church, I often secretly studied the minister, as he stood in the pulpit. How handsome he was, dressed in his formal dark suit, the light shining on him, turning him into an angel from heaven. This particular Sunday, I fantasised, wondering what it would be like to be the minister's wife. Suddenly I realised he was looking at me, holding my gaze. Embarrassed, I quickly pulled my eyes away and tried to concentrate on the service.

Under the covered porch, he greeted everyone by name as they left the church. Shaking my hand, he said, "Be extra careful on the streets of Dundee, especially after dark. A young woman can't take too much care."

I assured him I'd take his advice, and requested an appointment with him in four weeks, which would be my next day off work.

"Now, let's see what can be arranged," he smiled. His black wispy hair straggled over his brow, as he reached into the pocket of his jacket and retrieved a little red notebook. Flipping quickly through the pages, he ran his forefinger down the last page he opened.

"Well now! Hum-mm, how would the twenty-seventh of February suit you, Roselyn?" He smiled softly. "Perhaps you'll join my sister and me for afternoon tea at the manse?" His face broke into a beaming smile. "She bakes the most delicious scones and pancakes, and her preserves? Why, they're out of this world. Never mind, you'll sample them yourself."

I was overwhelmed at the unexpected invitation, and for once in my life, was at a loss for words. "I'll be most honoured to join you, Reverend Valente," I stuttered out. "At what time should I arrive?"

"Let's say two o'clock."

"I'll be there at two sharp."

"Good!" he beamed. "I'll look forward with anticipation."

Well, bless my soul! If I didn't know better, I'd swear he was flirting with me. Mother was fit to be tied. She did her best to catch my eye, but I ignored her overtures. Wild with curiosity, she leant over my shoulder as we descended the steps leading to the red chipped path below, whispering in my ear.

"Well! What was all that about?"

"Nothing that would interest you, Mother!" I answered flippantly. She stomped off in the huff, her nose in the air. Father gave a sheepish smile and held out his arm. Mother linked hers through his and off they trotted a few steps ahead of me, the tail of her silver fox swaying back and forth.

It had been a heavy service, with the minister pounding on the pulpit and his husky voice ringing out. As we walked down the path to the latch gate, I took a deep breath, filling my lungs with cold fresh air.

As a rule, my parents and I take a walk along the Common after church. Unfortunately, the wind had changed direction and the sky was fast becoming heavy with black clouds blowing in from the east. The sun that had shone so majestically through the stained glass windows of the church moments before, blinked intermittently through the clouds. A unanimous decision to go straight home was indeed the right choice to make.

No sooner had we turned down the cow-path than Julia, our neighbour's daughter, came running towards us frantically. She looked very pretty with glowing cheeks, and glossy blond cluster curls tied back in a bunch.

"Mistress Carey, Mistress Carey!" she shouted hysterically, at the top of her voice, as she approached, her eyes flashing sparks of fear. "Oh Mistress Carey!" she sobbed.

"In the name of heaven, Julia, calm down." Mother spoke firmly, reaching out to take her hands. "What's the matter?"

"Oh Mistress Carey!" she sobbed, "It's my Ma. There's something wrong with her. She sent me to fetch Doctor Scott, and said if I met you, to ask if you'd come quickly to her aid. Oh, Mistress Carey, please hurry, my Ma's in terrible pain. I think she's dying."

Julia was so upset she was stuttering, her whole body shaking. Mother put an arm around her shoulders. "There, there, now pet, don't cry. You come home with Roselyn and me." Turning to Father she said, "Larry, please run and fetch Doctor Scott, sounds as if it's Jenny's time." He did as she bid without question and hurried, post- haste, to fetch the doctor.

Mother thrived when she was in control and of course, this was no exception. She had a look of determination as she braced herself. "All right girls, let's go, we've no time to waste." Reaching out, she took Julia's hand and went down the cow-path, as if her life depended on getting there quickly.

I followed close on their heels, my thoughts miles away. Jenny Burkes was expecting her third child on the seventeenth of February. But by the sounds of things, the unborn baby had a mind of its own, and had no intention of waiting till then. I was shocked that Julia didn't seem to know her mother was pregnant. After all, she was thirteen and ought to have known.

Tam and Jenny Burkes had been born in Tayport, but had left the district shortly after they were married, fifteen years before. A friend of Tam's had enticed him to take a job in the shipyard at Clydebank, convincing him he'd make a fortune there. Full of ambition, and without a care in the world, off they had gone! But alas, they had soon discovered that Tam had been financially better off working in Dundee.

Jenny hadn't been able to settle on the west coast and after lots of soul searching they'd decided to return to Tayport. Tam was happy to pick up where he had left off in the Dundee shipyard.

It was a time when things were booming in Dundee, mainly due to the jute industry. Ships were being turned out by the dozen to carry canvas and linen produced in the mills to ports all over the world. All the canvas used to cover the pioneer wagons in North America was woven in the Dundee jute mills. Most of the world's whaling ships were built in the Dundee shipyard. This meant plenty of work for the shipbuilders.

Tam and Jenny had flitted all over the place but had eventually found "Jimora", the pretty grey granite cottage next door to us. Mother and Jenny had soon become friends. I've often heard Mother say, "How wonderful it is to have such trusted neighbours."

CHAPTER
10

Julia Panics

When we arrived at the Burkes' house, Jenny was in a state of disarray. She was pacing back and forth in the hallway, tears trickling down her puny face. It was obvious she was in severe pain. She gave a nod and a half smile the moment we entered the house, and spluttered out, "Thank God you're here, Liz!" Reaching out, she touched my shoulder, saying, "You too, Roselyn, you too!"

Julia's eyes were like saucers. She ran over and flung her arms about her mother. "Everything will be all right now, Ma," she sighed, "Mistress Carey and Roselyn are here."

"It certainly will, pet, it certainly will." Jenny forced a smile. I could tell from her face she was far too fatigued to be bothered, and could've seem Julia far enough.

Mother made herself useful. She put her arm around Jenny's shoulders and led her over to the bed. As Jenny went to climb into bed, she cringed, letting out an unearthly scream. For the first time in Mother's life, she didn't know what to do. I intervened, talking calmly to Jenny and settled her down.

"Let's you and I make a cup of tea, Julia." Mother suggested.

"Good idea, Mistress Carey. We can make enough for everyone. My Ma and I were baking all day yesterday. There's lots of food in the larder."

Mother winked, giving me a knowing look, as she led Julia from the room.

Jenny was plainly exhausted. The moment Mother and Julia were gone, she gave a big sigh and turning to me, stuttered out, "Oh Roselyn, I'm getting far too old for this caper."

"Come on now Jenny, you're not that old." I began to massage her back. "How old are you?" I asked out of curiosity.

"Thirty-four, on October the twenty-ninth, if God spares me."

"Well, I'd never have guessed, I thought you were only thirty. Never mind, you'll forget about this pain as soon as the baby's born," I smiled, trying to cheer her up. "You'll feel like a spring chicken, all over again. I can picture you now, sitting up in bed, pillows piled high behind your head, cradling your little bundle of joy in your arms."

"You're right, Roselyn, you're right, I'll be the proudest mother in the whole wide world."

"When did your pains start?" I asked, wiping the perspiration off her brow.

"About half past six, a little after Tam and Michael left. Tam believes in leaving at the crack of dawn when he goes fishing, you know." She raised her head, glancing at the clock before confirming her statement. "Yes, that's right, half past six!"

"And have you no inclination to push, Jenny?"

"None at all. The pains have been strong now for more than three hours, and I don't seem to be making any progress. I had short labour with Michael," she went on to say, "four hours, and boom, it was over. But dear, oh dear! It was a different story altogether when Julia was born - two full days of intense labour. God help me, it was a nightmare. Of course, they say the first's always the worst."

Suddenly, she cringed, pulling her knees up to her chin. "Oh God! Oh God! Oh God!" she puffed, from the depth of her stomach. Reaching out, she grabbed my arm, digging her nails into my flesh.

I stiffened, biting my lip as her nails sank deeper and deeper.

When the pain had passed, she released my arm and asked for a glass of water. "I've got a terrible thirst, Roselyn, I could drink Loch Tay dry!"

"I'll get you some water straight away." I sprang to my feet, and went directly to the kitchen, closing the bedroom door behind me.

I put a cold wet cloth on my arm to ease the pain in it. "I wish I had more knowledge of childbirth," I mumbled to myself. Sister Tutor skimmed over childbirth and its possible complications. That wasn't enough for me to make a sound diagnosis. I could only hazard a guess. I guessed the baby was either in transverse position, or it was too big for Jenny to deliver. I didn't want to face up to the third possibility, that the baby might be dead.

"How is she, Roselyn?"

"I'm not sure," I answered calmly, and turning to Julia asked her to run over and fetch my black bag from our house. "It's on the top shelf, in the back hall press. You'll have to stand on a chair to reach it." Mother hurried to the hall and fetched the house-key from her purse. Julia took off like a whirlwind.

"What in heaven's name's the matter, Roselyn?" Mother asked, full of concern, "why the urgency to get your bag? Is there something you're not telling me?"

"No, no! I just want to take Jenny's temperature and check the baby's heart rate. I need a thermometer and stethoscope to do so."

"Oh! Thank God that's all it is," she said, putting her hand to her heart and giving a sigh of relief. "For a minute I thought that..."

The door flew open and in burst Julia, huffing and puffing, bag in hand. "Is this it, Roselyn?" she gasped.

"Yes, that's it, thank you!" I took the bag and went straight to the bedroom.

Jenny was having strong contractions. She was gripping the bars of the bed and muttering through clenched teeth, "This is torture, Roselyn, simply torture!"

Her face looked as if it was ready to burst and perspiration was dripping off the tip of her nose. Her temperature was a bit high, but I was relieved to learn that the baby's heart rate was normal.

"Would you like a nice bed-bath, Jenny? It would help to cool you down!" I smiled encouragingly, handing her the glass of water.

"Oh yes, Roselyn, that sounds wonderful," she smiled and took the glass of water from me to drink the lot. "I'm so hot and sticky, I swear, I must be mingin'." She returned the empty glass to me.

I went into the kitchen and filled a basin with warm water. Mother, anxious to help, brought a towel, wash-cloth and soap.

Jenny was crouching down, hanging on to the bedpost. "Oh dear, oh dear!" she moaned. "What's keeping Doctor Scott? Is he never going to get here?"

"Come now, Jenny," I sympathised. "Let me help you back into bed. I'm sure the doctor will be here any minute." I was in the midst of wringing out the face cloth, when the door flew open and in bounced Julia, smiling from ear to ear.

"Mistress Carey and I made you a nice cup of tea Ma," she bubbled crossing the room, tray in hands. "We thought it would cheer you up, help you to feel better."

"Oh Julia, pet, how thoughtful of you. Put it on the dresser, I'll enjoy it when Roselyn is finished."

As Julia turned to leave, a violent surge of pain brought Jenny to her knees, and she let out the most unearthly groan. Well, needless to say, Julia went into hysterics. She ran tear-drenched out of the room. I chased after her, and putting my arm around her, tried to comfort her. "Your Ma's going to be all right, Julia! Please don't worry." She wriggled from my embrace, and dashing into the kitchen, flung herself on an easy chair.

"My Ma's dying!" she sobbed. "Can't you see that, Roselyn? She's dying!"

I threw up my hands in exasperation and returned to the bedroom, leaving her in Mother's care.

"Jenny!" I snipped, the moment I entered the room. "Why haven't you told Julia you're having a baby?"

"Oh Roselyn, I couldn't, honestly, I couldn't! I was too embarrassed. She'd have asked too many questions that I couldn't begin to answer. Admittedly, I was wrong and now I regret not telling her. She thinks I'm dying, and there's no convincing her otherwise. Oh, poor Julia, my poor wee lamb!"

"She'll have to be told, Jenny, and the sooner the better," I snapped. Her face flushed and, lowering her head, she began to cry. I immediately regretted my shortness.

"Would you like me to tell her, Jenny?" I asked apologetically.

Slowly raising her head she gave a gentle, "Would you please, Roselyn? You'll do a much better job than I ever could."

"As soon as I'm finished here, I'll have a word with her."

"There's a box of talcum powder in the top drawer of the chest of drawers. I've been saving it for this occasion. Would you fetch it please? I may as well smell nice too."

"Of course!" I got the powder and gave it to her. Upon opening the box, she lavished puff upon puff of heavily scented talc all over her body. The fine dust swirled up in clouds, causing me to sneeze.

"Not too much," I complained jokingly, putting my handkerchief to my nose. "Trying to get rid of me, are you? There now, how does that feel?" I smiled, popping a fresh gown over her head. I still felt a little guilty for having been so abrupt.

"Wonderful, simply wonderful! Thank you, Roselyn."

I quickly gathered up the things I'd been using and went directly to the kitchen with only one thing on my mind - Julia.

She was curled up on an easy chair, cuddling Tiger, the family cat. Her eyes were red-rimmed and swollen, her nose as red as a cherry. She was without a doubt a pathetic sight, but all she needed was to hear the truth.

"Well!" she snapped. The moment I entered the kitchen. "Is she dead yet?"

"Julia, I've already told you, your Ma's not dying. As a matter of fact, she's doing rather well, under the circumstances."

"Circumstances? What circumstances?" she snapped.

Smiling softly, I sat on the arm of her chair, taking her hand in mine. "Your Ma's not dying Julia. So you can put all that nonsense out of your head once and for all. She's having a ... "

"But she's in agony! How can she be in so much pain, if she's not dying?"

"She's having a baby, Julia, your Ma's having a baby. It's your little brother or sister trying to get out of her tummy that's causing all the discomfort. As soon as the baby's born, she'll be fit as a fiddle. Meantime we must be patient, and try to make her as comfortable as possible."

"She's having a baby?" She swallowed, eyes popping out her head. "I'd no idea she was having a baby. To tell the truth, I thought she was just getting fat and ugly."

"Oh, Julia, I'm surprised at you! How could you think such a thing? Your Ma will be slim and beautiful again in no time. But she's going to need all the love and support you can give her. Don't you think it'll be lots of fun, helping to take care of a brand new baby?" I poked her playfully.

"But why didn't she tell me herself, Roselyn?"

"Well, some mothers find it difficult to discuss such delicate matters with their children. I'm sure she didn't mean to hurt you or anything. She just couldn't pluck up enough courage to tell you. But believe you me, had she known what you were thinking, she'd have found a way. Perhaps she was hoping the baby would arrive when you were at school. Now, wouldn't that have been a lovely surprise to come home to?"

She didn't respond straight away. Then, suddenly, her face lit up, and with a smile that stretched from ear to ear, she burst out, "Hurray! A baby!"

"What time are you expecting your father home?"

"Oh, there's no way of telling. When my Da and Michael go fishing, they forget to come back. They left at the crack of dawn. I doubt if we'll see them much before midnight."

"Well! I think they're in for a big surprise when they do get home."

When I returned to the bedroom, Jenny was resting quietly and Mother was sitting on a chair by her bedside, flipping through a book. Jenny's contractions had evidently stopped.

"Is it possible she's been having false labour, Roselyn? She hasn't blinked an eyelid for the past half hour." Mother whispered under her breath, tiptoeing across the room to put the book on the dressing table.

"I don't know, Mother, I really don't. I'm very frustrated."

"I know you are, lass," Mother sympathised and patted the back of my hand, a worried frown on her face.

"Why don't you go home and prepare your tea, Mother? I'll stay with Jenny till the doctor arrives." The words were no sooner out my mouth, when there was a frantic rapping on the front door.

"That'll be Doctor Scott now," Mother said, springing to her feet, scurrying off to answer it. But it wasn't the doctor. It was Father, red-faced, and gasping for breath.

"Doctor Scott's out of town," he huffed. "His housekeeper doesn't expect him to be back till after five. But she's going to let him know he's needed here the moment he returns. How's Jenny?" he asked, as soon as he'd reported the bad news.

"She's resting quietly at the moment, Larry," Mother told him as she removed her coat from the coat rack and put it on. "Roselyn's going to stay with her until the doctor arrives. I'm going home to prepare the tea." She popped her head around the kitchen door, "How would you like to have tea with us, Julia? You can even stay overnight, if you wish."

Julia didn't need any coaxing. She dashed upstairs to get a nightdress and quick as a flash, slipped into her coat. Smiling from ear to ear, she left with Mother and Father.

As I stepped back into the bedroom, Jenny stirred. "There's another pain coming, Roselyn," she cringed. "Where in heaven's name, is that doctor?"

"He's out of town, Jenny, he's not expected back till five o'clock. Let me take you to the hospital. You'll get proper help there. You really can't go on like this!"

"Hospital!" she bellowed, almost choking on the word. "Never! I wouldn't go to a hospital if my life depended on it. Oh, please forgive me for sounding so ungrateful, Roselyn. But I've known people who've gone into the hospital and that's the last anyone ever saw of them. No, no, a thousand times, no! No hospital for me, I'd rather die in my own bed. Besides, I have proper help right here, where I am."

"Oh no you don't, Jenny. I'm not a doctor, I'm not even a midwife."

"Here's another pain coming," she winced, grabbing my arm, the fear of the unknown clearly in her eyes.

The following hours were hell on earth for her. Finally, about quarter past five the doctor arrived. Upon examining her, he beckoned me to the kitchen. "The baby's in transverse position, Roselyn. I fear the cord may be around its neck. I'm going to have to turn the baby back to the normal position. If that doesn't work, I may have to perform an emergency Caesarean section. Will you assist me?"

"Oh, Doctor Scott!" I gulped. "I'm sorry, I have to catch the last train to Dundee this evening. I'm on duty at six o'clock tomorrow morning. My mother would be happy to assist you, I'm sure."

"Good! Send her over at once." He dashed back to the bedroom, closing the door.

I grabbed my coat and bag and hurried home to summon my mother. She left immediately, leaving Julia in Father's care. Father was always good with children and when I left they were playing hangman.

Allan and I had to run all the way to the railway station, just managing to catch the train by the skin of our teeth. Gasping for breath, we plonked ourselves down in a seat by the window, toward the front of the train.

CHAPTER
11

Birthday
Celebration

A bright winter moon stood high in a clear sky, its beams reflecting on the glassy water. The train swayed from side to side as it rumbled slowly across the Tay Bridge from Wormit to Dundee. We sat in silence enjoying the privacy of our carriage, hypnotised by the awesome view. From our lofty perch, we could see out to the mouth of the river where Bell Rock Lighthouse flashed powerful rays out to sea, warning ships' captains of the great perils lurking beneath the rock-infested water surrounding it. To the southwest there are two other lighthouses flashing in sequence to Bell Rock, one at East Lights and one at West Lights.

Street lamps, lining the esplanade, stood to attention like sentries guarding a fortress. The jute fortress! The Law, lurking in the background watched over its people. The all-knowing, all-seeing Law! Dundee's natural landmark, that was once an active volcano, long since extinct; much loved and much admired by proud Dundonians, through the centuries.

Dundee was a garrison town, and had been since before the days of William Wallace, when Scotland had been a great threat to the English throne. The town crawled with English soldiers, looking for an easy catch. No young woman in her right mind would be seen on the streets of Dundee after dark.

"Do you think your parents will take Catherine?" Allan inquired, breaking the silence.

"I haven't the foggiest idea! I know my Mother thinks she's getting too old to have a five-year-old underfoot. But who knows? She could change her mind. I'm sure they'll make a decision by the end of the week, hopefully the right one."

"I hope they do take Catherine, it'll make things easier when it comes time for you to leave home."

"For me to leave home?" I swallowed, wide eyed. "But I've no intention of leaving home. What a silly thing for you to say, Allan."

"Well, you know what I mean – when you leave to get married."

"Married? Who said anything about me getting married? Whom might I be marrying, pray tell me?"

"Me, of course, silly! Who else?"

"But I haven't had a proposal," I teased. I tilted my head back and looked down my nose at him. The least he could do is to make a formal proposal.

"Fiddlesticks! You know perfectly well we're going to get married. And don't worry that pretty little head of yours. You'll get a proposal, on bent knee at that, when the time's right. Then we'll be together forever and ever."

I looked at him with deep sadness in my heart, "Oh Allan!" I gasped, "I feel so perplexed when you talk about forever. I ... I ... feel - oh, never mind, it doesn't matter."

"Sweetheart! What's the matter?" He took my hands in his and kissed them. "We've had this discussion many times and you've never reacted like this. You know perfectly well we're meant for each other and we'll always be together."

That uncanny feeling of sadness that I had experienced earlier came over me again. It was as if I was having a premonition. I felt I was somehow going to lose him. "Allan Dearest." my voice trembled. "My spirit is deeply troubled, so deeply troubled!"

"Roselyn Carey, I'm surprised at you! Come, let's see your pretty smile." He slipped his hand gently underneath my chin and lifted my head, kissing my brow. "Come now!" he insisted. I looked up into his eyes, smiling sweetly.

"That's my girl! Now, don't you feel better already?" He teased.

"Yes, much better!" I wiped my eyes with my handkerchief and blew my nose.

Allan had an incredible knack of lifting my spirits from the depths of despair to the height of tranquillity. He had a sensitive personality and always knew instinctively exactly what to say. But no matter, the feeling that I was going to lose him continued to haunt me.

The train came to a halt with a jerk as we prepared to disembark. I lost my balance and went flying into his arms.

"Well! How's that for fate?" he laughed cheerfully, "didn't I tell you we're destined to be together. Well, didn't I?"

"Oh Allan, you're the limit!" I laughed. Hand in hand we ran along the platform, skipping up the stairs, and out of the station into Union Street.

That day was my Aunt Nell's sixty-sixth birthday. She had invited Allan and me to join her for tea, to celebrate the happy occasion. We were anticipating a pleasant evening of chitchat and laughter.

It was a strenuous climb to the top of the hill where Nell lived. She had rented the tiny flat a year before, when she'd retired from her position as cook in Crawley Manor, a stately home in Perthshire.

Nell had been widowed more than thirty years previously. Willie, her late husband, had been drowned in a mysterious accident at sea. When the accident had occurred, it was rumoured that he had got into a fight with a friend over a gambling debt and had been accidentally knocked overboard. Unfortunately, Willie couldn't swim. It had taken Nell years to recover from the shock of the tragedy.

Huffing and puffing, we finally reached the top floor, four flights up. Allan pulled the shiny brass bellpull and leaned against the banister to catch his breath. A moment later, the door flew open and there she stood, short and plump, with a round rosy face, exactly as one pictures a cook. Her eyes were dancing with delight and a smile lit up her whole face.

"Come in, come in!" she welcomed us with open arms. "It's so good to see you. Here, give me your coats and make yourselves comfortable by the fire." She ushered us to the living-room before trotting off to hang our coats in the hall press.

We sat on easy chairs, one at each side of the hearth, holding our hands in front of the blazing coals. "I didn't realise I was so cold," I gave a shiver.

"Me neither." Allan agreed pulling a shivery face.

"I hope you have good appetites," Nell said, as

she entered the room. She was carrying a tray on which there was a half-bottle of sherry and three crystal glasses. "I've spent all morning in the kitchen, preparing things." She was bursting with pride. By the waft of something hot and savoury drifting from the kitchen we knew we were in for a treat.

"This'll warm the cockles of your hearts." She cheerfully filled the glasses with nut-brown sherry, handing Allan and me a glass each. With the remaining glass in her hand, she sat on the stool and put the tray down on the floor.

"Well, here's wishing you many happy returns of the day, Nell!" Allan raised his glass in her honour. I followed his lead, and promptly presented her with a box of chocolates.

"You didn't have to bother with anything for me." She flushed, as she ripped the paper off the box, eyes sparkling with delight. "Why, these are my favourites! You knew that, didn't you, Roselyn?" She continued to prattle as she removed the lid and offered us a chocolate, first popping one into her own mouth.

"My goodness Allan, you're getting taller each time I see you. You must be about six feet!"

"Six and one inch to be precise," I piped up.

"Well fancy that!"

Nell was bubbling as always. She listened intently to our latest news as we chatted back and forth.

"Something smells good, Nell." Allan declared, sniffing the mouth-watering aroma escaping from the kitchen.

"It's steak pie, Allan!" she beamed, "Roselyn told me it's your favourite dish." Turning to me she added, "I made a lovely sherry trifle for you, Roselyn. I know you'll enjoy that."

"But I like steak pie too," I protested.

"Then perhaps Allan will give you a few crumbs off his plate," she countered raising her eyebrows and excused herself to check the tatties. Just as she was about to leave the room, Allan asked what the latest news on Mary Ann was. Well, that was all Nell needed. She stopped dead in her tracks and her eyes lit up, as if she had been waiting for the cue.

"Oh, wasn't that a terrible state of affairs!" she declared, full of concern. (Gus Henderson was Nell's next-door neighbour.) "Gus spent the entire weekend searching for Alex, bless his heart. He went from door to door in the Cowgate, questioning the neighbours. And you'll never guess!"

"What?" we burst out simultaneously eyes popping. "Alex wasn't even in Dundee when the crime occurred! He was away in London, looking for work. He didn't return until early Saturday morning, totally oblivious to what had happened to his wife. Poor Alex is fit to be tied. Gus is at the infirmary with him this very minute, visiting Mary Ann. Gus said that Alex couldn't imagine anyone having reason to stab Mary Ann. He's in for the shock of his life, when he sees her. According to Gus, her face is so badly swollen, she's unrecognisable and her body's covered with cuts and bruises. Oh good Lord, look at the time, it's nearly half past seven," she declared, glancing at the clock. "The tatties'll be boiled to mush. You'll have to eat and run tonight, I'm afraid." She scurried off to the kitchen.

Allan and I talked quietly, enjoying each other's company. We had just swallowed the dregs of our sherry, when Nell popped her head around the door and announced, "Tea's ready."

She served a delicious meal: steak and kidney

pie, chapped tatties and neeps, followed by a generous helping of sherry trifle and, of course, a nice cup of tea to wash it all down.

While we were sipping our tea, she went on non-stop about the weekend's events, so much so that at the first opportunity, we excused ourselves quickly and thanked her profoundly for sharing her special day with us.

"It was my pleasure," she responded with a smile, helping us into our coats. As she went to close the door she invited us to, "Hurry back!"

Allan and I wasted no time. We hurried along Albany Terrace, down Law Road and along Panmure Terrace to my lodgings. Snowflakes were falling. Soon we looked like a couple of snowmen.

"You're just going make it by the skin of your teeth, Roselyn!" Allan commented, peeking at his watch.

It was mandatory that all nurses in training be in their residences no later than nine o'clock, at night. Our previous matron had been a student of Florence Nightingale's and had set out these rules. She had introduced a rigid training programme for women of good character and education. Prior to her appointment, the efficiency of the nursing department had been pitiful. A major problem had been the excessive alcohol drinking by night staff.

Since that time, the rules had been uncompromising and the nursing staff treated like criminals. So it was more than my career was worth to be brought before the Matron.

We smothered each other with kisses at the gate, the glow of the gaslight flickering on our snow-speckled faces. Allan sighed as he reluctantly tore himself away to catch the train home.

I gave the heavy iron gate a shove with my shoulder, latching it securely behind me and cautiously groped my way up the higgledy-piggledy steps to the front door. As I reached to put the key in the lock, I stubbed my toe. "Ouch!" I complained, tears rushing to my eyes. I pushed the door open, stumbling into the vestibule.

The sound of the soft chiming grandmother clock, in the hall, was the first thing I heard when I entered the house. I tiptoed quietly upstairs and slipped into my room. I was expecting Terren Dawn, my roommate, to be home. But to my surprise, she wasn't. "Where can she be?" I mumbled as I closed the bedroom door. "It's not like Terren to be late." Terren and I were good friends. We spent lots of our free time together. Often we would take a walk along the esplanade, our hearts filled with wonder at the indescribable panorama with the winding railway bridge as a backdrop. Or we might climb the Law. The view, from the summit was ever changing. Skies, with their different moods, always cast magical colours over the river. Heavily laden skies would foretell of imminent storms. The whole of the Tay estuary would take on a bleak greyness as the wind roared down the river causing utter turmoil on its way out to sea.

Our room was always a shambles. Textbooks were strewn all over the place. Notes and diagrams of organs we'd been studying were piled high on the desk. Hidden in a corner beside the wardrobe a laundry basket always overflowed with soiled laundry ready to be picked up by the laundry-maid, every Monday morning.

I hung my coat and hat in the wardrobe, slipped into my nightdress and took a textbook off the desk. With every intention of studying I flopped down on the bed, but the events of the past few days boggled my mind, making it absolutely impossible to concentrate.

My thoughts drifted to Annie and the thought of losing her, gave me a heavy heart. Although she was only my second cousin, we had spent every summer of our childhood together. And Catherine, an innocent little child was about to lose her mother. It didn't bear thinking about. I couldn't imagine the world without my mother in it. I was altogether lost in thought when suddenly the door flew open and in bounced Terren.

A breath of spring, is what she is. Her glossy black hair swings below her shoulders and big black eyes shine like deep mysterious pools. Her lips were so bright they almost matched her bright red Tammy. Her empathy and compassion for others made her unique. I've often thought, if I had a sister, I'd like her to be just like Terren.

"Roselyn," she gasped the moment she entered the room. "Guess what?"

"What?"

"Jerry and I got engaged! Oh, Roselyn," she breathed, "I feel as if I'm walking on a cloud. I'm so happy!" She was bubbling with excitement as she threw her coat on the bed and came toward me. "Wait till you see my ring!" she declared ripping the glove off her hand. "Well! What do you think of it?" she asked, waving her ring finger underneath my nose.

"Oh my!" I exclaimed, leaping out of bed. "It's gorgeous, absolutely gorgeous! I wish you good health to wear it, Terren. May I have a wish, on it?"

"Of course you may." She immediately removed

the ring and handed it to me. Slipping it onto the third finger of my left hand, I turned it towards my heart three times, and after making a wish I returned the ring.

"Well! What did you wish for?"

"Terren Dawn! You know better than to ask such a thing." I grinned. "Have you and Jerry set a wedding date?" I changed the subject.

"Certainly! We're getting married on the second of June. I've always wanted to be a June bride! Oh Roselyn! I can hardly wait! I can picture myself, walking down the aisle of St Paul's Cathedral to a fanfare of trumpets, God's golden sunshine streaming through the stained glass windows, reflecting all the colours of heaven on Jerry and me. Do you think I'll make a pretty bride?" she asked wistfully, admiring herself in the mirror and pulling a lock of hair down about her oval face.

"Of course you will. Why wouldn't you?" All of a sudden my arms were covered with goose bumps and an intense feeling of sadness engulfed me as I watched her. She undressed in silence and slipped into her nightie; she slung her robe over shoulders and put her outdoor clothes in the wardrobe. She came over and sat on the edge of my bed, taking my hand in hers. "Roselyn!" her husky voice spoke. "I'd like you to do me a big favour." She paused momentarily, clearing her throat and nervously biting her lip. "I'd like you to be my bridesmaid, please say you will!"

"Bridesmaid?" I gulped, eyes popping, "of course I will, I'd love to. I've always wanted to be a bridesmaid, but no one has ever asked me."

"Until now!" she chirped, cheerfully.

"That's right, until now!" I happily agreed. But the sadness within my heart persisted and I found it difficult to shake off. This should be a happy day but my feelings were of sorrow and loss.

"Jerry's going to ask Michael Young, one of his medical friends, to be best man. And we're hoping my cousin's daughter, Angela, and Jerry's nephew, Gordon, will be our flower girl and page-boy. Oh Roselyn! I can picture the little darlings, can't you? They'll be perfect for the role!" In a subdued tone she continued. "I've another favour to ask of you." She hesitated.

"Well? Out with it, out with it!" I egged her on, forcing myself to be excited for her. I took in a deep breath as a feeling of tragedy flashed through my mind, then instantly - it was gone!

"I was wondering if you'd design and sew my wedding gown? I know that you're extremely busy with finals coming up in April. But I thought perhaps your mother would help with the sewing. She's so good at those things. What do you think?"

"Why, Terren, you know I'll do it, it'll be an honour. And I can safely speak for my mother. I know she'll be tickled pink. As far as time's concerned, I'll just have to make time, won't I?" We looked at each other and burst out laughing. "What style of dress are you thinking of having?"

"Oh, I don't know. I'll leave it up to you to suggest something. I've no imagination when it comes to fashion."

We made tea and got out the biscuits and sat on the edges of our beds.

"Well, I picture you in something soft and flowing. Very elegant; high around the neck, and falling in soft folds from underneath the bust. A long train is a must and, on the waistline at the back, a huge bow to emphasise your slenderness. Similar to the style the Princess Royal wears and looks so lovely in. What do you think?"

She opened her arms wide and grinned. "It's all up to you, Roselyn!"

By the time every detail of her wedding plans had been addressed, we were exhausted.

CHAPTER

12

The Blunder

Sister Phillips, the head nurse, drew me a cutting look when I entered the ward five minutes late the following morning. She was sitting poised in a high-backed swivel chair, arms spread out, hands gripping the edge of the desk. She'd already started to brief the day staff, who, like me, were just coming on duty. They all stood to attention, their hands clasped firmly behind backs. They were gathered around her like a swarm of bees. They were listening intently to her instructions.

I squeezed between two of the nurses who had made room for me. Try as I might, I couldn't concentrate on what Sister was saying. My thoughts kept wandering to the weekend's events. I wondered what decision my parents would make about Catherine.

Sister was talking in a monotone, her voice sounding like a distant echo, as she discussed each patient's chart in great detail. Finally, she rose and proceeded to distribute duty lists to each nurse in turn.

"Nurse Carey!" she bellowed when it came my turn. "You didn't hear a word I said, did you? Isn't it enough that you were late for roll call, without standing there staring into space?" A sadistic grin came over her face as she shoved a duty list into my hand. "This should bring you down to earth."

"Thank you, Sister," I replied, and started to walk away.

"By the way, I want you to prepare Mistress Bailey's body for the morgue."

I was almost speechless, but managed to breathe out, "Certainly, Sister."

"Now don't forget to put her dentures in," she added, as I turned to walk away.

I knew it. I knew it! I knew she'd get me for being late. I hate dealing with the dead and she knows it. Still, I'll do the job well, and perhaps it'll raise my standing in her eyes. Since the first day I'd come to this ward, she had done her utmost to make my life miserable. Of course, she treated most of the other nurses in the same way, so I had no right to complain.

I hurried to the sluice, filled a basin with warm water, grabbed a wash-cloth, tucked a roll of cotton wool underneath my arm and returned to the ward. Behind white screens lay the lifeless body of Mistress Bailey, her nose pointing in the air and a new penny on each eyelid to keep her eyes closed. I hummed a tune to keep my mind off the ghastly job in hand. Once I'd stuffed all the necessary cavities with cotton wool, I sighed with relief.

"Now, where in the world are her dentures?" I mumbled, remembering Sister Phillip's instructions. I searched everywhere I could think they could possibly be. I, shook the bedcovers, looked inside the locker, and even emptied the locker drawer. "Where on earth can they be?" Suddenly, I spied them underneath the bed. "Thank heavens!" I whispered as I crawled under the bed to retrieve them. Giving them a good scrub, I quickly put them in her mouth. No sooner had I done so, than Peter, the night porter, entered the ward wheeling a stretcher.

"Ha! I see you've got her ready! Good lass!"

"Yes." I smiled, handing him a release form to sign. Together we transferred the body from the bed to the stretcher. Peter immediately threw a white cotton sheet over it and left.

Relieved that the gruesome job was over, I began to strip the bed. To my horror, when I lifted the pillows to remove the pillowcase, there, wrapped in a piece of gauze, were Mistress Bailey's dentures.

"Heavens almighty!" I gasped, "What have I done?" I lifted the parcel off the bed and discreetly slipped it into my pocket. My heart was pounding, my face flushed and my hands were shaking.

Totally puzzled, I didn't know what to do. "Now, if these are Mistress Bailey's dentures whose did I put into the corpse's mouth?"

"Wakey, wakey! Rise and shine, ladies!" the piercing voice of a first year nurse rang out as she entered the ward pushing the tea trolley. She went from bed to bed, arousing the patients with a cheerful, "Good morning, ladies!" and serving them a mug of hot tea.

Mistress Skelly, the woman in the next bed to where I had been working, was rummaging frantically through her things. She even got out of bed, shook the pillows and pulled the covers back. Finally she burst out, "Nurse Carey, you didn't happen to see my teeth, by any chance, did you? I put them on my locker, before settling down last night, and I can't find them any-where"

I froze, took in a deep breath, and in a firm tone said, "As a matter of fact, I did. I know exactly where they are, I'll fetch them."

Butterflies fluttered in my tummy. Now I would have to visit the morgue, a place I dreaded. I hurried from the ward, taking with me the soiled linen to deposit in the laundry hamper at the ward door.

I fled blindly along the corridor and skipped down the back stairs, two steps at a time, glancing over my shoulder occasionally to make sure no one saw me. The moment I stepped out into the courtyard, a strong gust of wind blew around the corner of the building, knocking me off balance and almost onto my face.

It was dark and the dimly lit walkway leading to the morgue seemed endless. Nevertheless, I continued to battle against the wind. As I approached the door, I spotted Peter. He was stooped over, fiddling with the lock. The minute he heard my footsteps, he stopped what he was doing and shone his lantern in my direction.

"Oh Peter! Peter!" I gasped rushing forward. "Thank heaven you're still here. I was afraid I might miss you."

"Why Nurse Carey!" he blurted. "What in the world are you doing down here, and without your cloak at that! For heaven's sake lass, you'll catch your death of cold."

"I'm such a fool Peter!" I sobbed, "I've gone and put the wrong dentures in the corpse's mouth. Sister Phillips will crucify me. I'll have to correct my error before she does. Oh Peter! Peter!" I burst into tears.

"Take it easy, lass, take it easy," he sympathised, taking my hand. "There's no need to get your self worked up. I'll exchange them and no one will be any the wiser. Do you have the correct set with you?"

"Yes! Yes I do!" I replied with a sniffle, fumbling in my pocket to retrieve the gauze parcel. With a shaky hand I handed it to him.

Before I knew it, we were inside the eerie building. It was black, pitch black! The strong odour of death hung heavily in the air. I put my handkerchief to my nose against the sickening smell, while Peter fumbled in his trouser pocket for a match, to light the gas mantle. I was petrified, I really don't know why I was so afraid. I've prepared lots of dead people for the morgue. I know there's no danger. But many nurses tell gruesome stories about bodies suddenly sitting up and eerie sounds coming from their mouths. I suppose I'd let my imagination run riot. It seemed an eternity before the mantle was finally lit. Distorted shadows danced on the whitewashed walls as Peter crossed the room to the marble slab, on which lay Mistress Bailey's body. He pulled the sheet back to open her mouth.

"Damn it to Hell!" he blasted, giving me a start. "I can't open her mouth. You'll have to help me nurse."

My bones rattled, my teeth chattered, as I moved to Peter's side. "Here, Nurse!" he ordered. "Press down on her chin. I'll force her upper jaw." I was shaking like a leaf. I couldn't bring myself to look at what I was doing. Nevertheless, I followed Peter's instructions.

"That's the ticket, lass!" With a jerk, he removed the dentures and replaced them with the correct ones. "There you are, Nurse Carey," he grinned, handing them to me.

"Oh Peter, Peter, you're a sweetheart!" I threw my arms about his neck, the moment we were outside the building. "Thank you! Thank you!" I danced around him. "I couldn't have done it without you!"

"Anything for a bonny lassie!" he smiled, flirtatiously. "Be off with you, before you're missed," he patted my bottom. "Now remember, Nurse! Mum's the word!" he put his forefinger to his lips.

It seemed as if I'd been gone for hours, but only

ten minutes had elapsed. I galloped up the stairs, and went straight to the sluice, scrubbed those dentures and returned to the ward.

"Here we are Mistress Skelly! I apologise for taking so long. You'll have to take better care of your things. Lucky for you, I knew where to put my hands on these!"

"Ah, Nurse Carey!" she gasped. A smile lifted the corners of her lips. "You're a sweetheart." She took the dentures from me, swirled them in a glass of water, popped them into her mouth and she declared, "That's better. Now I'll enjoy my tea."

I was quietly amused, and wondered if she'd have been so delighted had she known where they had been only moments ago.

White screens were around Mary Ann McKinley's bed, evidence that she was in serious condition.

As soon as I'd finished my tasks, I slipped behind the screens, crossed my fingers and hoped no one saw me. I was curious. I wanted to examine Mary Ann for my own satisfaction. I couldn't believe my eyes. I've seen some horrifying sights in my day, but this was by far the very worst. Her face was black and blue and swollen so badly, no one would have recognised her. I lifted the chart off the bottom of her bed and quickly scanned the page. A slight improvement had been recorded.

Morning rounds began promptly at ten o'clock, no matter what. The ward had to be spotlessly clean by then, the cleaning and polishing dutifully done by the nursing staff.

Professor Mulligan, the resident consultant, accompanied by Sister Phillips, headed the procession. Student doctors and staff nurses followed closely on their heels. One could hear a pin drop as the cavalcade paraded around the ward, stopping briefly at each bed to discuss the patient's progress, or decline, whichever the case may be. When they reached Mary Ann's bed, Professor Mulligan gathered the students around him and under his breath said, "Now, here's a young woman who would have died, if not for the excellent surgery I performed. We'll observe her closely over the next few days, and discuss her progress again at the end of the week. I'd like to remind you, that where there's life there's hope, and we're duty-bound to do everything in our power to save a life, whether we consider a case hopeless, or not. This woman is a typical example." He moved to the head of the bed and, taking Mary Ann's bandaged hand in his, asked how she was.

She peered out through swollen eyes, and in a faint little voice replied. "I'm fine, Doctor!"

As he was leaving, I overheard him telling the students he expected Mistress McKinley to be well enough to be transferred to a convalescent home in a fortnight. I couldn't believe my ears, she didn't look as if she'd be going anywhere for a long time, if ever. But he's the specialist, he should know.

Later that day, I was on my way to the sluice when Sister Phillips intercepted me. "Nurse Carey!" she touched my arm. "There's someone at the reception who wishes to see you."

"Someone to see me?"

"Yes, madam, to see you. And you know perfectly well you're not allowed visitors. However, it might be important. You have my permission to go down and find out. Just finish what you're doing and take ten minutes."

I sped along the corridor as soon as I was free, quickly running downstairs. "Perhaps it's Allan," I thought. "No, it won't be Allan. He'd never come to the hospital. When I entered the waiting room, I was surprised to see my mother. She rose from the chair and crossed the room.

"Roselyn!" she stuttered, reaching out to take my hands. "I hope you're not angry with me? I'd some errands to run in the town, so I took the opportunity to come talk to you.

"Mother!" I snapped, interrupting her. "You know perfectly well I'm not allowed visitors."

"Yes, I know, but this'll only take a minute, I didn't think you'd mind! I wanted you to know we're taking Catherine." Tears teetered on her eyelids as she spoke. "We're not adopting her though" she spluttered, "we've decided to be her legal guardians."

I could tell she was excited and that she was looking for my support. I regretted having jumped down her throat.

"That's wonderful news, Mother!" I said, squeezing her hands. "Have you told Annie yet?"

"Father has written, to both Annie and Jim, explaining our reasons for not wanting to adopt Catherine. But letting them know we'll be happy to take her when the time comes."

"Good! I'm sure you've made the right decision. But why aren't you adopting her?"

"Well! We think it's important for her to keep her own family, to be part of her background - don't you agree?"

"Yes! Yes, I do! You're right! By the way, I've some exciting news too. Terren and Jerry got engaged, and plan on getting married in June. And you'll never guess."

"What?" Her eyes grew wide.

"Terren asked me to be her bridesmaid."

"You said you would, I hope?"

"Of course! I'll write later in the week, giving you all the details. I must fly, Sister Phillips will persecute me all day if I'm not back soon."

"Oh, don't tell me that woman's still giving you a hard time?"

"She certainly is!" I glanced at my watch, as I bent to kiss her brow. "Oh, I almost forgot to ask about Jenny? What did she have?"

"Dear, oh dear, Roselyn, I was hoping you wouldn't ask. She gave birth to a lovely baby boy last night. He weighed in at nine pounds eight ounces."

"Wonderful."

A sorrowful look came over her, "Roselyn, the baby could be retarded. Doctor Scott said he won't know for certain for about a year."

"Retarded?" I couldn't believe my ears. "I suppose the prolonged labour had a lot to do with it?"

"Exactly! The doctor had to perform an emergency Caesarean operation. He told me the umbilical cord was slowly strangling the baby. Poor wee soul! Oh Roselyn!" she gasped. "I could never be a nurse! All that blood."

"How's Jenny taking it?"

"Oh, you'd be sorry for her. She is devastated. Tam's not helping the situation. He told her they'd have to place the baby into an institution. If she doesn't obey his wishes, he's going to leave home. Needless to say, Jenny's fit to be tied."

"Oh, I can just imagine."

"She puts a lot of faith in you, Roselyn. She said she'd love to have a talk with you. Get some advice from you. I told her you wouldn't be home till the end of the month. That's right, isn't it?"

"Yes, unfortunately. But tell her I'll write. I really must go now, Mother." I kissed her brow and left.

I stopped in at the duty office, where Gus was sitting quietly at his desk doing some paper work. Poking my head through the office window, I whispered, "Hello there, Gus." not realising I might startle him.

"Oh! My goodness, Nurse Carey! What a fleg you gave me! What brings you down here?"

"Oh, it's a long story Gus! I thought you'd like to know I checked on Mary Ann this morning. She's going to be all right."

"Thanks be to God! I've never stopped praying since she had the accident. Come to think of it, it wasn't an accident, was it? It was assault. I'll take a run up to see her before I leave. Thanks for bringing the good news, Nurse."

Sister Phillips was standing outside the ward door waiting for me to return, her arms folded over her large bosom and a scowl on her plump face. "Well, well, well! So you finally decided to come back?" She snarled as I approached. "You've overstepped it this time, madam," she said, eyes red with anger. "How dare you abuse a privilege? It's Matron's office for you." She grabbed me by the scruff of the neck and pushed me along the corridor towards Matron's office. I was so humiliated.

"But Sister Phillips." I protested.

"Don't 'Sister Phillips' me, Nurse."

"Oh, please, Sister, I beg you! I'll do anything you ask. But please, please, don't have me reprimanded by Matron! I apologise for taking so long, but my mother brought some good news and I lost all track of time."

She stopped abruptly, looking me in the eye. "So we're afraid of Matron, are we? Sounds like you've been rebuked by her before."

"Oh, no! I haven't, honestly! But I'll do anything to keep a clean record."

She hesitated, considering my plea. In the most authoritative manner, she said. "Very well! There'll be no time off for you, till the middle of March." She shoved me towards the ward. "Now, get back to work and let's have no more of your insolence."

I was livid! That would mean I wouldn't see Allan till then. My first impulse was to run as far as I could. That wouldn't have solved anything. So I swallowed my pride and obeyed her.

The days that followed flew by. I was engulfed by work during the day and my studies in the evening. By the end of each day, I was only fit to collapse on my bed exhausted. My life revolved around my work and I tried to meet every challenge with a positive attitude. But there were times when I wondered how long I could endure the pace.

One evening towards the end of February, I opened a letter I'd received from Allan.

Dear Roselyn,

Seems like forever since you were home. I've missed you terribly! Many things have taken place this week. I don't know where to start. First, let me tell you the bad news. My Granny's suffered another stroke. She was taken to St Andrews General, on Sunday. It doesn't look good. The doctor attending her gives the family no hope of recovery. I know this news will sadden you, sweetheart, but you must be brave! Now, the good news! I've applied for a position with International Times, in London. I submitted details of my qualifications to the editor and hope for an interview. The position, Assistant Editor, was advertised in last week's paper.

Of course, we'll have to discuss the probability of me having to move to London – something we're not going to enjoy. But it would only be for a short time. As soon as I get settled, I hope you'll join me.

I was speaking to your mother in the newsagent's the other day. She was telling me about their plans to take Catherine. She sounded extremely enthusiastic. She seems to be resigned to the idea of having a five-year-old underfoot.

Let me know when you're getting some time off and I'll come to Dundee to accompany you home. I'm longing to hold you in my arms, Roselyn! You are my life, and without you my world's an empty place.
Love, Allan.

The news about Granny Ethel made me so sad. Even though she hadn't been well for several years, it was still a shock. I fell asleep on top of the bed, clutching the letter in my hand.

I'd arranged to take two days off work, from the sixteenth of March, to accompany my parents to visit Annie. Of course, I was also excited and looking forward to tea with the minister.

At last the day of freedom dawned. At half-past three in the afternoon I signed off duty and ran all the way up the hill to my lodgings. Totally out of breath I stepped into the house!

In the bedroom I was surprised to find Terren lying fully dressed on her bed. She was fast asleep. "Terren. Terren! Wake up, Terren!" I roused her with a shake. "You're supposed to be on duty in ten minutes. Terren! Waken up!" Slowly, her eyes opened, and in a hoarse voice, she whimpered,

"Oh Roselyn. I think I'm coming down with

influenza. Would you write a note for the office? I'll sign it. Perhaps you could drop it off on your way to the train station?"

"Of course. Let's get you out of those clothes and into bed." I undressed her, and slipped a fresh nightie over her head. Then I went directly to the kitchen, and made her a hot lemon and honey.

"Here, drink this down!" I ordered, handing her the cup. "This'll sweat it out, and I'll be back Sunday evening before nine. Let's hope you're much improved." She sipped on the drink and by the time I was ready to leave, she was fast asleep again.

CHAPTER
13

Visiting Annie

llan was waiting at the gate when I stepped out of the house. His eyes shone with delight and he beamed the moment he saw me. It had been over a month since I'd had time off and more than a week since I'd received the bad news about his granny.

"You look wonderful Roselyn." he sighed, giving me a big hug. He slipped his arm around my shoulder and hurried me down the brae. I dropped Terren's note off at the office and we continued down the hill to the railway station.

"I had forgotten how lovely you are," he smiled contentedly.

"I'm happy to see you too, Allan. What's this?" I asked, pinching his waistline. "You've lost weight. What on earth have you been doing to yourself?"

"Well! I've had a ton of work to get through and with running back and forth to the hospital to see Granny, I haven't had time to myself, and no time to eat."

"Oh, Allan! I'm so sorry! Of course you haven't!

How is your granny? Has there been any improvement?" Sorrowfully, he looked me in the eye. "She'll never get better, you know, Roselyn. It's only a matter of time now." He was choking on the words. "Visiting has been restricted to family members. Unfortunately, you won't get in to see her. Just as well. It's better for you to remember her as she was. Oh God, Roselyn!" He burst into tears. "I'm going to miss her terribly." His voice trailed away in a muffled sob.

I didn't know what to say. I'd never seen Allan in such a state before. I put my arm around him and gave him a squeeze. "I know you're going to miss her, Allan, I know you are."

We sat on the train to Tayport in silence, holding hands.

When we arrived in Tayport, we walked along the shore to West Lights. A ray of sun broke through the clouds and died almost instantly. The sky quickly became covered in heavy black clouds and it turned out to be a miserable grey evening. We walked in silence. There was no need for us to talk.

My parents were delighted to have me home after such a long absence. It was a wonderful feeling to be home. We chattered back and forth catching up on all the latest gossip. Mother must have been up all night baking. The table was laden with all my favourite pastries. I had to discipline myself not to eat too much.

Allan tarried a while, not leaving until well after ten o'clock. When we kissed goodnight, in the hallway, he promised he'd escort me back to Dundee on Sunday evening.

My parents and I were up at the crack of dawn next morning in order to catch the half past seven train to Dunfermline. It left from Wormit, a two and a half-mile walk from our house.

We arrived at Jim's house a little before nine o'clock. It was a row house typical of those in all the mining towns of Fife. Before Father could ring the bell, Jim flung the door wide open. "Come in! Come in!" he welcomed us with open arms.

"Annie's been on heckle-pins all morning waiting for you to arrive!"

The mouth-watering aroma of ham soup wafted the moment Jim opened the door. He ushered us to the kitchen, where Annie was propped up in the recessed bed, mounds of pillows behind her head. There was a faint flush of excitement on her otherwise pale and gaunt face.

When we had entered the room, the antique brass ornaments on the mantelpiece caught my eye. They shone with the brightness of a new pin. It was obvious Annie was a meticulous housekeeper.

A glimmer of light flickered in her sunken eyes as she opened out her arms to greet us. "Aunt Liz! Roselyn!" She gasped, taking our hands, "it's so good of you to come." We embraced her gently by kissing her brow and pulled chairs over to sit at the bedside.

"Ahhhh! If it's not my favourite uncle!" she chuckled softly at Father. He gave her a big hug and spoke a few words of affection to her. She started to sob. Father, plainly didn't know what to do and quickly spluttered out, "I suppose I'd better give your father a hand, otherwise I'll never hear the end of it."

Jim served morning rolls spread thickly with butter, a good old cheese and, of course, a strong cup of tea. When we had finished eating, Jim asked Father to join him on his daily walk. "I've Annie's medicine to collect from the chemist and if we take our time, we can meet Catherine and accompany her home from school. She'll like that." He slipped into his jacket, put on his bonnet and turning to Annie, said, "I know you girls have lots to discuss."

As soon as they had gone, Annie sighed, "Thank heavens Father had sense to give us some time to ourselves." Poor Annie. Her coughing made it difficult for her to carry on an uninterrupted conversation. "I want to take this chance to talk about Catherine's future, Aunt Liz." The moment she mentioned Catherine's name, Annie burst into tears. "Oh, Aunt Liz! Aunt Liz!" she sobbed. "Life's so unfair, isn't it?" There was a note of anger in her weak voice - and no wonder!

Mother got up and cradled Annie in her arms. "It certainly is, pet, it certainly is. There's no doubt about it. Here, take this." She handed Annie a handkerchief with which she wiped her tears.

"I'd so many wonderful plans for my wee Catherine," she sobbed, "I've been saving up since the day she was born to give her a good education, so she could make something of herself." She choked and couldn't say any more. Tears trickled down the crevices of her cheeks, dropping one by one, like tiny pearls, onto the soft eiderdown.

I dried her face with my handkerchief, then fluffed up her pillows to make her more comfortable. "Would you like me to brush your hair, Annie?" I asked.

She smiled softly, nodding approval. She handed me the hairbrush. "Would you plait it please, Roselyn? It's much easier to keep when it's in a plait." As I was brushing her hair, she and Mother continued their delicate conversation.

"Now listen, Pet," Mother said, "whatever you want us to do for Catherine, just let us know. We'll gladly do whatever it is you want."

"I know you will, Aunt Liz! I know you will! My main concern is that she gets a good education. That's the one thing I truly want for her."

"Well lass, you can put your mind at rest. I promise we'll do that. Meantime, how would you like us to take her every other weekend now? It would give her the opportunity to get to know us. Your poor father could do with a good rest. What do you think?"

"Aunt Liz, whatever you want to arrange is all right with me. As you say, my father would get a rest. So would I, for that matter. I love Catherine, with all my heart, but, oh dear, oh dear, she doesn't half tire me out these days. Yes, Aunt Liz! It's a wonderful idea!"

"Well! Now that's settled, how would you like a nice cup of tea?" Annie's eyes lit up. All her worries had been resolved. Now she could relax.

"I thought you'd never ask," she answered jokingly. "I'd love a cup of tea."

"How is Allan, Roselyn?" Annie inquired, when Mother had gone to put the kettle on.

"Oh, he's very well. Working away like mad, as always. He sends his love, of course. Oh! By the by, he asked me to give you this." I rummaged in my bag for the envelope and gave it to her.

"What is it?" she exclaimed, ripping the envelope open and slowly removing the card. "Oh, my goodness, would you look at this?" she gasped. "Did Allan do the painting?"

"Yes. He did. And he did it just for you! It's his impression of a summer sunset on the River Tay. He wrote a poem for you, Annie. It's inside the card." I reached over and opened the card.

"Will you read it to me please, Roselyn!"

"Of course." I coughed to clear my throat.

'Once there was a rosebud
Growing on a vine
Happily it grew into
A Rose so fine
But alas, the day came
When God plucked the rose
He put it in His garden
Where it ever grows.'

She held the card to her heart, not able to speak. "Tell Allan it's beautiful, Roselyn. Absolutely beautiful!" I reached over and squeezed her hand. There was no need for words.

"Have you and Allan made wedding plans yet?" she asked when composed.

"Heavens, no! He hasn't even proposed yet. Well, not properly." I answered bashfully, raising my brows. We burst out laughing.

I told a couple of hospital jokes, to cheer her up. Her weak laughter will remain in my memory until the day I die.

"Here we are!" Mother said cheerfully, setting the tray on Annie's lap. After a sip, Annie's eyes widened, and with a twinkle in her eye, she uttered, "Oh, you've been up to your old tricks again, haven't you, Aunt Liz?"

"Of course! It's spiked with a nip of brandy. Now drink it down. Drink it down, it'll do you the world of good."

We talked quietly about everything under the sun to keep Annie's spirits high. When she'd finished the tea, Mother removed the tray and Annie flopped back against the pillows and gave a sigh.

The soft chiming of the clock on the mantelpiece struck twelve. Five minutes later, the door flew open and in burst Catherine, cheeks glowing, hair windswept to a fluffy mess. She made a beeline for Annie's bed, dropping her satchel, gloves, and hat on the way. She flung herself into her adoring mother's arms. My heart ached as I watched the pair embracing.

"Say hello to your Aunt Liz and Roselyn! They've come a long way to visit us," Annie told her.

Catherine didn't raise her head, but gave a muffled hello into her mother's bosom.

"She's not as shy as she'd have you believe," Annie told us. "There's no holding her back once she gets going. She's quite the social lady when she wants to be one." Annie was bursting with pride.

"My mother's dying, you know!" Catherine announced, raising her head. I could've strangled her! I looked at Annie sorrowfully. She lifted her head and gazed into my eyes, weakly shrugging her shoulders.

Jim put a tureen of ham and pea soup in the centre of the table and beside it a plate of fresh bread. "Come on then, lad and lasses," he gestured. "Enjoy the soup while it's nice and hot."

On a tray, he set Annie's dinner, and in a vase a single rose completed the setting. A faint smile flickered over her ashen face and her sunken eyes looked adoringly into her father's.

"Now, you mind your manners, Miss," he said to Catherine, as he took his place at the table. "Don't be giving your mother and me a showing up."

We kept the conversation light and airy, throwing in the odd joke here and there. Annie was always included in the conversation.

Following the soup, Jim served a generous helping of Eve's pudding smothered with pouring custard. I love Eve's pudding.

Mother and Father had seconds of everything. No wonder they were putting on weight. I didn't have as much, I wanted to watch my waistline.

"Good heavens! Look at the time," Jim said suddenly, glancing at the clock. "We'd better get moving or you'll be late for school, Catherine. That'll never do, will it?" he teased as he popped her hat atop her head.

Catherine was reluctant to leave but Mother assured her she'd be coming to visit us soon. She was clearly tickled pink at that idea, bless her little heart. She ran over to the bed and gave her mother a hug. She left all smiles, hand in hand with her grandfather and her Uncle Larry.

I cleared the table and washed and dried the dishes, while Mother sat quietly chatting with Annie. When the men returned, we indulged in another cup of tea and a wedge of cream sponge.

Our visit with Annie was short but sweet. All too soon it was time to say good-bye. We were well aware that it could be the last time we'd see her alive. That made it even harder to tear ourselves away.

We had left Jim's in plenty time to catch the two o'clock train from Dunfermline back to Wormit.

When we arrived back it was still and the sun shone, so we decided to walk home along the riverbank. The grass verges along the way were lined with crocuses in a multitude of colours. How lovely it was. Mother and Father were exhausted by the time we arrived home and went directly upstairs to their room to rest.

Not in the least bit tired, I was anxious to see Jenny's baby. I quickly ran a brush through my hair, put a little cream on my lips and splashed rose-water all over my neck and wrists. That felt better. My shortcut to Jenny's was a quick leap over the garden fence.

She seemed delighted to see me. "Why, Roselyn, come in, come in." She welcomed me with a beaming smile and taking my hand, led me to the wicker basket that was sitting close to the fireplace. The baby, wrapped in a white lacy shawl was asleep.

"Oh Jenny, he's beautiful!"

"Isn't he, though? He's just perfect, so he is."

Leaning over, I put a new half crown into his tiny hand. "What are you going to name him?"

"Kenneth James, after Tam's father." Then sadly she declared, "Aren't looks so deceiving, Roselyn?"

Lost for words, all I could do was pat the back of her hand.

"Would you like a cup of tea, Roselyn?" she asked, perking up and wiping a tear from her eye.

"Sounds wonderful!" She scurried off to the kitchen. I stood at the basket watching Kenneth as he slept peacefully. He looked perfectly normal to me. Jenny returned presently, cups and saucers and tea pot, milk and sugar all set out on a nice tray. She placed this down on a small table and went out again, to return with a plate of fruit cake.

"Oh Jenny! If you only knew how much I need this nice cup of tea," I said, as she handed me a cup.

"Me, too," she sighed. "I'm so thankful to you for taking the time to come over, Roselyn. I know how busy you are. I've been longing to have a chat with you. But first, let me thank you for writing. Your kind words certainly gave me strength."

I sat, sipping the tea, nibbling on fruit cake, while Jenny poured her heart out.

"What would you advise me to do, Roselyn?" she asked at last. "Tam won't have anything whatsoever to do with Kenneth. He hasn't laid eyes on the poor wee soul since the day he was born. He said the imbecile - that's what he calls Kenneth - will have to be placed in an institution. And if I don't abide by his wishes, he's going to leave home." She covered her face with her hands and burst out crying. Tears escaped through her fingers, trickled down her arms and dripped off her elbows.

I realised that anything I might have said at that precise moment would be falling on deaf ears. I sat quietly on the arm of her chair and put my arm around her. "There! There! Jenny! Try to be brave. No one knows for certain if Kenneth's brain-damaged. Doctor Scott was compelled to let you know there's the possibility. Everything will work out, I'm sure."

She raised her head and, looking me straight in the eye, asked, "What would you do, if you were me?" She had put me on the spot and was anxiously waiting for a reply.

"I honestly don't know what I'd do. I pray to God I'm never put to the test. But given the facts, I think I'd wait and see; as far as Tam's concerned, keep him at a distance for a few weeks. Perhaps he needs time to get used to the idea Kenneth may be 'different'. I'm sure he'll come around, Jenny. And who knows, he might even grow to love little Kenneth. Miracles do happen, you know."

She wiped her face with the crumpled handkerchief she'd been fidgeting with, and after pondering what I'd said for a few moments, with a quivering lip said, "You know, you might be right, Roselyn."

By the time I left she was in a much happier frame of mind, laughing and joking as she ushered me to the door.

Mother and Father didn't attend church that Sunday morning. They were too overwrought from the ordeal of the day before. Allan came over to accompany me to church. He wasn't happy with the idea of me having to go alone. It was a brilliant sunny day, typical of the time of year, but there was still a nip in the air.

Very often our church was half-empty, but that Sunday it was packed full. Perhaps the lovely weather was responsible for the good turnout.

CHAPTER
14

Tea
At The Manse

Allan and I took a slow walk home after church. We were full of joy, invigorated by the glorious sunshine. We picked up pebbles and found that we still had the knack of skimming them along the water's surface.

After a light dinner of cold ham and bread, we sat quietly on the window seat watching ships sailing up the channel and entering the Dundee harbour. Gulls squealed as they dove into the river, to soar heavenwards with mouths full of fish. Further along the shore, a group of schoolboys was playing football on the grassy embankment. They were having a wonderful time by the sound of their shouting and yelling.

To join the minister for tea I wore my red coat, with matching hat, and a pale pink floral dress. I was so excited. "What an honour to receive an invitation to tea with the minister." I whispered to myself.

Allan accompanied me to the manse, leaving me at the gate. As he bent to kiss me he assured me he'd be back for me at four o'clock sharp.

I was curiously nervous when I pulled the gleaming brass pull-bell. While waiting for the door to be answered, I took the opportunity to admire the cultured garden abundant with crocuses poking their little heads up through the soil. Daffodils, I thought, would soon be replacing the brave little winter soldiers. The grey granite house, sparkling in the sunlight, seemed to be in good condition, despite widespread rumours it was much in need of repair. The leaded windows glittered.

The door swung open. And there, dressed in a light grey pullover, pale blue open-necked shirt and charcoal flannels, stood Mister Valente.

My mouth almost fell open at the sight of him. I could hardly believe my eyes. I didn't expect the minister dressed in such casual attire. I'd only ever seen him in formal clothes. I'd always seen him as an angel from heaven in church and had no idea he was so masculine. My heart began to beat rapidly the moment I first saw him!

. "Roselyn, I'm delighted to see you. Welcome to my humble abode." He bowed, gesturing with a sway of his arm. "My, you do look lovely in red," he said as I stepped into the vestibule. He helped me out of my coat and hung it on the coat rack. He took my hand and led me into the magnificent entrance hall, with its beautifully carved oak staircase.

"Patty's delighted you accepted my invitation. She's always happy when I have guests. She loves to entertain."

"That's nice." I said for something to say.

"We only do it occasionally."

I was taken aback when he slipped his arm around my shoulders, to usher me into the living room. He made me feel so important.

French windows looked out to the picturesque garden with its beautiful ornamental fishpond. On the opposite side of the room a rugged stone fireplace embraced a welcoming fire. Red and yellow flames leaped in chaos, disappearing up the chimney.

"Come, sit by the fire, Roselyn," he suggested, and tucked a soft velvet cushion behind my back as I sat in the chair. I could hardly contain myself. My eyes followed him as he moved about. I felt dwarfed sitting in the massive easy chair. He brought a footstool, and lifting my dangling legs rested my feet on it. He sat in a high-backed, Queen Anne chair, on the opposite side of the hearth. Our eyes met and for a split second his eyes held mine. He smiled softly. I blushed feeling a little self-conscious. But, oh, how I was enjoying the attention he showered upon me.

No sooner had we settled, than the living room door swung open, and in bounced a smiling, rather short and round woman in her early thirties. Light brown wispy hair straggled over her forehead, and a pair of horn-rimed spectacles teetered at the end of her pug nose. She carried a large tray, upon which a waist-expanding selection was laid out. Mister Valente had talked about her cooking a few weeks before. Pancakes, scones, strawberry jam and fresh cream.

"Roselyn, I'd like you to meet my sister, Patty," he said, rising from his chair. She put the groaning tray down on the coffee table. "Patty, this is Roselyn."

"I'm delighted to meet you, Roselyn," she said, shaking my hand vigorously. "You'll have to excuse me for a moment, I forgot to bring the milk." She stepped out the room, closing the door quietly behind her. The minister immediately lifted the teapot and proceeded to pour the tea.

"I'll do that, Ralph." Patty blurted out the moment she re-entered the room with the missing jug of milk. "My brother's been excited for days at the thought of you coming for tea. If he's told me once, he's told me a dozen times, how pretty you are. If you'll permit me to say so, he wasn't exaggerating." She smiled softly, as she handed me a cup of tea. "Let me get a little side table to put that on." She crossed the room and brought over a small table and set it in front of me. "There, that'll be better than trying to balance everything on your lap," she said, offering me the cake stand.

"My goodness! Everything looks so delicious, I don't know what to choose." Deciding on the raisin scone, I topped it with strawberry jam.

"I'll leave you to enjoy each other's company," Patty said with a twinkle in her eye, "but I'll pop in to say goodbye before you leave, Roselyn." She crossed the room and closed the door quietly.

I knew that Patty thought I was there for a strictly social visit. Perhaps I was wrong.

Not knowing quite where to begin, I blurted out "I've come specifically to seek your advice about something that's been bothering me for quite some time, Mister Valente." I nervously swallowed a mouth full of tea.

"Please, call me Ralph, Roselyn!" He smiled encouragingly. "And what is it that's bothering you, my dear?"

"Well, Ralph, I believe our house is haunted. A ghost visits from time to time. Oddly enough, it only comes when I'm home alone. When I try to discuss it with my parents, they flatly refuse to listen to me. They become extremely angry when I mention the supernatural. 'It's all in your mind!' they'll say, but I know it isn't. I thought, if I brought my problem to you, you'd give me a logical explanation, and advise me what to do."

He was evidently surprised. He seemed to be thinking as he fingered his chin. "Well, unless I know more of the details, it's difficult to give you advice. There are many troubled spirits roaming the earth, you know. When a ghost, as you put it, hangs around, there's usually a good reason. Sometimes it's because the person doesn't realise they have died. They carry on as if they're still living on this earth. It's also possible the spirit has unfinished business on earth. Your parents, could have the house exorcised."

"The house exorcised." I swallowed. "Heavens no! They'd never agree to that!"

"Well, you could have it done when they're out. It is, after all, your problem. It's you who hears the ghost."

"Oh no! No, no! I couldn't do such a thing, they'd never forgive me."

"Well then, you'll have to make sure you're never home alone. It strikes me though, Roselyn, you're the reason the spirit's there, in the first place."

"What?" I couldn't believe what he had said. "And why would I be the reason the spirit's there?"

"That's what you'll have to find out. When you do, you'll know how to deal with it." He got up and poured another cup of tea for me. "Perhaps it's someone who used to live in your house. It could be a spirit who's trying to communicate with you, for one reason or another. Meantime, let's relax, and enjoy what's left of the afternoon." He smiled shyly.

He brought a chair over and sat close beside me, taking my hand in his. I was flabbergasted. I froze to the spot. My first reaction was to pull my hand away, but somehow I didn't. I didn't want to. I wanted him to keep holding my hand. I felt the strong magnetism of this man and I was powerless to resist him.

"Roselyn," he said, his voice deep and husky with emotion, "you must be aware that I've admired you for quite some time."

"Yes, I know. I mean ... I don't know what I mean. I am very confused. I have thought you were looking at me closely in church, from time to time. But until this very moment, I wasn't sure."

"I was thrilled, that Sunday, when you requested an appointment with me. I couldn't believe my luck. I wasn't mistaken when I thought you were holding my gaze in church, was I, Roselyn? You were, weren't you?"

I was thoroughly embarrassed. I looked down to my hands, trying to hide my burning cheeks. But I couldn't lie to him. "Yes Ralph, I was," I whispered. "I didn't think you had noticed me."

"Didn't think I had noticed you? How could I not notice?" he laughed. "I can't keep my eyes off you when you are sitting in the pew, a vision of loveliness."

"I apologise, Ralph! I didn't mean anything by it. Honestly I didn't! It's just, well you look ... I thought .... Oh, never mind!" I got all tongue-tied trying to talk my way out of the situation.

He sighed, squeezing my hands while looking into my eyes. "I've got two tickets for The Beggar's Opera, playing at the Opera House in Glasgow. I'd be most honoured if you'd join me, Roselyn. The performance is a week on Saturday," he stuttered out nervously, "please say you'll accompany me."

My heart was fluttering at the idea of Mister Valente inviting me to the opera. I must admit, there had been many occasions when I had thought he was gazing at me in church. But I had dismissed the idea immediately. I could've sworn he had been flirting with me a few weeks before. Now I knew he had been.

My mouth dried up and drawing in my breath, I answered graciously, "It's kind of you to invite me, Ralph, and with all my heart, I wish I could accept your invitation. You must know I have a boyfriend."

"Yes, I know! I noticed him at church with you this morning. Allan Robertson, isn't it? I'm told you've known him since you were a child. Is it true?"

"Yes! Yes it is! I met him my first day at school. I was five years old."

"What a lucky, lucky man! But surely you realise that what you and Allan have is only puppy love; that's not real love, Roselyn."

My head dropped and I blushed to the core. My heart was beating so loudly Ralph must have heard it.

"Oh Roselyn, Roselyn!" he gasped. "If only you knew how much I desire you, how much I want you! I have endless, sleepless nights, just thinking about you. Dreaming! Holding you in my arms. Making passionate love to you." He hesitated, and blushed. "Please, forgive me for this outburst, but I just had to convey my feelings to you, otherwise I think I'd go crazy. I want you to know, if you ever break it off with Allan Robertson, please, please, consider me! I could offer you a beautiful life." He was kneeling at my feet, imploring me.

Speechless, I sat quietly still holding his hand, waiting for his next move. The feeling I had inside was so overpowering I could have jumped with joy.

He got up and bent over me and circled me in his arms. He kissed me softly. I responded to his kisses with alarming enthusiasm as he kissed me again and again. "Oh Ralph! Ralph!" I gasped, not knowing how to contain my joy. My whole body was trembling.

"Forgive me Roselyn! I didn't mean to upset you, Roselyn, dearest! Please forgive me!"

"No need to apologise, Ralph. I understand, really I do. I got carried away too. If things were different, I'd gladly accept your invitation to the opera." As I said the words, I knew I meant them with my whole heart.

"Sh. sh." He put his forefinger to my lips. We gazed into each other's eyes, momentarily, as if we had just made a vow. We broke apart and I said I felt it was time to leave. He coughed, covering his mouth with his hand and instantly changed the subject. We talked about the lovely weather as he escorted me to the door.

Patty came rushing to the hall when she heard our voices. "It was lovely meeting you, Roselyn," she smiled shaking my hand. "I hope I'll be seeing lots more of you."

It had been a most pleasant afternoon sitting talking quietly to Ralph, the glow of the fire flickering on our faces. Part of me wanted to stay forever but my loyalty to Allan made me feel I had to escape from the intense feelings that had engulfed us.

"The invitation to the opera still stands, if you care to change your mind, Roselyn," Ralph said, as he helped me into my coat. I couldn't answer. Then he quietly closed the door.

I couldn't believe what had just happened. I was distraught at my behaviour, but I couldn't control those powerful feelings. I was absolutely enthralled with Ralph's overtures and for the first time in my life, I felt like a woman.

Allan accompanied me to Dundee, as promised. Pangs of guilt jabbed my heart, as I remembered what had taken place at the manse. To think I had been overjoyed with Ralph's advances made me feel even worse. I had to admit I had enjoyed every minute, now I felt guilty. But I kept it to myself. The least said, soonest mended. What had happened between us had been wonderful, but I was determined that my feelings for Ralph would not change my feelings for Allan.

Hand in hand, Allan and I strolled along the esplanade. I couldn't imagine life without him. Everything was wonderful when we were together, and life was bright and sweet. Of course there would be losses and sorrows in the future, but no matter, it was a beautiful, beautiful world.

My room was in darkness when I arrived at the Terrace. I fumbled for a match to light the gas mantle. A movement startled me. Terren moaned, pulling the covers over her head.

"Is that you, Roselyn?" she asked softly.

"Yes, it's me, Terren," I answered wearily, putting my things in the wardrobe, "I'm sorry if I disturbed you. Are you feeling any better?"

Pulling herself up she leaned on her elbow and cupped her face in her hand. "I feel much better. I stayed in bed as you ordered, and Jerry made sure I didn't starve to death."

"Good. You certainly sound much better. Would you like a cup of cocoa and a piece of toast?"

"Oh, yes, please. Sounds as if that's just what I need!"

I undressed, slipped into my nightie, slung my dressing gown over my shoulders and went directly to the kitchen to make toast and cocoa.

When I returned, I sat on the edge of Terren's bed and laid the tray on her lap.

Sipping cocoa and nibbling toast, I brought her up to date with all my latest news - well, not quite all.

"Oh! I nearly forgot, Allan sketched some ideas I had for your wedding gown. Just wait till you see them!" I smiled, happily, handing her the pad.

"Goodness!" she gasped, eyes sparkling with delight. "What a fantastic selection. I'd no idea you'd give me such a fabulous choice."

She flipped through the pages again and again, biting her lip indecisively. "It's a choice between these two." She pointed out her choices. "What do you think?"

"You'd look lovely in either of them! But you already know my opinion. I prefer the style the Princess wears. Very sophisticated! That would be my choice."

"Then it's settled. The swan-necked style it will be."

CHAPTER
15

Granny's Funeral

S ister Phillips was on the rampage next morning, ranting and raving like a maniac. One of the pinkies (a junior nurse) had spilt a bucket of water on the floor. Sister was furious. She called the poor lass a dimwit in front of the other nurses. I sympathised with the girl and knew how humiliated she was, having once had a similar accident myself. The girl was so embarrassed, she ran out of the ward crying, covering her face with her apron.

"Well, don't just stand there looking at it, Nurse Carey." Sister barked. "Mop it up!"

I had often wondered what made Sister Phillips what she was. She was an absolute villain with the nurses. Yet, a more compassionate, loving nurse to the patients one couldn't wish to find. We nurses were convinced she was mad and in desperate need of mental treatment and should have been in an asylum. Unfortunately none of us knew how to approach the situation.

Later that day, when I was coming from the sluice carrying a basin of water, Sister came hurrying after me. "Nurse Carey," she gasped, "this telegram just arrived for you."

I thanked her, slipped the envelope into my pocket and continued with my work.

As soon as I had a free moment, I ripped the envelope open and read the contents:

GRANNY DIED 10 PM MONDAY. FUNERAL AT DUNDEE EASTERN CEMETERY 1 PM FRIDAY. ALLAN

A sharp jab of pain pierced my heart. The telegram fell to the floor as I ran to the lavatory. Blinded with tears, I locked myself in a stall.

"Nurse Carey! Nurse Carey! Are you all right in there?" Sister called, banging on the door. But I ignored her overtures and continued to cry.

"I asked if you're all right Nurse?" She continued to batter on the door. "Open this door at once!" she shouted sounding thoroughly exasperated.

I wiped my eyes and blew my nose. I pulled myself together and opened the door.

"You dropped this!" she said, waving the envelope under my nose. "I took the liberty of reading the contents. I'm sorry your grandmother has passed away. Please accept my condolences. Nevertheless, you're not paid to sit on the lavatory in a state of disarray. Return to work at once! Mistress Smith's in need of a bedpan."

I could've screamed. But I swallowed my pride and continued with my duties for the rest of the day, my heart breaking.

Next morning, as I was on my way to the duty office to sign in, I collided with Gus in the lobby. "My goodness, Nurse Carey, you're in an awful hurry! Is someone chasing you?"

"No! But there will be if I'm late for roll call."

He quickly nipped into the office and put the register on the window ledge for me to sign.

"By the way, how's your sister, Gus?" I asked out of politeness. His mood changed drastically.

"Sister! If you're referring to Mary Ann McKinley, she's no sister of mine! Oh! I beg your pardon, Nurse, I shouldn't have spoken that way to you. I don't suppose you've heard the latest news?"

"Latest news?"

"The sleekit wee rat has run away with her fancy man!"

"Oh no!"

"Oh yes! And would you believe it, he's the one who tried to take her life? Between you and me, Nurse, she'd better keep on running, because if Alex McKinley gets his hands on her, he'll bloody well strangle her."

Gus was seething. I regretted having made the inquiry. Without being rude I politely excused myself and made a hasty departure.

After morning briefings, Sister took me aside. "Nurse Carey," she spoke softly under her breath. "As you're aware, it's against hospital rules to get time off to attend a funeral, other than immediate family of course. However, I realise how upset you are over the death of your grandmother. I know exactly how you feel, having lost my own a month ago."

"But Sister Phi ..."

"Will you please be quiet, and allow me to finish? I've decided to stretch the rules and give you permission to attend the funeral. Now, try to get ahead of your duties before Friday and I'll cover for you for an hour."

"You will?" I couldn't believe what I was hearing. "Thank you very much, Sister."

She stomped off leaving me dumbfounded. I nearly let slip it wasn't my grandmother. But I shut my mouth and said nothing.

Friday dawned sunny and bright. Unfortunately squalls were blowing up the firth, bringing with them dark clouds and spoiling the hope of uninterrupted sunshine.

I waited at the cemetery gate for the cortege to arrive. It began to rain, lightly at first, but before I could take shelter it came pelting down. I was so forlorn.

My thoughts turned to the evening Granny had said she was lonesome for her Geordie. I had no doubt she was reunited with him now in their heavenly home. Sheltered by a huge weeping willow, I waited patiently. Just as the hearse arrived, it stopped raining, and the sun burst out through an opening in the clouds, bringing with it the most beautiful rainbow. I followed close behind the procession as the horses pulled the carriage slowly, stopping at the grave side. Allan, surprised to see me, hurried over the moment his coach came to a halt.

"Roselyn," he gasped, "what a surprise! It's so good of you to come. How did you manage to get time off?"

"It's a long story, Allan, I'll tell you about it some other time." We moved to the side of the grave, holding hands. His parents acknowledged me with a nod.

The service was short but appropriate, and when Granny's body had been laid to rest, the Robertsons thanked me for attending. They invited me to join the family at a private reception, in the Queen's Hotel. I thanked them but of course, had to decline.

Allan offered to accompany me to the hospital. I convinced him his place was with his family on such a sad occasion. "Then I'll meet you at the railway station in Tayport tomorrow to escort you home."

Despite the fact that I had run all the way, it was nearly half past two when I arrived at the hospital. My heart was thumping as I ascended the stairs and sped along the corridor, gasping for breath.

And there she was, waiting outside the ward, arms folded over her gigantic bosom, eyes as large as melons; a scornful look on her plump face. She began to strut back and forth like a bantam cock, wringing her hands the moment she saw me. "Well, well, well! So you've finally come back!" Her voice was full of anger and although I tried to apologise she completely ignored me.

"I gave you permission to attend a funeral, surely it didn't take all this time. How dare you take advantage of my kindness?"

My head dropped. I was totally embarrassed.

A group of student doctors were arriving with their professor. I suppose she was displaying her authority for their benefit. Or perhaps she was just trying to impress.

"Excuses, excuses, excuses! I'm fed up with you and your feeble excuses. What have you to say for your boldness?" she blasted, maliciously.

"The funeral wasn't at the Balgay Cemetery. It was at the Eastern and as you know, that's much further away. I'm truly sorry, Sister, really I am, I ran all the way."

"Oh did you? Well, you didn't run fast enough.

'I'm truly sorry, Sister! I ran all the way!'"she mimicked.

"I'll make it up to you, Sister Phillips. I promise I'll work until six o'clock for the remainder of the week!"

She peered over the top of her spectacles. "Well! Since when did you have authority to set down terms to me?"

I was terrified of her, and she knew it. She ordered me back to work saying "I'll deal with you later, madam. Report to me before you leave this afternoon." I was nervous for the rest of the day and wondered what dreadful fate awaited me.

At half-past three in the afternoon, I stood trembling at her desk waiting for my execution. She was reading some papers, which she'd taken from a file lying on her desk. It seemed I'd been waiting forever before she spoke.

"I've been studying your file, Nurse Carey," she said at last, "I'm awfully impressed. You have an outstanding record, I can't believe it." Her attitude changed and she was sweet as could be.

"I apologise for being so hard on you, Nurse, perhaps we could make a fresh start?" She smiled sweetly, slipped the papers back into the folder and dismissed me. Well! You could've knocked me over with a feather. Here was I, thinking she was going to chop my head off, and she politely dismissed me. I was utterly flabbergasted.

Allan was waiting patiently on the platform when the late train puffed into the station that Friday evening. He was taking shelter under the overhang of the waiting-room building. For a fleeting moment I wished it had been Ralph meeting me. Quickly I dismissed those dangerous thoughts and ran to greet Allan with open arms. A sliver of moon, blinking intermittently through a cloud-scattered sky, was all that lit our way to West Lights.

Allan was dreadfully despondent. Not yet over the ordeal of his granny's funeral, I expected. We strolled along the dreary path in silence, each of us deep in thought. "I'll call for you at one o'clock, tomorrow, Roselyn," he whispered, and kissed me goodnight. He looked so lost as he waved from the gate, hurrying off and disappearing into the darkness.

CHAPTER

16

Catherine's Gift

My parents had retired for the night but Mother had left me a tray set with a snack. I sat quietly by the fireside watching yellow and red flames dancing in the grate, casting magical shadows on the ceiling. How comforting it was. My thoughts began to drift to Ralph. Immediately I could feel his lips on mine. A warm glow overwhelmed me, quickly replaced by a wave of loyalty for Allan. I knew that Ralph could never be a part of my life. When I finished eating, I went directly to my room, flopped on the bed fully dressed and fell fast asleep.

"Roselyn, Roselyn, wake up, Roselyn." A high-pitched, squeaky voice awoke me. I sat up and rubbed the sleep from my eyes and wondered where I was. And there, pulling at the eiderdown, was Catherine. I had completely forgotten she was coming.

"Get up, Roselyn! Get up!" she bubbling with excitement! "Come! Come quickly and see what I've got." She dragged me out of bed, leading me by the hand to the kitchen.

"Look, Roselyn!" She pointed to a basket on the

hearth. "Look! That's Pat! Uncle Larry and Aunt Liz gave him to me. And Roselyn," she gasped, "he's all mine!"

"Oh, Catherine! He's adorable!" I picked the little fox terrier up. Immediately, he snuggled his head underneath my chin and licked my neck furiously. "Hey, stop it! You're tickling me!" I protested with a giggle. Catherine laughed as I handed the puppy over to her. Her eyes sparkling with delight, she held him close and in a low, possessive voice, murmured, "He belongs to me, Roselyn, but you may borrow him sometimes if you like."

Mother and Father were beaming.

"Well, well, so it's started already has it? Just couldn't wait to spoil her, could you? Look at the pair of you, acting like a couple of overgrown children! And who's going to walk the dog?"

"She is!"

"He is!" They blurted out simultaneously.

Mother was quick on the defensive. She whispered under her breath, "the bairn had to have something of her own to love, Roselyn! Especially after her mother's gone."

While Catherine lay on the rug playing with her newly found love, Mother kept me company at the breakfast table.

"I was terribly sorry to hear about old Mistress Robertson dying." She struck up the conversation. "It's the road we've all to take, sooner or later, I suppose. It'll be Annie next, I expect."

"Mother! What a dreadful thing to say. Neither you, nor I, or anyone else knows who'll be next." I quickly changed the subject.

"Allan has applied for a job with a newspaper company in London."

147

"Oh has he? I suppose he'll want to get married, and cart you off to London. We'll never see you then."

"Don't be ridiculous, Mother, Allan hasn't mentioned anything about marriage."

She became rigid. She folded her arms across her body and said, "And perhaps he never will. He's not going to relish living in London all alone and, if it's not you, it'll be somebody else. I can't see him sitting around forever waiting for you."

I shrank back, stunned by her venomous outburst. My blood boiled at the bitterness of her words. "Oh Mother, Mother! You're so small-minded. I'm beginning to think you don't like Allan. Come to think of it, I don't believe you ever have."

I tried to comprehend her, reasoning but nothing she had said made sense. I had come to the conclusion she was jealous of my feelings for Allan, and mortally dreaded the day when I would no longer be with her.

"Roselyn," her voice mellowed and reaching over she gently touched my arm, "I didn't mean to upset you, lass, but it riles me that you don't give yourself a chance to meet anyone else. All you ever think about is Allan Robertson! There are lots of wonderful people in the world, you know!"

We cleared the table in silence. I offered to help with the dishes. "It's all right," she breathed, "I'll do them myself."

Deeply hurt at her behaviour, I didn't know what to say. Catherine broke the ice, suggesting she and I take Pat for a walk.

"Give me ten minutes to wash and change and we'll take him along the beach. By the way, I have a present for you, Catherine: pretty scraps I bought when I was in town last week, big, beautiful angels, to add to your collection. I'll give them to you when we return from our walk."

"Oh Roselyn, I love you!" she chirped, giving me a hug around the neck and dashing off to get Pat's leash.

When I returned, she was sitting on a chair in the back hall swinging her legs, looking like Little Miss Prim.

"Let's go!" And off we went, Pat almost pulling her off her feet. It was a glorious morning. The April sun was bursting through lightly scattered clouds. It radiated its thin rays over the entire countryside, now abundant with hosts of golden daffodils and pretty white narcissus.

As we gaily strolled along the beach a soft breeze brushed our cheeks, painting them pink.

"What's that you're singing, Roselyn?"

"Singing? Oh, I don't know, something my grandmother taught me when I was your age."

"Will you teach it to me?"

"Yes, but not today."

We threw a stick for Pat to retrieve. She commented several times, "He's the cleverest puppy in the whole wide world." Gales of laughter soared from her each time the dog retrieved the stick and dropped it at her feet. "I'll love him forever, Roselyn," she vowed.

Just as we were about to turn and head home, I was shocked to see Ralph hurrying towards us, with the ends of his fringed scarf fluttering in the breeze and the wide brim of his hat partially hiding his face. I watched him advancing speedily, pangs of excitement rushing through me.

"Roselyn," he gasped as he approached, "I noticed you as I was crossing the humpbacked bridge. I'm so happy to see you," he beamed. "I have a superb idea that I would like to share with you."

My heart was doing somersaults at the sound of his voice. Turning to Catherine I said, "Be a good little girl, Catherine, and take Pat home, I'll catch up with you."

"Okay," her little voice squeaked out, and turning homeward she skipped off throwing sticks for Pat.

"My goodness, Ralph, what is it that's so urgent?"

"Come over here a minute," he said taking my hand and leading me behind a huge mulberry bush. "I'm going crazy, for want of seeing you, Roselyn." He hesitated, biting his lip nervously. "What about coming to the manse once a month? In an official capacity, of course." he added quickly.

"An official capacity?" I gasped.

"Yes, for help to overcome your fear of ghosts. If you come to the manse, as I suggested, it would serve two purposes. It would give me the opportunity to see you, officially of course, and we could discuss the ghost."

"Ralph! I really don't think that's a good idea."

He put his forefinger to his lips, "Don't give me an answer right now, just think about it." He kissed my brow, leaving me speechless.

I hurried along the path to catch up with Catherine, feeling as if I was floating on a cloud and hand in hand, we walked the remainder of the way home singing happily.

Father was in the tool shed working on my bicycle. It had a puncture, which he was gallantly repairing. He assured me it would be ready in plenty time for my planned expedition with Allan that afternoon.

Catherine was thrilled at the idea of a bicycle ride. For some reason she was under the impression she was coming with us. "You have to be twelve to ride a bicycle on the main road," I told her kindly. "And I'm afraid you're not quite old enough!" She pouted, but accepted my explanation without question, running into the house and pulling Pat off his feet as she went.

I went straight to my room and sat on the rocker to consider Ralph's proposal. On one hand, I was as excited as could be at the idea of visiting him at the manse. On the other, I was drenched in feelings of guilt. What would Allan think if he ever found out? And how would I like it if Allan made an excuse to see someone else? But I convinced myself there would be nothing wrong with the minister talking to me. What a golden opportunity it would be to get to know him better. And, as Mother had said, Allan could meet someone while in London. Where would that leave me? No, there's nothing to stop me going to the manse. I quickly freshened up and put Ralph on the back burner for the time being.

Allan arrived promptly and was in a much happier frame of mind than he had been the night before. "Let's bicycle over to Windmill Park," he suggested.

"Sounds like a good idea," I agreed as I mounted my bicycle.

"Last one there's a rotten egg!" he chuckled, speeding away ahead of me.

Determined I wasn't going to be the rotten egg, I pedalled with all my might to catch up with him. I'm sure he deliberately let me win. We were both out of breath by the time we reached the park.

I spread out the tartan rug on the grass and set out the lunch Mother had insisted we take. What a feast we had! Roasted chicken legs, crusty rolls and fresh tomatoes from Father's greenhouse. Of course, no picnic would be complete without lots of lemonade.

Captivated with each other, the time flew by as usual. The main topic was the probability of him being offered the position with International Times. He was certainly excited, but at the same time he was anxious for my approval of his move to London. He gave me an extensive summary of the benefits, as well as the draw-backs. "The worst thing is we'll have to be separated for a while. Only until we can afford to get married," he assured me. "I'll come home as much as possible. Do you agree with that, Roselyn?"

"Of course I do, I'd never stand in your way, Allan, especially when it's your future that's at stake. You have my complete support. Let's talk about something else. I'm not looking forward to life without you."

A smile spread across his face as he took my hands. He pulled me down on the rug beside him and, gazing into my eyes, ran his fingers through my hair. "I love you, Roselyn."

"I love you too, Allan," I said, closing my eyes. Guilt engulfed me as thoughts of Ralph flashed through my mind. I felt so deceitful. I lay with my eyes closed, allowing the warm sun to play softly on my face.

For a while the day was crystal clear and the breathtaking view from the park seemed endless. Tall-masted ships leaving Dundee harbour on high tide was the only movement in the background, their coloured pennants flapping in the breeze. But the weather was ever changing and soon a strong wind began to blow up the firth and with it came rain clouds that blocked out the sun. We hurriedly packed up our things. Mustering all our strength, we had to pedal as fast as we could to beat the storm. As we turned down the cow path, we met Bob Wilkie walking his dog. "Roselyn Carey! Your father's going crazy, waiting for you to return, you'd better go straight home."

"Is something wrong?"

"Yes there is, but your father will tell you about it himself."

My heart raced as I sped blindly down the bumpy

path, all kinds of images whirling about in my head. I was standing in the vestibule, gasping for breath, before I knew it. In my panic I had left Allan far behind.

Mother and Father were all spruced up in their Sunday best. Mother was busy tying the ribbons of Catherine's bonnet. Father was buttoning up his jacket.

"Thank heavens you're back Roselyn, we've got to go to Dunfermline."

"Is it Annie?"

"No! It's not Annie, it's Jim! His neighbour sent a telegram, saying he's in hospital. Heart failure."

Mother was a wreck; I've never seen her in such a state.

"I'm going to stay as long as I'm needed, your father will be home tomorrow. There's a stew in the oven. Please don't let it spoil."

Her hands were shaking as she slipped them into her gloves. "Oh! By the way, don't worry about Pat," she told me, "he's at Bob's."

Mother and Catherine stepped outside the minute Allan arrived. I overheard her explaining the circumstances to him.

Father gave me last minute instructions. "Now don't forget to lock the doors before you leave for work, and drop the key off at Bob's." After hasty hugs and kisses they left.

In the living room, Allan lit a fire against the chill of the late afternoon. The kindling blazed and crackled cheerfully around the coals, casting shadows on the ceiling. Snuggling on the sofa we watched the smoke curling up the chimney, enjoying the situation in which we had unexpectedly found ourselves.

"My mother can't stay in Dunfermline indefinitely," I spoke my thoughts out loud, "and poor Annie - why, she's in no condition to be left alone. I hate to think what'll become of her, if Jim were to die."

"Your parents will probably bring her here."

"Oh I doubt that, we don't have enough room. Don't forget it wouldn't only be Annie. It would be Catherine as well. Besides, my mother couldn't cope. She has enough on her plate taking care of my father. I suppose poor Annie would have to be placed in a sanatorium."

"I expect you're right," he agreed. He arose up and crossed the room to make a cup of tea. His crisp hair was tousled from the bicycle ride from Wormit. He looked so very handsome.

"Roselyn, do you realise that this is the first time we've ever been in the house alone?" His husky voice broke into my thoughts.

Hesitating momentarily he turned about and came slowly across the room, his eyes focused on mine. Reaching out he took my hands in his and pulled me up on my feet. He stood gazing into my eyes for the longest time. Steeped in guilt, I could hardly look at him. He drew me close and kissed me, gently at first, then passionately as his lips explored my neck and nibbled my ear. I stiffened. I was surprised and reluctant to respond to his overtures. My thoughts went straight to my parents. How angry they would be at this behaviour.

I could feel the heat of his body penetrating mine, as if a fire had erupted within him. He reached for my breasts, and slipping his hand inside my blouse he began to massage me. I was quivering as his fingers skimmed over my nipples sending a tingling feeling throughout my entire body. I couldn't believe that Allan was doing this. He has never behaved like this before. I could've easily given in to him, but I stood fast.

"Oh, Roselyn!" he gasped, pushing me down gently on the sofa, kissing me violently.

Suddenly, Ralph's face flashed before me. "Oh God!" I gasped, "What are we doing?"

Slipping from underneath him, I stood to my feet. I was shaking like a leaf. "I'm sorry, Allan! I just can't bring myself to do this. Perhaps you'd better make the tea before we have regrets."

"Oh, Roselyn, Roselyn, I'm so sorry! Please forgive me! I don't know what came over me. Dearest, Roselyn, you know I adore you, don't you?"

"Yes Allan, I know," I smiled giving his hands a squeeze. The moment had passed.

We spent a lovely evening together but when it was time to leave he was reluctant to go. I knew he really wanted to stay. I wished he could have. I wasn't looking forward to spending the night alone. But behaviour like that could have led to something that would've discredited our names.

Before leaving, he helped me lock all the windows and bolt the back door. "One can never be too careful these days. Perhaps there's a bogie-man lurking in the bushes!" he teased, making scary faces and chasing me around the kitchen table. This was more like the Allan I was comfortable with. "Boo, boo, boo!" he bellowed. I giggled and squealed at the same time. "Now, bolt the door behind me," he ordered. I was amused at his concern and couldn't help but laugh.

"For heaven's sake, Allan, I'm a big girl and quite capable of taking care of myself."

He smiled, kissed me on the forehead and left. I closed and bolted the door. Resting my head against it, I sighed, thankful that Ralph's image had given me the courage to stop Allan's passionate embrace when it did.

CHAPTER
17

Encounter
with Ghost

T he moment Allan left, the house became like a morgue, so deathly quiet. As I moved about I began making as much noise as possible. I fluffed up the cushions and put away the dishes we'd been using.

In my bedroom I quickly changed into my nightie. "It's far too early for bed," I breathed, slipping into my robe. "Besides, what a crime it would be to waste such a lovely fire." Gathering up the quilt, I lifted a pillow off the bed and happily returned to the living room.

Wrapped in the quilt I snuggled up in Father's chair, pillow tucked in at my back, feet propped on the fender stool. Once again I attempted to read "A Tail of Two Cities", but I was tired and sleep soon overcame me.

The slamming of the front door awoke me and for a brief moment, I had no earthly idea where I was. "Is that you Father?" I shouted eventually, rubbing my sleepy eyes. But there was no reply. Footsteps came along the hall and stopped at the other side of the living-room door. Staring at the door I was expecting Father to enter, but he didn't.

"Is it you, Allan?" I shouted. "If it is, I don't think this is the least bit funny." Trembling, I stood up. "Allan! Is it you?" I demanded, hoping against hope that it was. There was still no answer.

"For heaven's sake, Roselyn," I mumbled to myself, "you're so stupid. How could it possibly be Father or Allan, the door's bolted?"

Terror gripped me, sending icy chills through my body. Maybe it was because I was alone that my imagination was running riot. I lifted Father's cane, which was propped up against the fireplace, and cautiously tiptoed over to the door. Leaning my ear against it, I held my breath to listen. But the loud beating of my heart made it difficult to hear anything.

I had to decide: was it my imagination, or, had I really heard the door slam? If someone had entered the house, were they standing on the other side of the door? "Who's there?" I called in a shaky voice. Still no answer. My heart continued to beat loudly and rapidly; I was certain whoever it was could hear it. Walkingstick clenched in hand, I was well armed to clobber whoever it was. I grabbed the doorknob and flung the door wide open. Zooooom! The cane was wrenched out of my hand and, with violent force, thrown across the room, hitting and smashing the window.

The impact sent excruciating pain up my arm and knocked me off my feet. For several moments I lay on the floor, stunned, not believing what had happened. Ignoring the pain momentarily, I struggled to my feet and peered into the darkness of the hallway. I saw nothing. There was nobody there!

"Oh God help me!" I shouted, my voice trembling with fear. I was so frightened I felt sick in my stomach.

The pain in my arm was so agonizing I began crying like a baby. After a few minutes, I pulled myself together and slammed the door closed. Leaning my back against it, I slid down onto my bottom. I sat there, for how long, I don't know. I was petrified.

I had thought of running over to the Burke's. But when I looked at the clock, I found it was only half-past two. I couldn't bring myself to disturb anyone at such an unearthly hour, and furthermore, I couldn't have left the room for a fortune. In due course, I did manage to pluck up enough courage to go to the kitchen to get a wet towel to wrap around my wrist. All the while, I had the strangest feeling someone was watching me. I restocked the fire and, wrapping the quilt around me, curled up in the rocking chair. The remainder of the night was spent troubled and restless. Finally, at the first light of dawn, I fell asleep from sheer exhaustion.

"Roselyn! Roselyn!" I was awakened abruptly by someone shouting and knocking on the window. Still half asleep, I rubbed my eyes and staggered over to see who it was. I sighed with relief. It was Allan.

"What's wrong with you, Roselyn Carey?" he shouted. "I've been battering on the door for ages. Anyone would think you're deaf."

"No, I'm not deaf," I chuckled, "I was asleep. Go around to the front door, I'll let you in."

His eyes went straight to my arm the moment he stepped into the house. "Good Lord! What happened to you?"

I threw myself into his arms and burst into tears. "Oh, Allan! Allan! It was terrible!"

"What was terrible?"

"You'll never believe what happened," I sobbed, and explained the events of the night before. "You do believe me, don't you?"

"Of course I believe you, why wouldn't I? Anyone else, no, but you, I believe." He led me to the kitchen, his arm around my shoulder, and sat me down on a high-backed chair. "Where are your slippers?" he asked noticing my bare feet.

"They're down at the side of the rocker, in the living-room." He went to fetch them and when he returned, knelt down and put them on my feet.

"Now, young lady, you go and get dressed. I'll make your breakfast. After breakfast, I'll take you to the doctor. That arm needs attention."

It was even painful to walk. Each step I took sent jabs of pain up my arm. In the doctor's surgery, Doctor Scott lifted his spectacles off the desk, putting them on to examine my arm.

"And what have we here?" he asked gently removing the sling. The pain was so severe I nearly fainted. "Ah, ha!" he said looking over the top of his spectacles, your wrist is broken. "What happened?"

I blushed with embarrassment glancing over at Allan, staring out the window. Perhaps he was wondering what I was going to say. The doctor waited patiently for my reply. "Well then! What happened?"

"I was fooling around with my father's cane and somehow or other, this is the result." I blurted out.

"Hummm." he sighed and removed his spectacles. He polished them and frowned. "You don't say!" He carefully bandaged a splint on my arm and advised me not to do heavy lifting for at least six weeks. "I want you to rest that arm of yours completely for at least a fortnight." He wrote a note to the hospital administrator and gave it to me!

As we were leaving a look of amusement came over his face. "Now let's have no more fooling around with your father's cane," he smiled as he closed the surgery door.

"Well, well!" Allan quirked, "now you know how to wangle time off work. All you have to do is get a ghost to break your wrist."

"Oh, Allan!" I gasped indignantly.

He offered to take the note to the hospital. Needless to say I readily accepted his offer.

I was still badly shaken from the frightful experience, so Allan stayed with me until my father returned, late that evening.

"How's Uncle Jim?" I inquired, as Father removed his coat.

"It was a false alarm! Acute indigestion is all it was, however, the doctor's keeping him in hospital for a few days, just to be on the safe side. Your mother's staying with Annie until Jim gets sent home."

"In the name of heaven, what happened to you?" he blurted, noticing my bandaged arm, and in the same breath asked why I wasn't at work.

I told him the story from the time I heard the door slam to the walking stick being wrenched out of my hand.

"Oh come on, Roselyn, you really don't expect me to believe that. Now, what really happened?"

"I told you already." Bursting into tears I ran to my bedroom slamming the door.

Before he retired for the night, he brought me a cup of cocoa and a piece of toast. As he turned to leave the room, he said, "Perhaps a good night's sleep'll clear your head."

I couldn't believe that my father, of all people, disbelieved me. He had always been more open minded than Mother. I hated to think what she would have to say.

The rain, battering against the windowpane, awakened me just before dawn. It had rained all night and was still as heavy as it had been the night before. I decided to keep out of Father's way and stayed in my room. In the late afternoon, Allan dropped in. He had already delivered the doctor's note to the hospital.

"I ran into Sister Phillips at the duty office. She sends her condolences and hopes to see you back to work soon." He laughed, raising his eyebrows.

"By the way I've done some research on this house Roselyn, seems you're not the only one who's had an encounter with a ghost here." Smiling curiously he handed me a clipping from an old newspaper. It read:

Captain Cook Roams Again.

Thomas Cook, a retired sea captain who died in the late seventeen hundreds, has been seen roaming the coast road in the vicinity of West Lights. The young woman who reported the sighting had vacated the house she had been renting there more than twenty years before. She said the ghost of Thomas Cook had haunted her in the house to the point of insanity, believe it or not!

"I'm flabbergasted, simply flabbergasted! But I detected scepticism in the reporter's closing remarks. Didn't you Allan?"

"Yes, definitely, but it doesn't alter the fact that you were attacked, presumably by the ghost of Thomas Cook. If it's the last thing I do, I'll get to the bottom of it." He took the clipping and slipped it into the inside pocket of his jacket.

"Allan, I'm terrified in this house, especially when I'm home alone! I was terribly hurt at my fathers' reaction when I told him what happened to my wrist. He doesn't believe me, Allan. Oh Allan, what am I to do?"

"Don't worry! He'll believe you by the time I'm finished."

"Isn't it strange that no one else in the household's bothered by the ghost? I wonder why?"

"That's exactly what I intend to find out. Now, I must run, I've a million things to attend to before I go to Edinburgh. I'll be gone for a couple of days, but I'll be back on Friday." He kissed me, tapped my nose and left.

Mother arrived just in time for dinner. She was anxious to know what had happened to my arm.

I told her the story exactly as it had happened. Well, she flew into a rage. "Good God Almighty!" she bellowed. "That settles it, Larry," she said, turning to Father and throwing up her arms. "She'll have to see a doctor. Heavens, people will think she's raving mad, if this rubbish leaks out. Let's face facts, Roselyn! It's all in your mind. Furthermore, I'm fed up with all your deranged stories. Now, what really happened?"

I stomped off to my bedroom enraged, shouting over my shoulder. "I've already told you."

For the next few days my parents were silent and distant and treated me as if I were insane. Especially Mother. She wouldn't even talk to me. But father mellowed. He brought my meals on a tray. He tried to get me to admit that I had made the story up.

It didn't stop raining for the next three days and being confined to the house greatly added to my feelings of dejection. Oh, how I longed for Allan to return. Hopefully, when he did, he would have more details about Thomas Cook.

With Allan away, I took the opportunity to study. During the time I was confined to my room, Pat was a great comfort. He was the only one in the household who accepted me the way I was. He spent his time curled up in a ball at my feet.

There was lots of time for thought. I thought a lot about Ralph and his suggestion to have the house exorcised. After the terrifying experience I'd had, I was inclined to agree with him. I would have him do it as soon as possible.

As always, Allan kept his promise. He was bubbling with enthusiasm when he returned. "Just wait till you hear this," he gasped excitedly, "I've got tons of exciting news about your ghost. Just listen to this:"

Captain Cook, better known to the locals as 'Auld Cookie', had been the original owner of Rose Cottage, located at West Lights. He had built the house for his young bride, in the seventeen hundreds. Her maiden name had been Rose MacFarlane, hence, Rose Cottage.

Ecstatically happy at first, they were blessed with two healthy children: a son, Albert and a daughter, Rose. However, while Thomas was on one of his long sea voyages, lonely Rose had fallen in love with a wealthy sheep farmer from the Highlands. She left Tayport to live with her new love, taking the children with her. It was the scandal of the decade.

When Thomas had returned and found his family gone, he went berserk and had spent months searching for them, to no avail. Brokenhearted he eventually gave up and was last seen walking into the river at high tide. Before anyone could reach him, he was swept away."

"Goodness me. I can't be ..."

"Just a minute!" he interrupted. "I'm not finished! Captain Cook's spirit continues to roam the area and confuses every young woman who lives in the cottage with his Rose. So you see, Mistress Carey," Allan said, turning to Mother, "Roselyn isn't crazy."

"My God!" she drew in her breath. "You're every bit as bad as her, Allan. Surely you don't believe all that rubbish? It's just a fairy story, made up by the newspaper publishers for people like you; I really thought you had more sense."

Allan ignored her comments, and, looking me in the eye said, "You're not crazy, Roselyn." He handed Mother the newspaper. "Please read this, Mistress Carey. Perhaps you'll see things differently. Your daughter's intelligent and she doesn't imagine anything."

She glanced nonchalantly at the paper, "Hum," she grunted, returning it to him and making no comment. She and Father shaking their heads, trotted off to the living-room. I was furious, on the verge of tears.

Allan, put his arm around me, "Don't let them upset you, sweetheart."

The moment Allan had left, I went to my bedroom and kneeling at my bedside prayed for God's help. Little or no sleep came my way that night, I was so upset. When I got up next morning, I sat quietly in my rocking chair, trying to reason with myself. Out of self-pity, I told myself I shouldn't have mentioned anything about the ghost to my parents. I should have kept it all to myself. I could have easily concocted a story of how I broke my wrist. But it went against the grain to lie.

A week the following Monday, I returned to work. Sister Phillips was in one of her rotten moods. "So! We haven't to do any heavy lifting, have we not?" she said sarcastically, upon reading the discharge note.

"That's correct Sister, I've to rest my arm as much as possible for another four weeks."

"Well, I have no use for an invalid in this ward," she said scribbling a note and handing it to me. "Take this to Sister Wotherspoon in Ward two. There's no lifting there, well, not nearly as much."

Happily, I pranced along the corridor and skipped downstairs to the medical ward to deliver the note to Sister Wotherspoon. Although I'd never met her, she couldn't possibly be the terror Sister Phillips was.

She was sitting at her desk doing paperwork

when I entered the ward, and as I approached she looked up and smiled. "Good morning, Nurse!"

"Good morning Sister Wotherspoon, my name is Roselyn Carey," I introduced myself, holding out my hand, which she politely shook. "Sister Phillips asked me to give you this." I smiled, handing her the note.

She read it quickly and said, "Well my dear, there's lots of work down here that doesn't require lifting. I don't think you'll damage your wrist dosing out the medicines, will you?"

From that first moment, I knew we were going to be friends. She mothered me and made my working day a pleasure.

"I prefer you to work regular hours while you're recuperating, and there will be no weekend work until your wrist is completely healed."

I couldn't believe my luck. My tattered faith in my superiors had been restored by the kindness of Sister Wotherspoon.

CHAPTER
18

A Sad Day

I t had been more than a week since I'd last seen
Terren. She was on night duty, I was on days, and
for one reason or other we hadn't connected. One
evening in early April when I entered our room, she was
already in bed. Her drawn face and sunken eyes told me
she wasn't at all well.

"What in the world have you been doing to yourself, Terren?" I demanded.

"Well, to tell the truth, Roselyn, it's taking longer
to get over this bout of the influenza than I'd anticipated. I've got no energy whatsoever. All I want to do is
sleep."

"What's Jerry saying about it?" I inquired while
putting my cloak in the wardrobe.

"Oh well, you know Jerry. All he says is, I don't
eat properly and don't get enough fresh air. What a nerve
he has. He knows perfectly well we nurses have to eat
on the run, and rarely get time to sleep, let alone fresh
air."

"Well, I really think it's about time you consulted
your doctor. He'll prescribe a tonic that'll pick you up

and stimulate your appetite."

"I've been thinking of doing that," she answered, closing her eyes. Slipping beneath the covers she pulled the sheet over her head

I lay on top of my bed that night, Ralph predominantly on my mind. My heart was filled with joy whenever I thought of him. I pictured him in the clothes he had worn that Sunday I'd had tea at the manse. Oh! How handsome he is! Olive complexion and eyes like deep mysterious pools. I tried so hard to shut him out of my mind. But in spite of myself, I couldn't. He seemed to have an unyielding hold on me!

Next morning I awoke with a start and was engulfed in a feeling of deep sadness. Allan was so loyal, and here I was having loving thoughts of another man. "It has got to end," I told myself, "it's all very well being friends with the minister, but that's where it has to remain: good friends."

Terren was feeling a little better by the following Saturday and decided to go shopping for the material for her wedding gown. Because of her recent illness, she'd changed her mind about shopping in far away Edinburgh. Instead she invited me to accompany her on a shopping spree in Dundee. As luck would have it, she found exactly what she wanted in Daniels. Ivory satin and fine Belgian lace was the order of the day. We had a wonderful time making the choices. Browsing about the aisles, we decided to try on hats. We laughed and giggled when we saw ourselves in hats with veils and hats with feathers. What fun!

A treat to lunch, compliments of Terren's father, boosted our flagging spirits. Terren chose to dine at the Royal Hotel. "'Might as well do it in style," she said as we happily climbed the red-carpeted stairs. The cheery head waitress ushered us to a table by a window overlooking the High Street. "You ladies can have fun watching out of the window," she smiled, pulling out a chair for Terren to sit on and promptly handing us a menu.

We chatted back and forth over a cup of tea. Terren confessed she still wasn't feeling very well. But she thought she'd feel much better once the wedding was over.

"What I need is a good rest, Roselyn," she confided. "We're going to honeymoon in the Channel Islands. I'll get lots of rest then and hopefully lots and lots of beautiful sunshine. Oh no!" She covered her mouth with her hand.

"What! What is it? What's the matter?"

"I've let the secret out. I've told you where we're going. That's supposed to be bad luck."

"That's rubbish!"

"Jerry insists that I retire when we get married. He'd like to start a family straight away."

"But what about your nursing career? If you retire when you get married, you won't be able to finish your training."

"I know!" she sighed, gazing out the window, a faraway look in her eyes. "I really don't care about that any more."

"What? I can't believe you're saying that, Terren. You were absolutely thrilled at the idea of being a nurse. You only have another year to do then you'd be a fully-fledged nurse. My goodness, you should be ecstatically happy, and look at you! You're as miserable as anything! What's really bothering you, Terren?"

"Oh, I'm happy enough, Roselyn, really I am. But, for some unknown reason, I have the strangest feeling it'll never take place."

"That what will never take place?"

"The wedding."

"The wedding?" I gulped, "how can you think such a thing? You're a perfect match, so right for each other. Of course the wedding will take place, silly. Come on, cheer up now, and give yourself a shake!"

"Oh don't misunderstand, Roselyn. It's nothing to do with our feelings for each other, or whether or not we're right for each other. It's this feeling I get deep down inside that haunts me and try as I may, I just can't shake it off."

"Oh Terren! It's only pre-wedding butterflies that's wrong with you. Lots of young girls about to give up their maiden name experience it." Her face lit up and a smile lifted the corners of her lips.

"You really think that's all it is?"

"Of course!" But as we were speaking, that awful feeling of sadness came over me again. Instantly I pushed it aside. We parted company at the top of Castle Street that Saturday afternoon, Terren to return to our lodgings and I to catch the two o'clock train to Tayport.

I stopped in at the manse on the way home to make an appointment with Ralph. I rang the doorbell and a moment later the door swung open. There stood Ralph, smiling from ear to ear at the sight of me. "My goodness, Roselyn! What a lovely surprise! Do come in please." He outstretched his arms taking my hands in his. "Let me take your coat?"

"No, no, I'm not staying, Ralph. I've given a great deal of thought to your suggestion about coming here for help with my visions of ghosts. I think it's a superb idea."

His eyes lit up and his face burst into a beaming smile. "When would you like to come?" he asked softly.

"Tomorrow afternoon around two o'clock, if that's convenient?"

"Of course it is! It'll always be convenient for you

to come here. Ralph Valente at your service." He gestured with a bow and a sway of his arm.

"Oh Ralph, please don't tease." The sound of his voice sent my heart pounding. "You must understand it'll be an official visit."

"Of course! Until tomorrow then." He smiled as he closed the door softly.

I hurried down the cowpath and convinced myself that the meeting with Ralph next day would definitely have to be an official visit, nothing more.

Mother and Father were delighted to see me, surprised that I'd arrived in time for tea. They made a big fuss, as always. Mother took my cloak and bag, scurrying off to hang the cloak in the press. Father busied himself pouring a glass of sherry.

"That'll warm you up," he smiled, handing me the glass of rich amber liquid.

"What's that terrible noise?" I asked as I headed for the living room.

"Oh, it's only the wee lass trying to play music for Pat."

In the living-room, Catherine was perched on the music stool thumping away on the pianoforte. Pat was sitting on the floor by her side, howling his head off.

"What in the world's going on here?" I asked, poking my head around the living-room door. Catherine, bursting with pride squeaked out, "Pat can sing, Roselyn, just listen to him! I taught him all by myself!"

"Oh, is that what he's doing? I'd never have guessed! I didn't know dogs could sing." I laughed. "I'd better leave you to it, then." I returned to the kitchen.

Mother was dying to see the satin. She was all eyes as I carefully undid the parcel.

"Goodness!" she gasped. "That is beautiful! It must have cost a fortune." She admiringly fingered the heavy bridal satin.

"It did. Terren's father wanted her to have the very best."

"Well! He won't be disappointed with this, it's absolutely exquisite. And the lace! Why, I've never seen the like."

"It's Belgian lace, Mother."

"Oh, is it! I should've known that." She flushed, a little embarrassed that she hadn't known. "How is Terren keeping? Is she feeling any better?"

"No, not really! I'm very concerned about her. She's lost a ton of weight and her complexion is awful. She's white as a sheet! I've taken the liberty of inviting her and Jerry for the weekend, in a fortnight's time. Didn't think you'd mind, Mother. It'll be a nice change for her, lots of fresh sea air. And, with a bit of luck, lots of sunshine. You'll have her dress ready for a fitting by then, won't you, Mother?"

"Of course! But Roselyn, we don't have enough room to accommodate two single people."

"I know that, but I thought perhaps Terren could have the guest bedroom, and Catherine can sleep with me. Allan's offered to put Jerry up at his parents' place."

"Oh well, in that case, there's not a problem."

We prattled away, forgetting the time and didn't sit down to tea until well after six o'clock. The crumbs rolled down my chin when I bit into Mother's freshly baked sultana cake. It was so good to be enjoying Mother's home baking again. I had two thick slices of cake and a wedge of cream sponge. Simply delicious.

"Where's Allan tonight? Is he not coming over?" Mother asked as we were clearing the dishes away.

"He's gone to London for a job interview. Remember I told you he has applied for a job with

International Times? He'll be back in a couple of days."

"Yes, I vaguely remember you saying something to that effect."

Father was sitting in his rocking-chair, reading the evening paper, his feet propped on the fender stool. He jumped to his feet, discarding the paper, the moment Mother and I had finished our chores. "Well, are my girls ready for another sherry?" he cheerfully asked.

"Certainly!" Mother declared without hesitation, as she sat heavily in her favourite chair.

"How about you, Roselyn? Would you care for another?"

"No thanks. I promised Catherine earlier I'd read her a story before she goes to sleep. Then I think I'll go to bed."

"Suit yourself." he answered, crossing the room and giving Mother hers.

Looking adoringly into his eyes, she took the glass. They were so contented sitting at the fireside, enjoying each other's company. It's a joy to see my parents so happy together.

Catherine listened intently as I read the story, 'Teeny from Troon', the little orphan girl who lived in a bewitched cottage with her grandfather. But soon her eyelids became heavy and sleep overtook her halfway through the story. She looked like a cherub lying on the soft pillow.

I bent down and kissed her brow and tucked the quilt around her. Tiptoeing over to the light, I turned the gas down to a peep and quietly slipped out of the room.

Raindrops were trickling down the windowpane when I awoke on Sunday morning. "I hope the rain isn't on for the day." I mumbled, as I threw the quilt back and slipped out of bed. I had awoken with a violent headache – the kind that makes you want to beat your head against a brick wall. When I have such headaches, they'll magically disappear as soon as I eat. I went to the kitchen and cooked a breakfast of scrambled eggs, thickly buttered toast and, of course, a mug of strong tea. Sitting quietly by the fireside, my breakfast on a tray on my lap, I was enjoying catching up on all the news in the Saturday paper. My parents and Catherine were away to church so there were no distractions. I had stayed home on account of my headache. I'd just swallowed the last mouthful of food when there was a persistent knocking on the front door. I hurried to open it. There standing on the doorstep was a handsome young telegraph boy.

"Telegram, Miss!" he announced the moment I opened the door. He handed me an envelope. "Will there be a reply, Miss?" he politely asked.

"No, no reply, thank you. But just wait a minute." I scurried off to my bedroom and fumbling in my purse took out a threepenny bit and gave it to him.

"Thank you kindly, Miss!" he smiled doffing his cap as he left.

I propped the telegram up on the mantelpiece, shovelled some coals on the fire and cleared the dishes away. Grateful my headache had lifted, I was dying to get a breath of fresh air. The rain had stopped. I stepped out into a beautiful sunny morning. The moment I put my foot out the door a familiar voice called, "Roselyn! Roselyn!"

"Why Jenny, what a surprise!" I gasped. "My goodness, you're looking well."

"I'm feeling wonderful, Roselyn," she beamed. "I took your advice, you know. And you'll never guess?"

"What?" I asked enthusiastically.

"Tam has done a complete turnaround. Now he won't let the wind blow on Kenneth. Between you and me, I think he's feeling guilty after the way he treated the poor wee soul when he was born. Just look at Kenneth, Roselyn." She beamed, wheeling the pram closer to the fence. Lifting Kenneth out of the pram, she handed him to me.

"Oh Jenny, he's beautiful! How heavy is he? He feels like a ton."

"Not quite." she laughed. "But he does weigh almost twelve pounds now. And it's no wonder, he has an appetite like a horse."

Julia came bounding over when she heard the commotion. "Can I take Kenneth for a walk, Ma?" she blurted out excitedly. "Please, Ma?" Jenny smiled serenely, raising her eyebrows as she reached over to take Kenneth from me and put him back in the pram.

"As you can see Roselyn, I have a willing helper." Julia seemed proud as Punch, as she wheeled the pram up the garden path and out the gate.

"It does my heart good to see you all so happy, Jenny."

"Thank you, Roselyn. But please excuse me, I must go. I'll get the beds made while Julia has him out. Have to make hay while the sun shines!" She smiled happily and left.

Briskly, I walked around the garden, filling my lungs with fresh air, before returning indoors. How exhilarating!

The clock on the mantelpiece struck two as I entered the house. "What's keeping them?" I mumbled, keen to know what the telegram said. "They should've been back ages ago."

The front door flew open and in bounced Catherine, moments ahead of the others. She made a beeline for Pat's basket where he was curled up, fast asleep. Lifting him she smothered him with kisses. The poor little thing was still half-asleep as she leashed him up and dragged him out the door.

Mother and Father were lively and bubbling, chatting away happily. They went upstairs to put their Sunday coats into the wardrobe. Mother was tying her apron strings when she entered the kitchen. Father was close on her heels, Sunday papers in hand.

"This telegram arrived while you were out." I gave it to him the moment he entered the kitchen.

"You should've opened it, Roselyn," he commented ripping the envelope open.

"It'll be the news we've been expecting, I suppose." He quickly scanned the page then handed the telegram to Mother, who in turn passed it over to me:

ANNIE EXPECTED TO GO ANY MINUTE. PLEASE COME AT ONCE! JIM

Silently we looked from one to the other. Then Father said, "Okay Liz, better pack a bag," he suggested, glancing at the clock. "We'll have a quick bite, and if we hurry we'll catch the four o'clock train from Wormit to Dunfermline."

With all my heart I wished I could've gone with them. Unfortunately, I had obligations at the hospital. As soon as they had left, I tidied up the kitchen and ran over to Bob's to explain our current crisis, taking Pat with me. "Don't worry about the dug," he said, "he's nae bother. He can stay with me as long as is necessary." I thanked him gratefully and left.

Dressed for my nursing, I ran all the way to the manse, for my appointment with Ralph. My heart gave an enormous leap of excitement when Ralph opened the door and invited me in. Beaming, he put his arm around me and led me out to the back porch.

"You look lovely, even in your uniform," he said,

giving me a squeeze. I felt weak at the knees and I was melting at his touch. What a wonderful feeling it was.

We sat on the porch, soaking up the late afternoon sunshine, enjoying a cup of tea and dainty sandwiches prepared by Patty. I poured out the ghost story from start to finish. He listened intently as I spoke, his gaze fixed on me.

"Well, Roselyn, it seems to me that Thomas Cook's got it in for you. Are you sure your parents wouldn't allow me to exorcise the house?"

"They certainly wouldn't. But I would! We have a wonderful opportunity to do it today. They've gone to Dunfermline."

"Good! Then let's go as soon as you've finished your tea." He excused himself and went upstairs to get his things. When he returned, he was carrying his Bible.

"Are you ready, Roselyn?"

"Yes!" I swallowed the last mouthful of tea. In the vestibule Ralph helped me put my cape on. As we stepped into the garden, he bent down to pick a beautiful golden daffodil. Handing it to me, he said "It matches the colour of your hair perfectly, Roselyn!" I was flustered! The feelings I had for him saturated me. But I controlled myself and took it from him with a shaky hand.

We chatted happily as we hurried down the cow path. I felt proud to be out with the minister and wondered what Mother would have said if she had known what we were up to.

Ralph waited in the garden while I ran over to Bob's for the key. "Sorry to keep you waiting Ralph," I apologised. "I should have my own key, but for some silly reason my parents only have one." I opened the door and invited him in.

He set about his business at once. I watched intently as he moved from room to room. He was saying prayers that I'd never heard before.

"Well, that should do it!" he declared at last, quickly gathering his things. "If that doesn't work, we'll have to think of something else."

I returned the key to Bob. I hurried back to Ralph who was waiting on the gravel path. Beaming with delight, he offered to escort me to the train station. Of course, I accepted his offer. Our conversation flowed so easily that it seemed no time at all and we were there. He left me at the main entrance to the station. I was greatly relieved he didn't linger there. Plainly he was eager to know when I'd be home again.

CHAPTER
19

Engagement

*I*n the privacy of the carriage I gave some thought to my feelings for Allan, and compared them with the fantastic pleasure and indescribable feelings I'd experienced with Ralph. I decided since I'd known Allan practically all my life, I couldn't bring myself to hurt him. He had to be the man for me.

My thoughts drifted and I became extremely depressed at the thought of what was happening to Annie. Although we'd been expecting the bad news, the blow hit hard. And the worst was yet to come. My heart ached for Catherine, poor little thing. A ray of sunshine bursting through the carriage window compelled me to move to the opposite side of the compartment. The view to the South was breathtaking, especially at that time of year. The Fife hills were thickly carpeted with an uninterrupted stretch of bright yellow daffodils. What a spectacular sight. Although my heart was heavy with grief, I couldn't help admiring such awesome beauty.

The next couple of days dragged by. Routine duties at the Hospital were boring. Sister Wotherspoon must have detected sadness in my eyes, as I went about my daily tasks. In the late afternoon on Tuesday, she invited me to sit at her desk. "What is it that's troubling you, Nurse Carey? You seem extremely downhearted."

"Oh! There's lots of things bothering me, Sister," I answered, on the verge of tears.

"Such as?" she persisted.

I explained Annie's illness and the obligations my parents were about to inherit.

She reached over and squeezed my hand. "Never mind, Nurse, I'll arrange some sick leave for you. It won't hurt the hospital to do without you for a few days, but it'll do you the world of good to be with your family in their hour of grief. Just finish what you're doing and you may go. Report for duty next Wednesday morning."

"Sister Wotherspoon!" I sighed, "you're so considerate! How can I ever repay you?"

She smiled softly, "Your compassion for others is payment enough, Nurse."

When I arrived at the duty office, Gus was being his usual witty self, laughing and joking with the nurses, as they came and went. When I approached the office window, he spluttered out, "Nurse Carey! How are you? Why so gloomy?"

"Well, Gus, a bucketful of sunshine would certainly go down well."

"I know exactly what you mean."

"How has the world been treating you?" I inquired, while signing the register.

"Oh, fair to middling, Nurse, fair to middling. I must tell you the latest news though," he said with a grin and proceeded to speak about his sister. "She's living down in Yorkshire with her fancy man. But, listen to this!" His face broke into a beaming smile. Folding his arms he leaned his head through the open window and whispered, "Alex has a lass!"

"You're joking."

"No, I'm no joking." His eyes were dancing as he spoke.

"Well good for Alex!"

"He met the lass at a ceilidh in Farfar. Love at first sight, it was. Agnes is her name, Agnes Kerrigan, and what a beauty she is! Hair as black as a raven's, and beautiful sea-green eyes. Oh yes, she's a beauty all right. When she and Alex got talking, he found out that she's the wife of Mary Ann's fancy man. Would you believe that, Nurse? It's certainly is a small world, isn't it?"

"Yes, it is, there's no doubt about that."

"Well, well, what's going on here?" A familiar voice drew my attention as a pair of hands grabbed me around the waist. Letting out a yelp, I quickly turned around. "Allan, oh, Allan," I gasped, "what a lovely surprise. When did you get back? What brings you here?" I asked all in the same breath.

"Checking up on you of course, what else?"

"Oh! Then I'd better behave myself," Gus chuckled.

As soon as we were out of earshot Allan whispered. "Go and put on your best dress. We're going out for dinner."

"You got the job! Oh Allan, you got the job!" I was jumping with glee.

"Yes, I got the job! Now settle down! Settle down! I'll tell you all about it later. I've made reservations for seven o'clock at the Queen's Hotel. You'd better make haste if we're to make it."

"Oh, Allan, we'll never make it for seven."

"We will if you hurry. Come on, let's go!" He gave me a pat on the bottom.

He waited at the entrance gate while I went to change. A cat's wash was enough. I slipped into a pale blue cotton dress with a delicate daisy pattern. Just before leaving the room, I sprayed a little rose-water on my neck and wrists.

I was so excited. It was good to see Allan again. Skipping down the steps two at a time, all I could think of was how happy I was for him.

"Well," I blurted excitedly, "let's hear your wonderful news."

He tilted his head in a conceited manner looking down his nose, "You're looking at the assistant editor of the International Times!"

"Oh Allan! That's terrific!"

"And just listen to this," he went on, "I'm to have a full column every week for my own editorials, plus a yearly salary of two hundred and fifty pounds. What do you think of that?"

"Goodness me! And when do you have to start?"

"The first of August. Michael Young, the editor, wanted me to start sooner but I told him I'd lots of loose ends to tie up. Besides, I wanted to spend the summer with you, my precious one." He smiled, rubbing my nose with his and squeezing my hand.

At the Queen's, the head waiter led us to a window table overlooking the river. "I trust this is to your satisfaction, sir?" he said, pulling out a chair for me.

"It's perfect." Allan replied.

"Your waiter will be with you presently, sir." He handed us a menu, lit the candle on the table and left.

I glanced around the dining room. Tables were draped in gold coloured Irish linen. Red serviettes, and red roses cascading from a crystal bowl, completed the setting. Luxurious red velvet curtains, tied back with gold cords, framed the floor-to-ceiling windows. Tropical plants filled huge ornamental pots, placed tastefully about the room. A crystal chandelier cast an array of glittering colours. In the corner of the room a three-piece orchestra played a selection of romantic dinner music.

Allan pulled his chair closer to mine, and, taking my hands in his, kissed them. "You look lovely tonight, Roselyn, simply lovely!" His eyes were dancing.

"Isn't this a bit extravagant?" I said, scanning the room. "After all, celebrating a new job shouldn't warrant such splendour, should it?"

He smiled flirtatiously. "Well Roselyn, my dearest, I'm hoping we'll celebrate something far more important than a new job, tonight!"

The waiter arrived with a basket of dinner rolls, interrupting our conversation. He asked if we were ready to order.

"What would you suggest we have?" Allan asked.

"Well sir, I highly recommend the fillet of Tay salmon. It's served in a creamy hollandaise sauce. One of our chef's specialities."

"What do you think, Roselyn? What would you like?"

I quickly scanned the menu before deciding. Smiling shyly, I replied, "I'll have the salmon."

"Make that two," Allan said "and please bring a bottle of champagne."

"Certainly, Sir!" The waiter left taking the menus with him.

"Allan Robertson!" I gasped. "Are you out of your mind?"

"Certainly not!" arising from his chair he knelt on the floor at my feet.

"What, are you doing, Allan? Get up!"

He gently took my hands in his. "Roselyn Carey, would you do me the honour of becoming my wife?" I blushed knowing every eye in the room was on us. For a split second I thought of Ralph but instantly dismissed the thought. The sincerity in Allan's voice, and the love radiating from his eyes, made me oblivious to the onlookers.

"Yes! Oh Allan," I sighed, "Of course, I will."

He fumbled in the inside pocket of his jacket to retrieve a velvet box. Out of the box he took the most beautiful solitaire diamond I'd ever seen. "My Granny wanted you to have this, Roselyn. She entrusted me with it to give to you, on our special day. Of course, she was hoping to celebrate this day with us."

There was a tremendous applause from the onlookers, as Allan slipped the ring onto my ring finger.

"Oh Allan!" I breathed. "I'll treasure this till the day I die." Tears of happiness filled my eyes. My heart was bursting with joy.

"Good Lord!" I gulped, covering my mouth with my hand, once over the shock of it all. "What will my parents say?"

"No need to worry, sweetheart. I've already spoken to them; they gave us their blessing."

We set a wedding date for May the twenty-first the following year. That would allow Allan to get settled in his new job. I would sit the general nursing exams later that April and to complete the nursing course I'd do the midwifery course, beginning in September.

We had a wonderful time planning our future life together, that magical spring evening.

"My parents would like you to come home with me tonight, Roselyn. They're very excited about our engagement and want to celebrate with us. You may spend the night, if you wish."

"Oh Allan, I'm sorry, I can't, I've to catch the first train to Dunfermline tomorrow."

A look of such disappointment came over his

face, that I relented.

"Oh, never mind, if you promise to rouse me in plenty of time to catch the train, I'll come."

"I'll do better than that, I'll escort you all the way to Dunfermline."

We were bursting with joy, skipping down the red carpeted staircase, two steps at a time and holding hands. We ran all the way to the station and just caught the last train in the nick of time.

The Robertsons were bubbling with excitement. They greeted us with hugs and kisses the moment we arrived. "Come in, come in!" his father said, leading us to the living room. "What a happy occasion this is. It calls for a glass of champagne, does it not? No, come to think of it, it calls for two glasses of champagne. One to celebrate your engagement, and one to celebrate your new job, Allan." His face was radiant as he stepped over to a cabinet, popped a bottle of champagne and poured the drinks.

"Welcome to the Robertson clan, Roselyn," he said, as we all clicked glasses, "and the best of luck to you in your new job, Allan."

Mistress Robertson had a permanent smile on her face. "Have you chosen a date for the wedding, Roselyn?" she eagerly inquired, fussing over me.

"Yes, as a matter of fact, we have!" Allan butted in. "We're getting married on the twenty-first of May, next year. That'll give me the opportunity to get settled in London and give Roselyn the chance to complete her training."

"Next year," she gulped, "that's far too long to wait. For heaven's sake, we could all be dead and buried by then." The hairs on my arms stood up the moment she said that and I was overcome with that profound feeling of sadness.

"Mother! What a terrible thing to say. Let's change the subject, shall we?"

Sitting around the fireplace in the living room, we chatted over one glass of champagne, and then another. When I finally laid my head on the pillow, it was midnight. I drifted off to sleep, floating on cloud nine.

Allan awoke me at the crack of dawn as promised and off we went to catch the train.

During the last few days of Annie's life, while the death angel hovered, Jim and Catherine spent every moment with her. It was as if they were trying to cram a lifetime into the few hours left before she went to heaven. Annie had imagined great plans for her life with Catherine, but God saw things differently. In the end she was content to go, with the knowledge that Catherine would have a happy life with us.

The evening of the day she died, all the far-flung relatives arrived, appropriately dressed in solemn black. Perched on high-backed chairs around the room, looking like vultures, they waited in silence for the undertaker to arrive.

Sitting on my lap, Catherine nervously chewed the end of a pigtail. Swinging her legs back and forth, she silently viewed the solemn scene.

The gold damask curtains that framed the windows were drawn closed, as were all the curtains in the house. The soft-chiming clock on the mantle piece and the proud grandfather clock in the living room had been stopped at the moment of Annie's death. I simply detested such occasions. I'll never understand such morbid customs.

The heavy odour of death crept into the air, as Annie's lifeless body lay decomposing beneath the stark white sheets. A perfumed handkerchief to the nose was poor defence against the ghastly smell.

Mother continuously sprayed the room with lily of the valley perfume, always used to disguise the odour of death.

It seemed strange remembering how it had been when Annie and I were children. We were the best of friends, sharing our innermost secrets. She was - I was jerked back to the present, when the undertaker, accompanied by his young apprentice, entered the room carrying the coffin.

Catherine stiffened. Enfolding her tiny body in my arms I held her tightly. The atmosphere was tense and all but Catherine's eyes were focused on the undertaker. The coffin was placed on the floor beside the bed. Carefully, Annie's body, dressed in a white shroud, was lifted out of the bed and put into the coffin.

Catherine buried her tear-drenched face in my bosom. "I'm not going to look, Roselyn!" she sobbed. "Oh Roselyn, I'm not going to look."

"It's all right, you don't have to." I consoled her. She snuggled her head to my heart.

The undertaker and his assistant lifted the coffin and placed it on a trestle in the centre of the room. Four candlesticks were placed beside it, two at the head and two at the feet. The undertaker lit the candles and crossed the room to where Jim was sitting. He whispered into Jim's ear. Jim promptly arose, and the undertaker, taking his arm, led him over to the coffin.

Broken hearted, Jim stood staring at his beloved Annie's lifeless body. He put a white lily of the valley on her chest and bent over to kiss her. It was evident that he was trying desperately to curb his feelings. But grief overcame him. He buried his head in his hands and cried like a baby. Father stepped over and putting his arm around him led him out of the room.

My heart was aching for both Jim and Catherine.

How awful for them, having to endure this ritual.

Catherine straightened up. She tossed her head back and in a clear voice said, "I want to see my mother, Roselyn," she demanded, "I want to see my mother."

"Wheesht, wheesht now, Catherine! You may see her if you wish!" I put my arm around her and led her over to the coffin and lifted her up.

She took one look at the waxen face with its long pointy nose, sticking in the air. "That's not my mother!" she sobbed. "Oh Roselyn, Roselyn! That's not my mother!"

White handkerchiefs muffled the whispers that spun around the room. Mother, quick to the rescue as always, said, "This is no place for the bairn, Roselyn, take her to the kitchen."

In the kitchen, Jim was sitting by the fireside. He was sipping on a glass of whisky and staring into the fire when we entered. He was totally oblivious to Catherine and me.

Sitting quietly in the chair on the opposite side of the hearth, Catherine on my lap, I snuggled her into me. When she had calmed down, I suggested to Jim that she and I stay at the Inn and return to West Lights in the morning.

"That's a good idea, Roselyn," he spluttered out between sobs, "this is no place for the bairn."

In Catherine's bedroom I packed a change of clothes, nightgown and toiletries into an overnight bag. Upon bidding everyone goodnight we left.

Next day we enjoyed a leisurely breakfast of porridge, boiled eggs and toast, served in our room. After that, we caught the ten-past-ten train to Dundee and would, in due course, catch the three o'clock train from Dundee to Tayport.

Huddled in a corner of the carriage, Catherine gazed aimlessly out the window. She was deep in thought. Poor little soul, she looked so forlorn. I watched her intently for the longest time, wondering what was on her mind.

Suddenly, with a glint of light in her eyes, she chirped, "Is my mother in heaven, Roselyn?"

"Of course she is, Catherine, she most definitely is."

"Then there's no need to be sad. So many times she told me that God's in heaven and it's the most beautiful place you can ever imagine."

I smiled, and gently took her tiny hand in mine. "Catherine! Your mother was absolutely right. And to be with God in heaven is the greatest honour we can strive for. Hopefully we'll be reunited with your mother some day. Until then, we must get on with our lives."

She squeezed my hand and gave a big contented sigh.

West Lights was far removed from the trials and tribulations of the previous day. The balmy April breeze, blowing down the Firth, brought with it a multitude of heavenly fragrances to welcome us home.

All Catherine could talk about now was her beloved Pat. The moment we reached home, she slipped her hand out of mine and ran over to Bob's to get him.

"Let's take Pat for a walk, Roselyn." Pat was straining on his leash and panting furiously, his little red tongue hanging out. I had to smile to myself at their antics.

"What do you say we nip over to pay Allan a visit, Catherine? I'm sure he'd love to see how big Pat has grown. Perhaps we could invite him for tea."

She jumped with glee at the idea. Bounding off ahead of me she shouted over her shoulder, "I know the way to Allan's."

From that day on, yesterday's heart-breaking events were forgotten. She never brought up her mother's name again.

Allan was taken aback when he answered the door to Catherine and me. "Why Roselyn, what a lovely surprise! I didn't expect you back till Sunday. What are you doing back so soon?" he asked in the same breath.

"Oh it's a long story Allan, I'll tell you all about it some other time. Catherine and I have come to invite you to tea."

A smile broke out on his face as he leaned forward to cup my face in his hands. He kissed my brow and said, "I'd be delighted to come! Let me get my jacket."

Down to the common we went before going home. Catherine loved to play chase with Allan. We all had lots of fun. I made a huge fuss of Allan. In my own curious way I knew I was trying to make it up to him for my feelings for Ralph.

Mother and Father arrived home late Monday afternoon, exhausted from the ordeal of Annie's funeral. Needless to say, they made a big fuss of Catherine, pleased to find her in such high spirits.

"Aunt Liz!" she blurted out excitedly the moment they came in the house. "Roselyn said, she'll be my big sister, if I wish." Mother, smiling softly, asked if she would like that.

She looked at Mother and in a spirited voice, said. "Oh, yes, Aunt Liz! Roselyn and I have lots of fun and she even lets me sleep with her sometimes, don't you Roselyn? It's great having a big sister."

It was as if Catherine had always been part of our family. Obviously Mother and Father were delighted to have her. From what I could see, they were enjoying every minute.

After tea, Catherine couldn't wait to go out to the garden to play with Pat. She was bubbling with joy as she hastily fastened his leash to his collar. Turning to me she asked if I would like to come out to play?

I had to smile to myself at the sweet innocence. "Not this time, Catherine, perhaps another day."

While Catherine was out, Mother and Father took the opportunity to congratulate me on my engagement to Allan. "Your ring's absolutely magnificent, Roselyn!" Mother remarked holding my hand to examine it more closely. "Allan certainly didn't make a fool of you."

"It was his granny's ring, she bequeathed it to me."

Mother's eyes narrowed as her indignation rose. "What, you mean to tell me he didn't buy you a new ring? Well, you'll never have a day's luck wearing someone else's ring."

I was shocked at her attitude. She couldn't be serious. She had to be joking. But she was very serious.

"What does a ring have to do with luck, Mother?" I snapped.

"Oh, you'll find out sooner or later. I never thought that Allan Robertson was so stingy, but I might have known. Huh! A second-hand ring! I thought you meant more to him than that."

"Mother, stop it! How dare you speak of Allan like that? If I had wanted a new ring he would have gladly bought me one. I had very deep feelings for his granny and I still do. I'm proud to wear her ring. So there! What is it that disturbs you so, Mother? I really wish I knew."

Father intercepted. "Liz! For the love of heavens stop it. Forget about all that superstitious nonsense. Whether the ring's new or not makes no difference whatsoever. A ring is a ring, is a ring." He rose from his chair, folded his newspaper, and stepping over, he took my hand in his. "I wish you and Allan all the luck in the world, Roselyn." He bent and kissed me on the brow, and went back to his reading.

Catherine broke the silence when she barged in

gasping out, "Aunt Liz, Aunt Liz, come and see what Pat's doing."

Mother got out of her chair to answer Catherine's call and pausing in the threshold of the doorway, looked me in the eye, saying, "You mark my words. This'll not be the end of this. This is not a good beginning. Not a good beginning."

When I entered the lounge at my lodgings on Wednesday evening, my colleagues descended upon me like a swarm of bees. Nothing ever goes unnoticed at the residence, and my engagement ring dazzled their eyes. Each one in turn had to have a wish on it. Questions were fired from every direction.

"Have you and Allan set a date yet?"

"Yes we have. We're getting married on the twenty-first of May, next year."

"Is it going to be a white wedding?"

"Of course." My head was spinning by the time I got upstairs to my room. Quickly undressing, I jumped into bed and as I lay there I began to have doubts. Had I done the right thing, I wondered? Like always, Ralph came into my thoughts and a feeling of sadness saturated me. "Oh Ralph, please forgive me!" I sighed, closing my eyes.

CHAPTER

20

The Ball

Terren and I were well prepared for the exams. The written part commenced at nine o'clock sharp the following Monday and continuing until Thursday. The oral exam was to take place on Friday in Matron's office. This was the part we all dreaded. Seated on benches in the reception area, the nurses sat stiff and prim as they waited in silence for their names to be called. All looked pale-faced and nervous.

Mister Dallas, a retired consultant, was the examiner that day. He rose from the high-backed chair in which he had been sitting when I entered the office. He crossed the room, greeting me with a cheerful, "Good Morning, Nurse Carey!"

"Good morning, Sir!" I responded nervously.

He led me to the chair on the opposite side of the desk from his. "Please sit, Nurse Carey," he gestured with his hand.

Nervous as a kitten and stiff as a poker I sat on the edge of the chair.

"Relax Nurse Carey!" he smiled, resuming his seat. "I'm not going to bite you, I'm only here to ask you a few questions." He settled himself in his chair like a chicken getting comfortable in her nest. "Now, tell me what happens when the spinal chord is severed? What are the implications for the nurse? How would you treat such a patient if you were in charge of him?"

I coughed, clearing my throat. "Well the first thing that happens is ..." I gave him details as to what happens in such cases and all the nurse's responsibilities. I got into such a list of things that he had to stop me from going on and on.

He continued with more questions and all the time I was answering his questions he was jotting down notes. "Now tell me, what is consumption and how is it treated?" He peered over the top of his spectacles, making me feel more nervous than ever. In the back of my mind I was telling myself not to be afraid, but I just couldn't stop the fluttering in my heart.

"Consumption is a disease that can damage a person's lungs, or other parts of the body, causing serious illness. It damages the lungs so that the patient ends up with no ability to breathe." I thought desperately for things to say about this one. It seemed to me that no one knew much about this terrible disease. "The treatment for the disease is plenty of rest, fresh air, and good nutritious food. At the present time there is no known cure for consumption," I quickly added.

"Now, Nurse Carey, name four of the major organs of the human body."

"The heart, the lungs, the kidneys and the skin." I rattled them off, all in the same breath. I told myself that I had to speak more slowly in order to sound intelligent. When I rattled things off, I knew that I sounded foolish.

"Can you tell me what are the dangers when treating someone with a compound fracture?" He yawned as if bored by all this chatter. I sympathized with him. Indeed it had to be boring asking the same questions to young girls as green as myself.

"The main risk would be infection. It is important to keep everything clean near the patient and to make sure that all dressings are changed often. It is also important that the patient gets a good diet so that the bone can heal." And more and more about bone and flesh healing. Again he had to stop me. I didn't know if I was all wrong, or if he got the impression that I did, indeed, know my material and so he didn't have to pay attention.

"What can be done if there is infection?"

"If possible there should be drainage and if possible the wound should be left open to the air to help it heal." Now that I was getting into the questions, I was quite relaxed and almost enjoyed the battle.

He asked several more questions and again I rattled off answers and hoped that they were correct.

"Thank you, Nurse Carey, that'll be all. Would you please send Nurse MacDonald in?"

"Certainly!" I replied happily, relieved that the examination was over. I stepped briskly across the room, closing the door quietly behind me.

"Nurse MacDonald!" I spoke softly scanning the group. A plump, freckle-faced girl with carrot-red hair jumped to her feet. "Would you please go in now?" She timidly entered the office, closing the door.

Prancing along the corridor, I happily skipped down the wide staircase to the main hall. I had to admit the examination hadn't been half as bad as I'd imagined. I couldn't believe the professor had asked so few questions.

My heart was full of joy as I made my way up the hill to the residence. "How did you do?" I asked Terren the moment I entered the room.

"Oh God, Roselyn!" she sighed. "I thought I'd made a fool of myself. When the professor asked me to name the main artery of the heart, my mind went blank. I just sat there like a dummy for what seemed an eternity. Suddenly, out of the blue, I spluttered out, 'the aorta' - I felt so foolish! Such a simple question and my mind drew a blank. How did you do?"

"Well, I was as nervous as could be, but I didn't have a problem. Thank heavens I knew the answers to the questions he asked me. Perhaps they were easier than yours."

"That'll be right," she laughed. She seemed to be much improved. She had a little more colour in her cheeks and she was much more lively than she'd been for a long, long time.

Relieved that the general exams were over, we played in the room like a couple of schoolchildren. Of course, we were also excited about the Hospital Ball that was taking place that evening. Neither of us had ever been to a ball before and could only imagine what it was going to be like.

Our room was an utter shambles. Dresses were hanging on hangers on the outside of the wardrobe. Our white starched petticoats lay on our beds and a smoothing iron was warming on the gas ring, just in case we needed to do some touching up. Excitement made us hysterical. We danced about the room, singing at the top of our voices. "Hip, hip, hooray! Hip, hip hooray! Exams are over, now we can play! Hip, hip hooray!"

"Would you fasten these hooks for me, Roselyn? Terren asked, slipping into her dress. "I can't seem to reach them." Her dress was a delicate shade of eggshell, with flared cap sleeves. I fastened the hooks for her and, she in turn fastened mine.

My dress was a lovely coral colour, with matching chiffon stole. Mother had made it especially for the ball. I twirled in front of the mirror, admiring myself. I saw myself as truly elegant.

Allan and Jerry were waiting patiently at the gate, looking like a couple of penguins, dressed in their formal wear. The moment Terren and I stepped out the door, they gasped with delight. "Look at you!" they burst out simultaneously.

Linking arms together, we walked four abreast happily down the Infirmary Brae. We chatted excitedly all the way to the taxi rank outside the city churches.

The Inn on the Park was the best hotel in Broughty Ferry. Its fine cuisine was said to be fit for a queen.

The five-course dinner, served in the formal dining room, was scrumptious. A sliver of smoked salmon, garnished with a pickle or two, started us off. A bowl of Cullen skink and lots of fresh crispy rolls followed. The main course was wild duck in orange sauce, fresh vegetables and Parisian potatoes. Traditional sherry trifle, biscuits and cheese and of course, coffee, completed the meal. It certainly was a feast fit for a queen, but I was so excited, I hardly ate a thing.

After the meal had been served, a few couples drifted into the ballroom and stood around waiting for the music to begin. A crystal chandelier reflected a multitude of colours about the room creating a magical atmosphere. What a pretty picture it was.

French windows opened onto a trellised terrace and a beautiful garden full of spring flowers. Many couples chose to sit out on the terrace, enjoying their port, watching the rippling on the silvery river.

The moment the maestro announced the first waltz, a massive exodus to the ballroom took place. Without a doubt, everyone was in a lively party mood. Our group danced every dance, exchanging partners for some of the reels. Even the Matron, consultants and sisters whooped it up, not at all like the stuffed shirts they had appeared to be in the hospital.

I thought the ball was fabulous. I can't remember ever enjoying myself so much. Everyone seemed to have an equally wonderful time. The senior staff got drunker by the minute, and when Allan and I were ready to leave we also were a little tipsy. We waltzed our way along the platform in the railway station and caught the last train to Tayport from Dundee, just in the nick of time.

Snuggling in the carriage, we began to dissect the highlights of the evening. "Wasn't it hilarious when Sister Phillips fell on her bottom, while dancing with Professor Fairly? He's the Chief of Staff, you know. I was so embarrassed for her, weren't you Allan?"

"Yes, I was! But wasn't that her husband she was dancing with?"

"Husband!" I swallowed. "She doesn't have a husband. Who in their right mind would marry her?"

"Roselyn, what a nasty thing to say! Surely she isn't that bad? By the way sweetheart, cattiness doesn't become you."

"You're right, that was a nasty thing to say, I take it all back."

In the shimmering moonlight, the gravel crunched beneath our feet as we strolled hand in hand along the path to my home. The only sound in the still night was the lapping of the water gently kissing the shore and the echo of our footsteps on the gravel path.

"I wish I didn't have to leave you, Roselyn," Allan whispered, "I love you so very much. I just want to be with you all the time. It's going to be terrible when I have to go to London."

"I know what you mean, but time will pass quickly and it'll be New Year before we know it. I wish you didn't have to go, but you must." I said what he wanted to hear. He kissed me and left at once.

My parents were already in bed, so I went straight to my room. In my nightie, I sat at the dressing table brushing my hair. My thoughts of course drifted to Ralph. I knew he was going to be devastated by my engagement to Allan. It would put an end to all his hopes. But he was well aware of the situation from the beginning. I prayed to God that he'd understand. I jumped into bed and put both Allan and Ralph out of my mind.

A shaft of light streaming through a slit in the curtains awoke me next morning. It was already eight o'clock and I had promised Mother we'd get an early start for the market in Dundee.

Wrapped in my dressing gown, I went to the kitchen. Mother was out in the back garden hanging washing on the line. The sheets cracked as they flapped about in the wind.

Catherine was frolicking about on the grass with her canine friend. She was having a fabulous time. Her happy shrieks filled the air, as she threw a ball for him to retrieve.

Pat was a good little puppy, a bit on the shy side with strangers, but a brave little soldier whenever someone came knocking at the door.

Father was sitting at the fireside reading the

morning paper when I entered the kitchen. He jumped to his feet the moment I stepped into the room. "Good morning, Cuddle," he said and immediately began to serve my breakfast.

"Now that your exams are over, does that mean you're a fully fledged nurse?" he asked, as he poured out the tea.

"No, not at all. I still have the midwifery course to do. It starts in September, and finishes next April. But I'm considering taking the summer off. I'd like to spend as much time as possible with Allan, before he goes to London."

"Does your mother know any of this?"

"Good heavens, no. I hesitate to tell her anything these days, the way she's been behaving. I can just hear her, can't you? She'll go stark staring mad. I promised her a long time ago I'd look for a job on this side of the river when I finished my general training. I hate breaking a promise, but I'd much rather do midwifery in the Dundee Royal."

"Dear-oh-dear, I sympathize with you Roselyn. I'd be happy to break the news to her, if you like."

"Oh, Father, you're a sweetheart, you really are." I rose and gave him a big hug. "But don't say anything yet. Let's wait and see what I decide." I smiled softly, sipping on the hot tea.

"What ever you say, cuddle!" He smiled and went back to reading his newspaper.

Mother and I were excited at the thought of a day's bargain hunting at the market in Dundee. Father offered to mind Catherine. He had arranged to take her sailing with a friend who had bought a new sailboat. The boat was moored in the harbour at Crail, about fifteen miles down the coast from Tayport.

Catherine was delighted at the idea of going sailing. She shouted over the fence, letting the neighbours know where she was going, as she skipped up the path hand-in-hand with Father.

The market was in full swing when we arrived. All along the pavement, as far as Castle Street, the stalls were almost touching. Meat, vegetables, fish, buttons, bows, elastic and pins, more vegetables, toys, and last but not least, piles and piles of second-hand clothes.

"Haddock, fresh haddock! Arbroath smokie's! Two pairs for fourpence!" Fish Willie, a heavyset, rugged man in a striped apron, shouted at the top of his voice. He tossed the fish about on his dripping wet, fly-infested stall.

Along the front of the stalls it was thick with sharp-elbowed people, shoving and pushing each other as they ploughed their way to the tea tent. The tent was always packed with people when they'd finished shopping, enjoying a cup of tea, a mutton pie, or perhaps a soda scone thickly spread with butter. The women serving the tea were by no means hygienic. They swirled the dirty dishes around in a galvanized tub full of cold water and wiped them dry on their grimy aprons.

A charcoal brazier, which served two purposes, sat in the centre of the tent. Kettles of water were boiled to make the tea, and the hot coal kept the tent warm in the winter. A day at the market wouldn't have been complete without a visit to the tea tent.

Customers sat on benches chatting happily to each other as they enjoyed their weekly treat. Of course, like everyone else, Mother and I couldn't resist indulging, hygienic or not.

Children, wide-eyed, were licking on ice cream cones. Gentleman stood about in small groups chatting to each other, puffing on their pipes, waiting patiently for their wives.

We had the time of our lives rummaging through old cotton dresses piled high on the rickety stalls.

As we relaxed on the homeward-bound train, we chattered happily, content with our treasures.

In the house, Catherine came running, throwing herself into Mother's arms. "Oh Aunt Liz! Aunt Liz!" she sobbed. "I was so sick on that awful boat."

"Are you all right now?" Mother asked, full of concern, putting her hand on Catherine's brow, before removing her coat.

"Yes I am! I was all right as soon as I got off the boat. I didn't like sailing, Aunt Liz, I never want to do it again." She trotted off to the kitchen to get Pat. Suddenly she covered her mouth with her hand and began to cry.

"What's the matter, Catherine?" Mother and Father asked simultaneously.

"My tooth hurts." she sniffled.

"Oh dear me! Let's rub some oil of cloves on it, that should help." Mother went to fetch the bottle from the medicine cabinet.

"Will that make my tooth better, Aunt Liz?" she asked opening her mouth wide.

"It might! If it doesn't, I'll put some more on before you go to bed."

The toothache that bothered her all evening had been soothed by the oil of cloves and a hot water bottle that Mother had given her to take to bed. She had fallen asleep with her face resting on the bottle. The water in the bottle soon grew cold and the tooth started to ache again. Poor little Catherine wakened up to misery. Mother ran to the bedroom to comfort her, this time rubbing whisky on her gums around the affected area. Alas, the toothache persisted and early next morning, Father carted her off to the dentist to have the tooth pulled.

The following weekend Terren and Jerry came to visit, as previously planned. We travelled together on the train from Dundee to Tayport. In high spirits, we hadn't a care in the world and were acting like overgrown children, telling silly jokes and playing 'I-spy'.

CHAPTER
21

The
Wedding Gown

Allan was waiting on the platform when the train hissed to a stop in the station. He was beaming as he helped me alight and warmly greeted Terren and Jerry.

It was a glorious evening. The sun in the western sky was ablaze, giving prospects of fine weather to come.

My parents were delighted to have laughter about the house, after all the sorrow that had surrounded our family lately.

They had prepared a delicious tea. Father had baked a ham and egg pie – one of his specialities – and served it with mashed potatoes. By the look of the groaning table, Mother must have been baking all day. Lemon meringue pie, cream sponge, and sultana cake were but a few of the treats on the table.

I was reminded of old times when Tom used to bring Ella home for the weekend before they got married.

After tea, we lingered around the table, telling tall tales, each trying to outdo the other. Of course, Father won hands down as always, with his never-ending stories of exotic places visited while he was in the army.

After Allan and Jerry left, Father excused himself. "You girls must have lots to talk about. You don't need an old fuddy-duddy hanging around." He smiled as he left the room, taking his newspaper with him.

We huddled around the fireplace enjoying the smouldering embers, telling ghost stories, of all things, until all that was left in the grate was a pile of cinders.

The crowing of the cock at first light awoke me next morning. I became restless, turning the events of the day before over in my mind. I just couldn't get back to sleep. Slipping out of bed, I draped my dressing gown over my shoulders, and went to the kitchen to make a cup of tea.

I filled the kettle with water and put it on the gas ring. Lifting the ashes, I kindled the fire, and was about to set the table when Mother came into the room, yawning her head off.

"My goodness you're up early, Roselyn," she said in between yawns, "I thought you'd have a lie-in this morning."

"I intended to, but that damned rooster of Davie Mar's woke me at the crack of dawn. It's enough to wake the dead!"

I continued to set the table. Mother fussed about, filling the milk jug, adding sugar to the sugar bowl and putting them on the table.

"My goodness, Roselyn, what a shock I got when I saw Terren! You're right, she has lost a lot of weight. But surely it's not only pre-wedding nerves? I think there is something else wrong with her. She should consult her doctor."

"She has; he prescribed a tonic for her. To tell the truth, I think she's worrying too much about the wedding. I'm sure she'll bounce right back afterwards." As I said it, my arms became covered with goose bumps.

Another deep feeling of sadness came over me.

"I certainly hope you're right. She can't afford to lose much more weight. My goodness, there'll soon be nothing left of her."

Mother cooked a lovely breakfast. Porridge, bacon, eggs, black pudding and, of course, thick toast oozing with butter. I think she was trying to fatten Terren up.

Catherine was sitting on Terren's lap entertaining her, while Mother and I washed and wiped the dishes. I overheard her telling Terren about the clever things that her Pat could do. "And guess what, Terren?" she squeaked out, "he can even sing."

"Really? He certainly is a clever little dog."

"Let's get on with the fitting of the dress before the boys come," Mother interrupted, rolling her sleeves up as if she meant business.

"Can I watch, can I watch?" Catherine blurted out excitedly. "Please, please!"

"If you promise to behave yourself," Mother told her. "But I think perhaps you should get Terren's permission. After all, it's her dress."

Catherine looked at Terren pleadingly and before she could say a word, Terren said, "Of course you can, your opinion's important too."

Mother went upstairs to fetch the dress and joined us in the bedroom. Holding it by the hanger in one hand, she cleverly flared the skirt out like a fan with the other, showing the dress to its best advantage.

Terren gasped. "It's beautiful Mistress Carey!" She gently fingered the shimmering satin. "I'd no idea it would turn out to be so beautiful."

"Just wait till you see yourself in it." Mother carefully slipped it over Terren's head.

"Oh, oh, you look just like a princess," Catherine burst out, full of excitement, before the dress was half way over Terren's head. Although the dress was gorgeous, Mother had an awful lot of pinning to do to make it fit.

Terren's ashen complexion was greatly exaggerated by the ivory colour of the satin. Just as well it wasn't pure white, other wise she'd look like a ghost.

"Well, what do you think?" Terren inquired twirling around in front of the mirror.

"You look beautiful, Terren, but what's most important, what do you think?"

"I'm too excited to think, but it is beautiful, there's no doubt about that." She paraded back and forth and each time she passed the mirror took another look. Of course, Catherine was in her glory, walking behind her holding up the train and singing at the pitch of her voice, "Here Comes the Bride".

Allan and Jerry arrived promptly at ten o'clock, full of the joys of life. Allan had borrowed Patricia's bicycle for Terren, and Ian's for Jerry. It was a glorious morning, brilliant sunshine and not a cloud in the sky.

"St. Andrews, here we come!" Jerry shouted, at the top of his voice, as we sped along the Cupar road.

Because of the clarity of the day we could see an amazing distance. Sailing ships entering the mouth of the river looked like little toy boats, bobbing about on the horizon.

We pedalled with all our might, singing the latest songs in harmony and by the time we reached St. Andrews, we were certainly invigorated. Terren's ghastly complexion was replaced with rosy red cheeks.

Where should we picnic? Now this is the big question. Although the beach would have been the logical place, we agreed the sand would get into everything.

The Abbey was the chosen spot, but to picnic in the graveyard wouldn't have been my choice.

Terren and Jerry had never visited St. Andrews before. They were simply overwhelmed by the magnificent architecture. Jerry was particularly impressed with the university buildings. Set in their own grounds and overlooking St. Andrews Bay, the buildings were enough to impress anyone.

"If everyone's finished, I'd like to go," I said, packing up our things.

"I'll second that." Terren piped up. "I'm not at all happy, sitting here amongst the dead."

When we arrived at the beach, we parked the bicycles in the racks behind the old clubhouse.

Grains of sand oozed up through our toes as we ran barefoot along the beach, slipping and sliding all over the place. We splashed our feet in the icy cold water searching for seashells. The best shells are found when the tide is receding. A brisk breeze blowing in from the German Sea revitalized our spirits. It was breathtaking.

"Lets have a piggyback race!" Jerry shouted with glee. The words were no sooner out of his mouth when Terren leaped onto his back. I did likewise on Allan's. The boys took off at great speed, having difficulty keeping their feet in the slippery sand. Full of enthusiasm, Terren and I urged our imaginary ponies on. Allan was first to give up, throwing himself down, gasping for breath, and taking me down with him. Jerry soon followed suit. Our happy voices echoed gales of laughter that I would long remember. Exhausted, we spread ourselves out on the sand, letting the warm sun play softly on our tired bodies.

"Thank you, Lord, for this beautiful, beautiful day!" Terren sighed, "I will cherish it forever!"

We had all tired ourselves out and soon fell

sound sleep. An odd drop of rain woke us up. Rain clouds blocked out the sun. "Good heavens! We're going to get soaked!" Jerry said, jumping to his feet.

Slipping and sliding we ran as fast as we could to retrieve our bicycles. Giant rain pellets began to fall from the overcast sky. They fell sparsely at first, but moments later, the heavens opened up and torrential rain swept the countryside.

The journey home was nothing less than a nightmare. It required a great deal of effort to fight against the strong wind and heavy rain.

The boys went straight to Craigie Bank, while Terren and I carried on through the narrow winding streets of Tayport and followed the coast road to my home.

The delicious aroma of something hot, crisp and spicy wafted out the moment I opened the front door. It might have been gingerbread or perhaps ginger-snaps. But, whatever it was, made me hungry.

"Good heavens, would you look at you two!" Mother gasped, hurrying to fetch a couple of towels warming in front of a roaring fire. "You'd better hurry up and dry your hair. Get out of those wet clothes before you catch your death of cold." She was particularly concerned for Terren. "Hurry up now!" she said giving us each a towel. "Go sit by the fire and I'll bring you a cup of hot tea, that'll warm you up."

The rain had lasted a couple of hours but by late afternoon the sun burst out again promising a beautiful evening.

We were none the worse for the soaking we'd got. Later we decided to walk along the beach to meet our sweethearts. Wild flowers growing in abundance along the banks of the river were laden with raindrops, slowly evaporating in the early evening sunshine. Their heavy perfume mingled with the sweet smell of wet grass, sending out a heavenly fragrance that only occurs after rain.

Terren and I had only walked half way to Tayport, when Jerry and Allen came speeding towards us on their bicycles. They were overjoyed to see us looking more like their girls than the drowned rats they had left a short while ago.

"Come on, Roselyn," Allan called excitedly, skidding to a halt, "hop on!" he ordered. I sat sideways on the bar of his bicycle. Terren quickly followed suit on Jerry's.

Refreshed and happy, we rode merrily along the path, blasting out old sea shanties at the top of our voices. The balmy breeze blew through our hair and the sun shone its golden rays upon us. When we reached the end of the path, we disembarked to admire the configuration of the Tay Bridge.

"That's certainly a sight to behold," Jerry gasped. "It certainly is an engineering marvel, there's no doubt about that. I read in the local newspaper that the Queen's going to be crossing the bridge in June, supposedly to encourage people to use the bridge. Rumours that the structure's far too weak scare people off; something to do with the foundations. Have you heard anything to that effect, Allan?"

"Yes, I have, but let's face it, rumours are only rumours. It's the longest bridge in the world, you know."

"Yes, so I believe! How long is it, exactly?"

"It's a little more than two miles from Wormit to Dundee."

"That's amazing!" Jerry commented.

"The first train crossed over the bridge in September 1877. It was a glorious day. The bright, autumn sun stood high in the sky lighting the bright reds, golds and oranges of the Fifeshire Hills. But the formal opening didn't take place until nine months later."

"Allan and I witnessed the official crossing on June the first last year," I piped up, "didn't we, Allan?"

"Did you really?"

"We certainly did! We were among the crowd that cheered the special train carrying dignitaries across the bridge, including Sir Thomas Bouch, the engineer who designed it. He must have been proud."

"I remember every detail as if it were yesterday. Allan and I were so excited. We were fortunate enough to get a spot on the platform. Wormit was choked with people from all walks of life lining the railway banks as the train approached. Handkerchiefs waved, and loud cheering greeted it. School children waved their little flags. Many of the ladies waved their parasols, including me. As the train passed by, handkerchiefs fluttered from the carriage windows. It certainly was a day to remember."

"Of course, don't forget it was a historical event," Allan piped up.

"How did that make you feel, Allan? To be part of history, I mean?" Jerry asked, jokingly.

"Well, we're all part of history, are we not?" Allan replied smugly.

"I hate to break up this serious discussion," I interrupted, "but we'd better make tracks. My mother's expecting us at six. She'll be most annoyed if we're late."

Mother and Father were plainly happy to see us in such good spirits.

In the living room, Father poured a glass of sherry for everyone and raising his glass, toasted our guests.

Jerry was overwhelmed with the view from our living-room window. He stood there staring out to sea, totally mesmerised. "You know, Mister Carey, there are lots of people who'd give a fortune to have a view like this."

"I've no doubt there are! We consider ourselves very fortunate!" Father smiled proudly.

It was obvious that Jerry was enjoying his visit. He bombarded Father with questions about the shipping industry and the ships that frequented the Dundee harbour. He was flabbergasted to learn that most of the whaling boats in the world had been built in the Dundee shipyard.

Catherine helped Mother put things on the table. She was dressed in one of her Sunday dresses, covered by a pretty white apron trimmed with frilly lace made by Mother for the occasion. "You look just like a French maid, Catherine!" Allan teased. She giggled at the very idea.

"Tea's served!" Mother announced with a beaming smile.

"It certainly smells good, whatever it is, Mistress Carey," Allan said as he arose from his chair to go to the table.

"It's fish, I hope everyone likes fish." Mother's eyes scanned the guests.

Father sat at the head of the table and dutifully said grace. "For what we are about to receive may the lord make us truly thankful. Amen!"

I was proud of my parents. They had gone to a great deal of effort to make things nice for my friends. They served poached rainbow trout with mashed potatoes and peas. Eve's pudding smothered in hot custard followed. I'd guessed correctly about the spicy aroma; it was gingerbread.

In his element, as always when we have visitors, Father was the perfect host. He made sure that no-one's plate was empty and included everyone in conversation.

We huddled around the fireplace listening to his many tales of faraway lands. When Mother thought we'd had enough, she suggested a singsong. Each in turn sang their party-piece and helped those who had forgotten the words of their own special song.

Listening intently, Catherine's eyes sparkled with delight. Curled up on Mother's lap, she cradled Pat in her arms.

When it was time for Jerry and Allan to leave, Terren and I kissed our sweethearts goodnight underneath a star-filled sky. What a memorable evening.

CHAPTER

22

Terren Departs

When I entered the ward the following Monday, Sister Phillips was sitting at Sister Wotherspoon's desk. I could tell they had been talking about me by the way Sister Phillips eyed me the moment I entered.

She gestured with her forefinger, beckoning me to join them. "I was inquiring whether you are fit to return to the surgical ward, Nurse Carey?"

The thought of going back to work with her made me cringe, but I smiled and answered politely, "I'm quite sure I'll manage all right, Sister. My aim is much improved."

"Nurse Carey is being rather optimistic, Sister Phillips!" Sister Wotherspoon intercepted. "I think she needs another two or three weeks down here. I'll start to introduce some light lifting to strengthen her wrist. Of course, that's if you're agreeable?"

Sister Phillips flushed. I could tell she was furious. In spite of this, she agreed to Sister Wotherspoon's suggestion. "Very well, another three weeks and I want to see her back upstairs, whether she's ready or not."

She stomped off resentfully.

The moment she'd gone, Sister Wotherspoon leaned over the desk and whispered, "Much as I'd love to keep you, Nurse, you have to complete your clinical in order to complete your diploma."

"Yes I know," I smiled, "I'm aware of that. It was kind of you to get me some more time with you."

There wasn't much excitement at the hospital now the exams were over. No more lectures to attend. No exchanging of notes. And no more studying into the wee small hours. Everything was strictly routine.

The townsfolk seemed to be much happier, now that the weather had warmed up. It did my heart good to see such happy, high-spirited people.

Children were taking full advantage of the twilight evenings, playing in the street until long past their usual bedtimes. Boys played at pinners and boolies and girls played French ropes and hopscotch. Their high-pitched voices and laughter rang out, echoing in the air.

I had become accustomed to the Dundee people and their ways. I'd even come to like the town despite its foul smell of raw jute, chimney stacks, and dull three and four storey tenement buildings.

The outskirts of the town were far removed from the jute industry community of the downtown core. Lovely open spaces contained large mansion houses owned by the jute-mill barons and many local merchants. At that time, West Ferry, a suburb of Dundee, was regarded as the most affluent suburb in the world.

When the Town Council had learned that Queen Victoria was planning to cross the Tay Bridge sometime in June, they invited her also to visit the Albert Institute. She had not yet seen the magnificent building the town had erected in memory of her Prince Albert. And if the truth were known, the people of Dundee were upset that she hadn't.

Now that she was to be coming, all had been for-
given. Everyone was thrilled at the idea of the planned
visit. All kinds of wonderful preparations were being
made to impress Her Majesty. Schools were to be
closed, so children could wave their little flags.
Enthusiasm swept through the town as the day of the
royal event drew near.

Terren and I were planning to join in the happy
festivities surrounding the royal event. Of course, that
would depend on whether we could wangle a half-day off
work. Neither of us had ever seen the Queen in person,
so it would be the thrill of a lifetime.

On the morning of May the twenty-seventh, I
bumped into Sister Wotherspoon in the corridor. "Why
Nurse Carey, you're the very person I've been looking
for. I'm most concerned about your roommate, Terren
Dawn. I passed the time of day with her at the duty
office last evening. She sounds and looks dreadful,
please get her to see a doctor, the sooner the better."

"I've already tried to do that, she flatly refuses to
take any advice. I really think pre-wedding nerves is at
the root of the problem."

"'Pre-wedding nerves!'" she gasped. "For heav-
en's sake, Nurse, I credited you with more sense. If you
ask me, it looks more like consumption. But whatever it
is, I can assure you it's serious!" She walked off shaking her head.

The curtains were still drawn in our room when
I came off night duty next morning. Terren was sound
asleep.

"Terren! Terren! You were supposed to be on duty
twenty minutes ago. Terren?" I gave her a gentle shake.

"Oh, Roselyn, what time is it?" she moaned,
pulling herself up to a half-sitting position. "I feel terri-

ble! I've coughed the whole night long, and I feel as if there's a ton weight lying on my chest. My whole body aches." I quickly stepped over and put my hand on her brow. She was roasting.

"I'm going to fetch a doctor," I said, quickly throwing my cloak over my shoulders.

"Get Jerry, Roselyn!" she spluttered out. "Get Jerry!"

"You know I can't do that, it's against the code of ethics."

"Oh to hell with the code of ethics! I said, 'get Jerry'!"

I couldn't believe my ears. I'd never heard Terren speaking like that before. I ran all the way to the Infirmary, gasping for breath. I found Jerry in Paediatrics.

"Terren's not well, Jerry," I told him, "her temperature's sky-high. She wants you to come."

"I can't do that, Roselyn, you know I can't!"

"Yes I know! But she was adamant and insisted I ask you."

"I'll get Bill Gardener to go. He's an excellent doctor. You keep an eye on her until Bill arrives. I'll be there as soon as I've finished my rounds."

Huffing and puffing, I ran all the way back to Terren. Quietly opening the door, I slipped into the room. Terren was delirious, speaking in a childlike voice and thinking I was her mother.

I rushed to the bathroom, filled a basin with warm water, grabbed a washcloth and towel and returned to her bedside. I began sponging her down and continued to do so until Doctor Gardener arrived.

He examined her thoroughly and turning to me he said, "It's pneumonia in both lungs. She'll have to be moved to hospital. I'll send an ambulance at once. Keep a close eye on her until the ambulance arrives." He left, leaving me open-mouthed.

I sat on the edge of her bed looking down at her pale, gaunt face. A twang of pain stabbed my heart. It was at that moment I realised how seriously ill she was. If anything happened to her, I'd be the one to blame. I should've forced her to consult her doctor ages ago. Now, her ailments had developed into this.

I checked my watch continuously, praying the ambulance would arrive soon. It seemed to be taking forever.

At last the door flew open and in burst two attendants carrying a stretcher. It was like all hell had been let loose. In no time Terren was lifted out of bed, laid on the stretcher, wrapped in a blanket and taken off.

Jerry arrived just as they were leaving. "What's happening? What did Bill say was wrong with her?" he asked over his shoulder as he followed the ambulance crew out.

"It's double pneumonia, Jerry!" I called.

"Oh God, no. I'll keep you posted, Roselyn," he said and slammed the door closed.

Everyone was gone! Now I was alone in an empty room. I threw myself on top of my bed and cried my heart out. I must have fallen asleep. It was the wail of the one o'clock bummer, the horn from the jute mill summoning the workers back from their break that woke me. I sat upright on the edge of the bed, rubbing my bleary eyes and yawning.

I had a good wash and prayed that Doctor Gardener's diagnosis was wrong and she had nothing more than the after-effects of a bad bout of influenza.

I had dressed and gone down to the hall when Jerry entered.

He looked ghastly! I surged forward. Putting my

arm around him, I led him into the sitting-room. He sat on the sofa and burst into tears.

"So Doctor Gardener's diagnosis was right after all?"

"Yes, and Doctor McLaren confirmed his findings." Jerry sat staring out the window for the longest time with a faraway look on his face. Then, clearing his throat, he said, "I've sent a telegram to Terren's parents and have just received a reply. Her mother's arriving on the four o'clock train from Glasgow this afternoon. Her father will be arriving on a later train this evening. I can't get away to meet Mistress Dawn, Roselyn, I've an important meeting at three o'clock. I was hoping you could go to meet her?"

"Of course I will, Jerry!"

"I want you to tell her the truth, if she asks."

"And what might that be, Jerry?"

"Terren's dying, Roselyn!" He buried his face in his hands and sobbed.

"Oh, no! No, you must be mistaken! Surely there's something that can be done."

"It's double pneumonia, Roselyn, and other than a miracle, my darling Terren is going to die."

"No! No, no, Jerry, I won't accept that." Moving over, I sat beside him and encircled him in my arms while he cried his heart out.

As it happened, the Glasgow train was half an hour late arriving at the station. Pacing back and forth on the platform, I began to pray. "Dear God please, please, don't take Terren from us yet, she's so young. Please, God!"

"Roselyn, Roselyn, is that you?" A woman's voice jolted me back. It was Mistress Dawn. She looked so befuddled, windswept hair and hat tilted to one side of her head. She carried an overnight bag in one hand, umbrella and shopping basket in the other.

"Oh, please forgive me Mistress Dawn! My thoughts were miles away. Let me help you with these." Taking the overnight bag, I led her out of the station to the taxi stand.

"Andrew had an important meeting to attend in Renfrew this morning. He had already left when Jerry's telegram arrived. However, I sent word to him. He's arriving on the half past eight train this evening."

"What exactly is it that's wrong with Terren?" she asked the moment we were settled into the taxicab. "All Jerry said was, 'Come at once! Terren sick!'"

With a lump in my throat, I reached over and took her hand in mine. "Mistress Dawn!" I coughed nervously. "I'm afraid I'm the bearer of bad news. Terren is dying, she has developed pneumonia and there's nothing that can be done to save her."

Flopping back in her seat, she reached into her pocket for a handkerchief. "I tried to persuade her to see the doctor the last time she was home. But would she? Oh no! Not her! She's so stubborn. Thinks she knows better than everyone else, she does. Now look where it's got her."

"What has happened has nothing to do with whether she consulted a doctor or not, Mistress Dawn. It's because her resistance was low." I felt a need to defend my friend. "We'll just have to pray for a miracle."

"A miracle? Miracles only happen in the Bible, Roselyn!" she said bursting into tears. I left her at the foot of the stairs leading to the sickbay. I took her things to the room reserved for visitors and deposited them inside the door.

I ran up the infirmary brae to my residence. Into bed I crawled in order to get a couple of hours sleep, before going on night duty.

When I had finished work next morning, I couldn't wait to sneak up to the sickbay to see Terren. In spite of the fact that the sickbay was strictly out of bounds, I was determined to see her. Quiet as a mouse, I crept up the narrow staircase. Glancing back over my shoulders I made sure no one saw me. At the top of the stairs, my heart was pounding so loudly I could hear every beat. As I tiptoed towards the ward, the floorboards creaked with every step I took. I was hoping to persuade the nurse in charge to stretch the rules and allow me a few moments with my dying friend.

Terren was in a private room, an indication that she was seriously ill. I prayed to God her condition had improved. Surely all my prayers hadn't fallen by the wayside. Quietly entering the room, I held my breath.

Someone else was in the room. There was a large figure curled up on the bath chair. Looking closer I realised it was the sister in charge. Wrapped in her cloak she resembled a huge cat. Her loud snoring sounded like a cross-saw on a log. I was thankful she was asleep.

Tiptoeing over to Terren's bed I put my hand on her forehead. She was burning! There was a bowl of water sitting on the locker. In it I rinsed a washcloth and gently sponged her brow.

She looked so frail. Her eyes opened slowly and she gazed about the ceiling and the walls. Then she gradually focused on me. Long lashes fluttered on her pale cheeks, but opened wide a moment later. The hint of a smile curled the corners of her mouth. "Roselyn," she gasped, "I'm going to die, you know! I'm sorry to have made so much trouble for you. You've been a good friend, very kind to me. I don't know what I'd have done without you."

"Wheesht, wheesht, now Terren! Wheesht! Don't talk, you have to save your strength."

"What for?" she sighed. She pointed to the water jug indicating she wanted a drink. I poured a little water into an invalid cup and held it to her lips. She sipped slowly, but was far too weak to swallow. The water ran out, trickling down the sides of her mouth and her chin. But she thought she was drinking and that's all that mattered.

Death was set on her face. Her glazed eyes looked into mine and a lonesome tear ran down her cheek. "Roselyn!" she whispered. "I want to be buried in my wedding dress! I must look beautiful for Jerry. Promise me you'll see to that for me." Her voice sank a little lower and faded away in a muffled sob. She turned her face away from me and closed her eyes.

With tears in my own, I bent over and kissed her brow. "I promise you, Terren," I whispered, "I promise you."

"What on earth do you think you're doing?" an angry voice behind me demanded.

I nearly had a heart attack! It was the 'Cat'. She grabbed me by the scruff of the neck and pushed me out into the corridor. I desperately tried to explain to her that the patient was my roommate, but she wouldn't listen.

"I'll have you reported for this," she bellowed. "What's your name, Nurse?"

"Carey!" I stuttered out. "Roselyn Carey!"

"Well, Roselyn Carey! You know perfectly well, this floor is out of bounds. Only the patient's family has the right to be here. Unless by special permission."

"She has permission," a familiar voice rang out. "She has my permission."

"Why, Doctor Lynton!" she stuttered. Her attitude changed at once. Turning to me, she apologised profusely.

"Oh Jerry!" I declared. "Am I glad to see you!"

"I'll meet you in the lunch room in about fifteen minutes, Roselyn," he said, patting the back of my hand. Glancing at his watch, he disappeared quickly into Terren's room.

In the lunchroom, Jerry sat opposite me at the table. Looking devastated, he took my hands in his. "She's sinking fast, Roselyn," he gulped, eyes brimming with tears.

"I know, Jerry, I know! But we mustn't give up hope, must we?"

"There is no hope, Roselyn. She was far too weak to begin with," he mumbled. "I blame myself for not taking her to see a doctor long ago. I should've known there was something far wrong, but I suppose I was too close to her to realise it."

"Don't blame yourself Jerry! I could say the same thing! But, you know as well as I do that Terren was always such a stubborn person." I squeezed his hands.

"This might be a little premature, Roselyn, but Terren asked to be buried in her wedding gown. Does your mother have it finished yet?"

"Yes! It's only to be pressed."

"Did she tell you her wishes, Roselyn?" he asked, choking on the words.

"Yes, she did." I handed him a handkerchief to wipe his face. "She made me promise I'd see to it."

When Jerry and I parted company that morning, my heart was breaking. Thoughts of all my strange feelings flashed through my mind and I wondered if I had been having premonitions.

Terren slipped peacefully away in her sleep three days before what would've been her wedding day. She was laid to rest in her beautiful wedding gown, on the day she and Jerry were to be married. It was the saddest day of my life!

After the funeral, Allan and I strolled along the winding path to my home. At the front door he encircled me in his arms, holding me close. I closed my eyes and rested my head on his shoulder.

"Time will heal the pain you're feeling, Roselyn, and life will be bright and beautiful again, I promise." His loving eyes swept over my face. "Oh Roselyn, my precious, precious one! I love you so much!" We stood in companionable silence for the longest time.

At the tea table the following evening, Catherine walked around to the side of my chair. Leaning over, she whispered in my ear, "Will you take me to see the Queen, Roselyn? She's going to be crossing the Tay Bridge on the twentieth of June. Please Roselyn, will you?"

"Indeed I will not!" I snapped. "I've better things to do with my time." She ran over and buried her head in Mother's lap and cried. I was immediately sorry I had spoken so sharply to her. But at that moment all I could think of was that Terren and I had planned to go to see the Queen. Now she'd gone, I'd absolutely no desire to do so.

"You didn't have to talk to the bairn like that, Roselyn!" Mother said softly, after she had tucked Catherine into bed. "Why don't you give it some thought? You can't stop living because Terren has died," she whispered. "Anyway, it's not Catherine's fault."

Unable to sleep that night, I tossed and turned and finally, at midnight, I went to the kitchen to make a cup of tea and a slice of bread and butter. By the time I'd eaten, I'd made up my mind.

"I've decided to take you to see the Queen, Catherine!" I told her when I entered the kitchen next morning, "I hope you'll forgive me for snapping at you last night? I didn't mean to!"

"Oh Roselyn!" she breathed, "I know you didn't."

Standing on her tiptoes, she gave me a big hug around the neck.

Resentment that Terren had died consumed me. I couldn't think of anything else but Terren. Of course, now she was gone, another young nurse, Nancy Jackson, had filled her place in my room. This, I might add, took some getting used to. I felt so guilty I just couldn't take to Nancy, even though she was a lovely girl.

Reluctantly I had been thinking about my future at the hospital. I knew I had to do midwifery now that I'd completed the general nursing. But I couldn't make up my mind whether to do the course in Dundee, or join Allan and finish my training in one of the hospitals in London.

Chapter

23

Queen's Visit

The twentieth of June dawned bright and sunny. Catherine was so excited she was almost uncontrollable. "Oh Roselyn, Roselyn," she bubbled, "do you think the Queen will notice me?" Sitting smugly in the corner of the carriage, she was as pretty as a picture, dressed in her blue floral cotton frock, boating hat and white gloves.

To commemorate her visit, Her Majesty would plant a tree in the gardens surrounding the Albert Institute. In an open carriage she would travel along Dock Street, up Commercial Street, to the Albert Institute. Then back to the railway station via Reform Street, the High Street finally down Union Street to Tay Bridge station. She would rejoin the royal train and cross the Tay Bridge en route to London.

The hot sun beat down on us. Catherine and I were glad of our parasols. A massed pipe band marched down from Dudhope Castle to the railway station, blasting out rousing music to welcome the Queen.

The harbour was choked with three-masted ships and small fishing boats, all flying Union Jacks and Royal Scottish Standards. They were sounding their horns, adding to the excitement and merrymaking.

Children of all ages were waving little flags and dancing circles around their parents. Even the adults were acting like children, dancing jigs and reels. Some threw flower petals into the air, letting them float down at random on the crowds.

People from all walks of life gathered in the streets. Open carriages brought ladies and gentlemen in fine apparel to the station, just to get a glimpse of their beloved Victoria.

The noise reminded me of the day of the official opening of the bridge, although that was not on such a grand scale. It was so good to feel part of something exciting again.

"Oh Roselyn, I'm glad we came, aren't you?" Catherine asked, as we waited patiently in the waiting room, hoping to get a glimpse of the Queen the moment her train arrived.

On the platform, people were pushing and shoving trying to get closer to the barriers. "I didn't think there would be so many people here, Roselyn. I thought it would only be us." Catherine was disappointed that she had to share the Queen with other people.

Just as the royal train pulled into the station, the bells of the Old Steeple began to ring out in all their glory, 'God Save the Queen'. A twenty-one-gun salute was fired from the cannons in the Dudhope Castle grounds.

But, alas, all the cheering and merrymaking soon came to a halt when the people realised the Queen had changed her mind. Plainly she'd decided that she was not going to disembark. All she did was come to the carriage window and wave to the people who were standing on the platform waiting to greet her.

However, Catherine didn't know any better. She was ecstatic! She laughed joyously and waved her little flag at the Queen.

"This is certainly a day to remember, Catherine! Three cheers for Queen Victoria!" we shouted at the top of our voices as the train carrying the Queen pulled away from the platform, puffing out of the station.

"Oh Roselyn, wasn't she beautiful?" Catherine sighed, "and she looked straight at me and smiled."

The roads were badly congested with people and carriages, all trying to get out of town. It had taken longer than I had anticipated reaching Martha's Tea Room at the top of Castle Street. Before catching the train back to Tayport Catherine and I had a delicious cream tea - scones with clotted cream and strawberry jam.

It was threatening rain when we finally reached West Lights. We were fortunate to be home, for a storm came thundering down the Tay Valley from the west. The first drops of rain fell as we reached the front door.

Catherine ran into the house ahead of me, excitedly telling my parents how beautiful the Queen was. "She even smiled at me, Aunt Liz!"

Mother was in the midst of lighting the gas mantle. It cast flickering shadows on the gleaming brass ornaments on the mantelpiece. Father was putting the kettle on. But everything had to be postponed while Catherine reported her news.

It wasn't long before thunder cracked and flashes of lightning lit up the whole valley. I stepped over to the window to watch the storm rolling out to the German Sea. How eerie it was.

We all sat around the fire, drinking cups of tea, nibbling on biscuits that Mother had made to cheer us up.

"The storm's over, Roselyn," Catherine jumped out of her seat the moment the rain had stopped and run over to the window, "look Roselyn, the sun's coming out and there'll be a rainbow, won't there?" she squeaked.

"Yes, look, look, there it is." I pointed out the window, and sure enough there it was. The great bow in the sky stretched across the river from Tayport to Carnoustie. It arched up in a span of colour, as if it were reaching up to heaven. It was a spectacular sight.

We stood silently watching it and then, innocently, Catherine asked in her squeaky little voice, "Is there really a pot of gold at the end of the rainbow, Roselyn?"

Looking her in the eye, I smiled softly, "I really don't know - if there is, I haven't found it."

The weeks that followed were bitter. I was simply lost without Terren. Try as I may, I couldn't get her out of my mind, so I decided to take the summer off work.

Allan was very supportive of my decision. He was looking forward to spending as much time as possible with me, before he had to go to London.

Ralph's spiritual guidance was a great comfort to me after Terren's death. I don't know how I could have survived without his help. Of course he was devastated that I had become engaged to Allan. "I haven't given up on you, Roselyn," he had told me point blank, "I still think you'll have a change of heart." For some unknown reason Ralph seemed to have an incredible knack of tugging at my heartstrings. What he had said made me doubt the feelings I had for Allan. But I meant to stick to my guns. I kept a healthy distance from him, no physical contact, fighting a constant desire to have him touch me, hold me, kiss me.

One evening towards the end of June as I hurried to the duty office to sign out, I bumped into Jerry. This was the first time I'd seen him since the funeral. "I've accepted a position in the Glasgow Royal Infirmary," he announced. "I just had to make a move, Roselyn. I can't stand it here any longer. Nothing's the same without Terren."

"They say time heals all pain, Jerry."

"Yes, I expect it will." We shook hands and wished each other well. That was the last time I ever saw him.

Allan's parents had invited me to join them on their annual holiday to Tobermory on the Isle of Mull. John Robertson, Allan's uncle, and his wife Norma, had a sheep farm there.

"It'll give you and Allan the opportunity to spend some happy moments together before he leaves for London." Mistress Robertson had said.

Of course Mother wasn't at all happy with the idea. But after lots of persuasion she reluctantly agreed. I'm sure she was hoping she could persuade me to change my mind.

On the twenty-ninth of June I left the hospital on a two months' leave of absence. The only one who understood why I was doing this was Sister Wotherspoon. She invited me out for a farewell tea at the Royal Hotel the evening I left. She and I had become good friends over the past few months and we had a good old chinwag before parting. I felt a little sad, but the knowledge that I would perhaps be returning to the infirmary in September made me feel better.

Mother and I spent all our free time sewing clothes for the children at the orphanage. I was happy to have something to occupy my mind. And it gave Mother and me the opportunity to renew our friendship. All our differences were forgotten. Things between us were just as they had been when I was a child.

One morning in late July I was down on my knees in Mother's rose garden, lightly scratching the soil with a hand rake, after adding some manure. Catherine was mimicking me with the toy rake Mother had bought for her.

"Look, Roselyn," she gasped excitedly, pointing at the hollyhocks. Butterflies were clinging to them in droves. Wistfully looking around the garden, I noticed a spider spinning a beautiful pinwheel between the tiger lilies.

"Look what the spider's doing, Catherine," I said pointing with the rake.

"Oh! I don't like spiders. They make me shiver," she said, giving a little tremble and covering her eyes.

Suddenly, Pat began to bark and snarl, running to the gate. I turned to see what all the fuss was. Three tinkers had entered the gate and were boldly coming down the garden path, two men and a woman.

I quickly got up and grabbed Pat by the collar. He barked and barked, baring his teeth.

The woman was pushing a dilapidated pram, full of junk. For all I know, it could have been all their worldly possessions. She appeared to be in her late twenties. Burnt auburn hair tied back in a straggly knot framed her healthy-looking, wind-burned face. She was dressed in what was probably her Sunday best. The material, a faded shade of rose silk, was far too luxurious for a tinker woman to afford. It was probably a cast-off from one of the aristocrats. Her hands looked as if they belonged to a much older woman; hard work in the fields had left its mark.

"If you cross my palm with silver, I'll tell your fortune." The voice was sweet and crystal clear. It didn't sound like the voice of a tinker woman. Her voice whistled through the gap in her front teeth.

Excitedly, I sprang to my feet "I'd love to have my fortune told. Unfortunately I don't..."

Mother, having heard all the commotion, came rushing out. "We're not interested in all that rubbish," she bellowed, waving the back of her hand at the woman.

The elder of the two men was bent over and walked with the aid of two canes. Weather-beaten and unshaven, he looked as if he could have done with a good scrub and smelt like it, too. He stepped forward and began to plead poverty, begging for money for food.

"We've hardly enough money for ourselves," said Mother quick as a whip. "But if you care to wait five minutes, I'll bring you a nice bowl of lentil soup and some freshly baked bread."

"God bless you, lady," he smiled, "God bless you, we'd love a bowl of soup."

They settled themselves down on the lawn prattling away in tinker gibberish.

Catherine and I followed Mother into the house and helped her set up a tray for the tinkers. A smile stretching from ear to ear came over Mother's face as she carried the tray out to serve them a hearty meal.

"Oh, how they annoy me!" she complained when she re-entered the house, "they're forever pleading poverty. And if you ask me, they could buy and sell us."

It wasn't until later in the afternoon that Catherine missed Pat. "Where can he be?" she asked, glancing about the room and running over to look out the window to check the back garden.

"Oh, he'll be out the front," Mother said, "better go and fetch him in. While you're out there please bring in the dishes."

Off she bounded, only to return in tears. "My Pat's not there, Aunt Liz," she sobbed.

"Now, now, don't be getting yourself in a state! He'll have sneaked around the back when you were going out the front door." She dashed out the back door and returned tear-drenched and red faced.

"He's not there either; the tinkies must've taken him."

"Now Catherine, what would the tinkies want to take Pat for? They'll have left the gate open and he'll have run over to Bob's! Come, Roselyn," she said rolling up her sleeves, a thing Mother did when she meant business. "Let's go get him."

Of course, Pat wasn't at Bob's. In fact, he was nowhere to be found. We searched high and low, whistling and calling his name, but we couldn't find him anywhere.

"Maybe he followed the tinkies," Mother suggested.

"Oh no, Aunt Liz! Pat wouldn't follow the tinkies, he wouldn't do that."

"Oh yes he would, if they were feeding him; he'd follow Old Nick for a treat!"

"Then we'll simply have to find the tinkies," I suggested.

We trekked all over the place in the scorching heat, unsuccessful in our search. Catherine bubbled and booed all the way, convinced she'd never see him again.

"What now?" Mother sighed, exasperated.

"Perhaps by the time we get home he'll be sitting on the doorstep."

We had just crossed the humpbacked bridge when Father came, pedalling his bicycle furiously. "Eddie Lynch saw the tinkers on the Cupar road with Pat tethered to their pram," he huffed, "he thought we'd sold the dog. If I hurry, I'll catch up with them. Now don't cry, my wee pet, Uncle Larry will get your wee doggie back for you!" Turning to me he said, "By the way, Roselyn, the minister's waiting in the garden. He wants a word." He mounted the bicycle and sped off.

"What on earth does the minister have to say to you?" Mother asked, full of curiosity.

"How should I know?" I answered, my heart turning over with joy.

"Never, ever, trust the tinkers," Ralph said, rising from the bench and greeting us with a beaming smile as we approached. "They'd sell their own granny, they would."

"My goodness, Reverend Valente, it's so nice to see you. Would you like a cup of tea?"

"Oh no! No thank you, Mistress Carey, I just want to have a quick word with Roselyn, if I may, then I'll be off."

"Of course," Mother replied and she and Catherine went directly indoors.

"What in the world are you doing here, Ralph?" I gasped indignantly under my breath, avoiding eye contact with him. We took a few steps down the gravel path and sat on the park bench.

"To tell the truth, Roselyn, I really don't know what I'm doing here. I've tried to put you out of my mind, but it's impossible. Perhaps you could say I'm here to steal a moment in time with you."

"Ralph! You know I'm betrothed to Allan. You're making things very difficult for yourself. And for me too," I quickly added.

"And just how difficult am I making it for you, Roselyn?" he asked, looking me in the eye.

I blushed and looked down at my feet. I couldn't answer his question and said nothing. I wanted to shout to him that he was making it difficult for me to breathe because my body thrilled at his nearness. I wanted to shout with joy, but I managed to control myself.

"You're being dishonest with yourself. I know you have deep feelings for me. I've known it ever since you came to the manse for tea on the twenty-seventh of February, and I see it in your eyes every time you look at me. In your voice every time you speak my name!"

"Ralph, please! Don't do this."

"I know you're going along with this engagement business, because you don't want to hurt Allan Robertson. But that's no basis for a happy marriage, Roselyn." He took my hands in his and kissed them.

I could have died. That old feeling that I couldn't control came rushing back. Taking a deep breath, I spoke softly. "You're right, Ralph, absolutely right! I could never do anything to hurt Allan. He's been my friend for fourteen years, I'll always love him."

"There! You said it, he's your friend! People don't marry their friends, Roselyn."

I couldn't help noticing the desperation in Ralph's voice as he spoke. I very much wanted to throw my arms about him and tell him I cared. Oh how I cared! But I couldn't bring myself to hurt Allan.

We sat in silence holding hands listening to the water lapping against the shore and the loud squealing of the gulls. My heart was torn between Allan and Ralph. I didn't know what to do. "I really must go, Ralph," I whispered "Allan will be arriving soon."

He appeared to be so depressed as we slowly walked back to my home. After I had stepped through the garden gate he whispered, "I love you with all my heart, Roselyn!"

I almost gave in. I wanted to shout "I love you, Ralph!" But I pushed the deep feelings I had for him aside.

"I mean to have you, Roselyn; if it's the last thing I do, I'll have you. God has a way of working things out for people and I'm sure He'll do so for us." He paused for a moment, squeezed my hand and left.

"Well! What did the minister have to say?" Mother asked the moment I stepped into the kitchen.

"He wanted to talk about the ghost problem I've been having. I told him all about it, you know." My face was burning, I felt so guilty for lying to her.

"My, he's a handsome-looking man, don't you think?" she said, watching my face and waiting for my reply.

"Is he? I hadn't really noticed," I answered flippantly. "For heaven's sake, he's our minister, Mother."

She smiled coyly. I knew she suspected something, but she didn't know what.

Allan called fifteen minutes later, he was lively and excited. I greeted him with a kiss on the cheek. I felt like Judas. Hand in hand, we strolled along the gravel path towards the bridge. I had difficulty focussing on Allan and I kept turning over in my mind what Ralph had said. I could only think about Ralph.

It was a sultry day; one of those days when all you want to do is lie on the beach. But I was already nursing the sunburn that I had so foolishly acquired the week before. We found the perfect spot to relax in, underneath a large weeping willow on the embankment on the north side of the path. Sitting on the sweet-smelling grass, I curled my legs up under me and spread the skirt of my frock about the lawn.

Allan sat by my side, staring out over the river, elbows resting on his knees and face cupped in his hands.

The Tay Valley Yacht Club's regatta was well underway and from where we were sitting we had a bird's eye view of the exciting event.

"I'm going to miss all this," Allan said, scanning the magnificent panorama. "I'm beginning to wonder if I've made the right decision - about going to work in London, I mean. I truly don't want to leave you, Roselyn." He took my hand in his.

"Well, it's not as if it's the end of the world. If you don't like London, you can always come home. And please, Allan, whatever you do, don't worry about me. I'll be okay. Besides, I'll be fully occupied at the hospital. It'll be the New Year before you know it and you'll be home for that, won't you?" I smiled encouragingly.

He took me in his arms, his eyes searching mine as if he was trying to read my mind. Pangs of guilt engulfed me after what Ralph had said. I wanted to tell him about my change of heart but couldn't bring myself to hurt him. Perhaps he was just thinking about what had happened to Terren, and didn't want the same thing to happen to me. "I have the awful feeling I'm going to lose you, Roselyn," he said sadly.

"I know exactly what you mean, Allan." I touched his face with my fingertips. "I've had visions of some raven beauty sweeping you off your feet when you're away in London! All those lovely London lasses. Exciting. Beautiful. Glamorous. You'll forget all about little old me."

"Never! Oh Roselyn, never in a million years!" His eyes scanned my face. "You have absolutely nothing to worry about, darling. I've loved you since the first day I set eyes on you in the school playground, your pigtails tied up with bright satin bows. But never in my wildest dreams did I think you'd reciprocate my feelings."

"Allan! Don't you think our love is only puppy love? I ... think ..."

He covered my mouth with his fingertips saying "Sh. Sh. No, my dearest, of course it's not puppy love. No one will ever entice me away from you." He leaned over and kissed me, whispering in my ear "No-one else could ever fill my heart with so much joy." I stiffened, but he didn't seem to notice. The sound of the tide and the squealing of the gulls muffled the rapid pounding of his heart.

Father went zooming by with Pat sitting in the basket on his handlebars. Pat's ears were blowing back with the wind. "It's a long story," he shouted in the passing, "I'll tell you about it later."

Allan and I tarried a while. He wanted to make all kinds of plans for our future life together. But my heart was full of doubt. I didn't know what to do so I decided to do nothing. We sauntered home just in time for tea.

"Would you believe the tinkers were preparing to have a feast of dog?" Father confided the moment we entered the kitchen.

"I've heard tinkers do that," Allan said, "apparently they eat dogs, and cats too for that matter. They consider dogs and cats a delicacy."

"We're having tea in the back garden," Mother interrupted as she carried the teapot, sugar bowl and milk jug out to the garden on a tray. "Come, everything's ready," she said over her shoulder, "it's such a lovely evening it would be a shame to waste it."

We all took our places at the table in the back garden and caught the tail end of the Yacht race as we enjoyed our tea.

It sounded as if it had been a wonderful event. We could hear cheering and hand-clapping echoing across the river, as each boat went home to rest.

It was indeed a beautiful evening. We lingered in the garden, laughing at some of the funny stories Father recounted about the eating habits in different countries he had visited. Of course, the tinkers' intention to eat Pat had jolted his memory.

Allan and I left Mother, Father and Catherine in the garden. Off we went for a walk along the beach. Allan was content just being with me. We sat on a park bench and sang our favourite songs in harmony. I felt so deceitful. I tried to convince myself there was nothing between Ralph and me, only fascination.

But, as I lay on top of my bed that night I tried to work out why I was so intrigued with Ralph. I just couldn't help my feelings for him. He seemed to draw me to him like a fly to sticky paper. Perhaps it was because he was older? More mature? I tossed and turned for hours but came to no conclusions. I'd decided to let it all go until Allan left for London. Then I'd see how things worked out.

CHAPTER
24

Lammis Fair

The next few weeks were filled with preparations for the long journey to the Isle of Mull with Allan and his parents. A joyous air of expectation surrounded me and, with each day that passed, the pain that had been in my heart since Terren's death was slowly diminishing and I was beginning to be able to face life again with a positive attitude.

Ralph was constantly at the back of my mind, despite the fact I tried to push him out. I felt it was he I should be with, and not Allan. But arrangements had been made for me to accompany the Robertson family to Mull, so I decided to leave well enough alone.

Catherine had been a great comfort to me. She had helped me overcome the bitter feelings I'd had since Terren's death. She kept reminding me "Terren's in heaven beside my mother!" What a sweet, pretty and thoughtful child she is.

For some unknown reason Catherine was under the impression she was going to join Allan and me on our holiday. She was very upset when she learned she wasn't coming with us, and went about sulking for days on end. But she eventually accepted things.

In the living-room one morning, she was curled up on the window-seat staring out the window. "Look, Roselyn," her squeaky voice poured out, "look at that ship coming up the river. Do you suppose it's the Vikings coming to capture us? Maybe they'll sweep us up and take us to a far off land to torture us. Even tie us to a tree and stick spears into our hearts."

"Why, Catherine, what a vivid imagination you have. You have the makings of a clever little storyteller. But I'm sorry to have to inform you that is not the Vikings, it's a ship bringing raw jute from India to Dundee." I smiled softly patting her head.

"Raw jute? What is raw jute?" she asked, full of curiosity.

"It's the bark of Corchorus plants that only grow in India. The bark is stripped off the stalks and hung out on lines to dry in the hot sun. After that, fibres are teased out to make a soft fluffy material. The natives of India bundle it up and it's shipped over to the mills in Dundee. That's what raw jute is."

"What do the mills do with it, Roselyn?"

"Well, it goes through many processes such as spinning and winding and finally the yarn is woven into canvas. That foul smell in Dundee comes from raw jute."

"I didn't know that."

"Well, now you do!"

She sat quietly absorbing what I had said. "How would you like me to take you to Lammas Fair in August? It'll be in St. Andrews. I'll take you if you like."

"Lammas Fair?" she gasped, eyes like saucers. "Oh Roselyn, I've always wanted to go to Lammas Fair." She jumped up and threw her arms around my neck. "You're the best big sister in the world, Roselyn!" she declared. I left her sitting in the window-seat, lost in her dreams.

As I've already said, Mother wasn't thrilled at the idea of me going on holiday with Allan, even although she knew we'd be well chaperoned. However, she was gradually coming around and I was positive that by the time I had to leave, she would have accepted the idea.

The moment I entered the kitchen that morning Mother asked if I would mind nipping into Tayport to get a pan loaf and while I was there would I pop into the grocer's? "I need some cinnamon and a half pound of tea."

"Of course. Would you like to come into Tayport with me, Catherine?" I asked poking my head into the living room.

"No thanks, Roselyn, Aunt Liz and I are going to give Pat a bath in that old tub that's out in the shed." She was grinning from ear to ear.

It was a glorious morning with not a cloud in the sky. I walked briskly along the water's edge, filling my nostrils with the sweet smell of seaweed and admiring the awesome view.

When I turned onto Castle Street, I collided with Ralph. "Why, Ralph," I gasped in surprise. My heart leaped with an enormous surge of excitement and began to beat rapidly.

"My goodness, Roselyn," he breathed, every bit as surprised as I was. His eyes were dancing with delight. "You're the last person I expected to see this morning. I thought you'd gone on holiday with the Robertson clan?"

"No, we don't leave until tomorrow, we're taking the first train in the morning to Dundee. We'll catch a train to Glasgow, then another to Oban and from there the ferry to Mull. Phew! Sounds terrible, doesn't it?" He smiled at my comment.

"Would you care to join me for a cup of tea, at the bakery?" he happily inquired. "They have the most delicious cream cakes first thing in the morning." He smiled and waited for my reply.

"I'd love to, Ralph, I have the most uncontrollable weakness for cream cakes!" I raised my brows. "As a matter of fact, I was on my way to the bakery to buy bread."

I know I should've declined his invitation, but I couldn't resist the opportunity to spend even a few stolen moments with him.

We chose to sit at the table in the bay window overlooking Castle Street. The moment we sat down, the owner's daughter, Sally, came to serve us. She gave us a curious look as she placed the cake stand, laden with cream cakes, onto the table. However, without comment she returned moments later with the teapot, sugar and milk.

"I'm mad with jealousy! I'm not myself." Ralph blurted clear out of the blue.

"I beg your pardon?"

"You heard me," he said, "I'm mad with jealousy."

"What are you jealous of, Ralph?"

"The idea of you going on holiday with Allan Robertson."

"What? You have no reason to be jealous of Allan, Ralph."

"I don't know why you think that, I strongly believe fate brought us together this morning, so I could tell you exactly how I feel."

"Oh, Ralph, please stop it! I'm engaged to Allan. I have every right to be going on holiday with him, if I wish. Please don't torture yourself like this. You and I were both in the same place at the same time this morning by sheer coincidence. And now, we're enjoying a lovely cup of tea together. Let's leave it at that!" I reached over and squeezed his hand.

"You're right! I'm being unfair to you," he said sheepishly. "Let's just enjoy each other's company while we can. How do you like the cakes?" he asked changing the subject.

"They're delicious. Couldn't be better!"

"Have another?" he said, offering me the cake stand.

"Oh, no thank you, Ralph. I have to watch my waistline. You wouldn't like to see me fat, would you?"

"I'd take you any way you are," he smiled.

I felt so happy just being with him. I simply loved the attention that he showered upon me. He had a wonderful way of putting things that made me feel important. We couldn't stop staring at each other. Quickly changing the subject I asked how Patty was.

He smiled and replied, "She's well."

We chatted, laughing and enjoying each other's company, but I could sense an undercurrent.

"Bon voyage!" he said, as we reluctantly parted company. He shook my hand as if it were made out of crystal and then he took it to his lips and kissed it. His breath warm on my skin.

I hurried to the grocer's, got what Mother wanted and went straight home. My thoughts were still with Ralph.

Next morning everyone was up at the crack of dawn to wish me a happy holiday. Of course, there was no show without Punch, Catherine just had to be in the picture. You'd have thought by the way they were all carrying on, I was going to the other end of the earth. Mother and Father had tears in their eyes. Catherine was bubbling, and to my surprise, I was on the verge of tears myself.

"Oh, Roselyn," Catherine sobbed, "please don't forget to come back."

"Now, Catherine! How could I forget to come back when I've promised to take you to Lammas Fair?" I tickled her under the chin and she giggled.

Father slipped a few coins into my hand. "Just in case you run short," he whispered as he kissed me on the brow. They all stood at the front door, waving as I stepped into the waiting cab.

When I arrived at the railway station in Tayport, Allan was waiting at the gate. He greeted me with a hug and a kiss. He was so excited, like a little boy. His family was waiting on the train and the moment Allan and I entered the carriage the train puffed out of the station.

At the Tay Bridge station, Mister Robertson did a quick head count to make sure we were all there. He lifted his cases off the platform as the Glasgow train hissed into the station. Allan's eyes met mine and holding hands we waited eagerly for the train to come to a halt.

Everyone was as excited as could be at the thought of the long train journey, and noisily piled into the compartment causing a big commotion. We hardly had time to settle down when the train shook out of the station.

The journey from Oban to the Isle of Mull took two hours and thirty minutes by boat. The bright afternoon sunshine made the trip a most memorable experience.

We 'the children' as Allan's parents called us, spent the duration of the trip on the upper deck, admiring the scenery. They, on the other hand, enjoyed tea in the lounge with some American tourists they had met on board.

From some of the comments we overheard, we

were 'privileged' to be natives of 'such a beautiful country'. But we already knew that.

Patricia and Ian were overjoyed that I could join them. We were all very compatible and always had a wonderful time together. They were bubbling with excitement, telling me about the things that they'd planned to share with me on the Island.

The people we were going to visit were John and Norma Robertson, Allan's uncle and his wife. Those Robertsons had two children, Audrey and Derek. Audrey would be celebrating her twenty-first birthday the next day. Her parents had planned a surprise party for her. She had been down in Essex for two weeks competing in an equestrian competition.

Derek was twenty-five and he's the most handsome person in the world, according to Patricia. He was a veterinary surgeon and took care of the livestock on their farm.

Both Allan and Ian talked of Audrey with great admiration. "She's an excellent horsewoman, Roselyn," Derek informed me.

"Is she really?"

"Yes, and if you can't ride, you'd better watch out! Audrey's got no time for anyone who can't ride."

The moment Audrey's name was mentioned, Patricia got up and went to join her parents in the lounge.

"Attention, everyone! Attention!" The captain's voice came over the loudspeaker. "We're due to arrive in Tobermory in approximately ten minutes. Anyone visiting the Island for the first time is in for a wonderful treat."

Allan grabbed my hand and led me to the bow of the ship. He was indeed excited. "You've just got to see this, kitten," he said. And with great anticipation, we leaned over the bow-rail to get a better view. My eager eyes waited patiently to capture my first glimpse of Tobermory Harbour.

"Shut your eyes, Roselyn, shut your eyes!" Allan ordered excitedly, "No peeking now," he said, putting his arm around my waist. The boat slowly turned to port. "Okay! Open your eyes now!"

"Oh, my goodness!" I gasped. Never in my whole life had I ever seen such beauty. The sun was slowly slipping into the western sky, casting magical, golden shadows over the harbour. Quaint little houses were tucked neatly into the hillside in layered tiers. From the water's edge to the crest of the hill, the fairy tale picture was perfectly mirrored in the still harbour waters.

Brightly painted cobles lay randomly on the beach their oars propped against the sea wall. Two tired-looking fishing boats were tied to the jetty at the far end of the harbour. Their fishing-nets, tossed carelessly on the dock, waited to be mended.

Lobster traps were unloaded from another fishing boat by a tall weather-beaten fisherman. Dressed in long rubber boots, a bright green jersey and a red woollen hat, he was assisted by a boy who could have been his son. He had the same blond curly hair and bright blue eyes.

Allan held my hand, expectantly watching my expression as I captured the majestic scene. I wanted to store every detail safely in my mind, and keep it there forever.

CHAPTER
25

Tobermory

J ohn and Derek Robertson were waiting on the dock when the ferry arrived that evening. Waving like mad to draw our attention, they were shouting "Hey. Over here! Over here!" They had come in separate buggies to transport us to High Fields, their farm five miles south west of Tobermory.

After a brief, informal introduction, Derek suggested we'd better make haste so we would reach our destination while we were all alert.

John Robertson could have been Allan's father's twin. They looked so much alike, with the exception of their hair colouring. John was as blond as David was dark.

The long, uncomfortable, hoof-clopping journey seemed endless. It was dusk when we finally arrived at the farm. The two storey sandstone farmhouse was massive. Designed by a French architect, it had the appearance of a chateau. I couldn't wait till morning to explore the beautiful, cultured garden.

Norma Robertson was a pretty, petite woman in her late forties. Lustrous black hair framed her happy, wind-burned face. As soon as formal introductions were over, she ushered us into the most ornate dining room that I'd ever seen. She had prepared a feast fit for royalty. With the help of a maid, she served roast pig, which had been cooking slowly over an open spit for hours. I'd never before tasted pork cooked this way. Without doubt it was the most succulent pork I had ever tasted.

We all lingered around the massive dining-room table sipping on tea, chatting, laughing and joking into the early morning. The glow of oil lamps flickered warmly on our faces.

Everyone had a lie-in next morning, with the exception of John, Norma and Derek. After a hearty breakfast Allan and I ventured outdoors to explore the garden and the awesome Isle of Mull.

Norma, her hands covered in flour, called from the open kitchen window as we passed by, "Be sure to be back by six o'clock, Audrey's party starts at half past!"

"We'll be back long before that, Aunt Norma," Allan assured her. Holding hands, we strolled through the hay fields to the ridge and followed the rugged path down to the beach. A strong Atlantic breeze made it difficult to keep our balance so we carefully chose each step.

Patricia had planned to join us on our walk, but she had developed a splitting headache and decided to stay home. When we left, Ian, stripped to the waist, was relaxing on a deck chair in the back garden, sunning himself and reading.

"I'm glad we're going to have the day to ourselves," Allan said, smiling happily. I felt so guilty as thoughts of Ralph flashed through my mind, but I quickly dismissed them.

"Penny for your thoughts, Roselyn?" Allan asked, jolting me back to the present.

"I really don't think you'd approve of my thoughts, Allan," I said, quickly changing the subject.

Beautiful seashells were washed up on the beach. Agate and amethyst rocks in abundance were lying there, just for the taking. I could hardly believe my eyes!

"Oh, this is wonderful, Allan," I breathed, full of enthusiasm, the wind blowing through my hair.

"It certainly is, Kitten. Let's see who can find the biggest shell." Slipping his hand out of mine, he ran down to the water's edge. He removed his shoes and tied them together with the laces. He slung them around his neck. He rolled up the legs of his trousers and splashed in the ocean. How comical he looked, like an overgrown schoolboy. "How about this one?" he yelled, picking up a pretty shell and holding it up in both his hands.

"I'm coming over there," I shouted, slinging my beach bag over my shoulder as I ran to join him. I almost stepped on a hermit crab and let out the most unearthly scream.

Allan dropped the shell and came running to my aid, thinking I'd stepped on a Portuguese man-of- war or something. When he realised I was being a baby, he lifted me up and pretended to throw me into the ocean. Our screams and laughter filled the air, echoing our joy. It certainly was a fun day.

Audrey was arriving in Tobermory on the afternoon ferry. By the time we returned Derek had already gone to meet her in the cart to bring her home.

The guests arrived in dribs and drabs. Norma and John greeted everyone as they stepped into the massive hall, offering them a glass of champagne. There seemed to be an awful lot of people. Dressed in our fineries we mingled with the elite of the island. The honoured guests were getting merrier by the minute, as they waited for Audrey to arrive.

John and Norma had expected Derek and Audrey to be earlier. They were becoming concerned. John was just about to go searching for them, when wham! Audrey made her dramatic entrance.

She was so arrogant, such a real snob, that only a mother could have loved her. Full of her own importance, she mingled with the guests, sipping on a glass of champagne and making derogatory remarks about her fellow competitors.

There was no doubt in my mind that she flourished on other people's misfortunes. I had taken an instant dislike to her the moment she burst into the room so pompously. I could tell she was watching me from the tail of her eye as she moved about the room. Finally she came fluttering over, all la-di-da, and flinging her arms around Allan's neck, she kissed him on the lips.

Her lips were painted vividly, so red they looked as if they were bleeding. Her face was bronze with powder, her eyelashes so heavy with mascara she looked to me like a tart. I've never seen anyone wearing so much make-up. She wore long dangling earrings and around her neck a twisted gold and black necklace resembling a snake.

Before Allan could introduce her to me, I commented in a loud voice, "Why Allan, you didn't tell me you had a kissing cousin!"

From the startled look on Audrey's face I could tell I had embarrassed her - for the first time in her life perhaps. Allan was quietly amused, but Audrey, offering me a limp hand, said, "And you must be the little nurse from West Lights."

Allan intercepted, putting his arms around my waist, "Audrey, I'd like you to meet my fiancée, Roselyn Carey." Then with a smirk on his lips and a devil in his eyes, he said, "Roselyn, this is Audrey, my kissing cousin!" She shook my hand limply and stomped off with her nose in the air.

It was obvious from the attention showered upon her and the gifts she received that the birthday party was a success.

Next morning, Audrey came fluttering down ten minutes after everyone else had started breakfast. She was dressed in a startling royal blue suit with silver threads woven through the silk material. Over that she wore a black velvet jacket. She half-heartedly apologized to Allan over her breakfast porridge. "I'm sorry if I embarrassed you in front of Roselyn, Allan, I don't know what came over me." Turning to me she said, "Allan and I are not really kissing cousins. We're just very good friends." Then, in a hoity-toity manner she said, "You may come riding with us if you wish. That's if you know the head of a horse from its backside."

"I'd be delighted to join you, Audrey," I replied with confidence. But I could've swallowed my words the moment I'd said them. The only horse I'd ever ridden in my life was an old cuddy at Broughty Ferry.

"I don't recall saying I'd go riding with you, Audrey," Allan piped up, "perhaps Roselyn would rather do something else?"

"Oh don't be silly, Allan," she bellowed, "you always go riding with me when you come to the farm. Besides, Roselyn accepted my invitation. So there! I'll meet you both in the tack room in fifteen minutes."

Allan was furious, but he went along with Audrey's wishes to avoid a scene. Patricia touched my arm as we were leaving the dining room and whispered under her breath," I warned you about her and now you know. Good luck, believe me, you'll need it!"

The stables were situated some distance from the

house. As we walked there, Allan teased me about only ever having ridden an old cuddy, pointing out there was a vast difference between a cuddy and a horse.

He quickly gave me a crash course on riding, explaining how to mount, how to sit, how to hold the reins, how to make the horse move, and most importantly, how to make it stop. "But don't worry," he said, "you'll soon get the hang of it."

The groom had three horses saddled and waiting. They were so majestic standing there, tall and proud, cross-tied in the aisle.

Her ladyship was already dressed in her riding attire, when we entered the tack room. With her crop, she casually pointed to some old outfits that were strewn over a steamer trunk. "I trust you'll find something there to fit you," she said in a spirited voice.

Although I didn't like her attitude, I had to admit she was a beautiful young woman. Once she had mounted, she looked magnificent sitting high in the saddle, dressed in all her riding paraphernalia, her long auburn hair hanging beneath her cap. But I could detect sadness in her hazel coloured eyes. I'm sure she'd have preferred if I hadn't been there.

"I've given you one of our docile mares," she told me, as we rode slowly out to the meadow. I thanked her kindly for being so considerate.

"Come along, all!" she bellowed "Let's go!" She whipped her horse with the crop and both she and Allan took off like bullets and my horse followed at a slow walk.

The docile mare that she had given me may as well have been an old cuddy. After a few steps, the mare came to a complete standstill. Try as I might, I couldn't get her to budge. All she wanted to do was nibble on the sweet grass. It was obvious who was boss and it certainly wasn't me.

I heard Audrey's shrill laughter in the distance, and realized she had planned things exactly this way so she could be alone with Allan. She was exceedingly cunning!

I was annoyed at her tactics, but it was such a glorious morning I soon simmered down. I feasted my eyes on the beauty that surrounded me and breathed in the crisp fresh air. The meadow was ablaze with bright golden buttercups, huge daisies, purple foxglove and mounds of mauve thistles, sprinkled here and there. Around the edge was a border of bright green cedars. I'd never seen anything so pretty.

Suddenly, Allan came galloping at great speed through a clearing in the trees. "Are you all right, Roselyn?" he burst out as he approached. "We don't have to do this, if you'd rather not."

I almost said, "Let's not," but my pride wouldn't let me. "It's quite all right, Allan, I really do want to, I just can't get this darned horse to move, all it wants to do is eat grass."

"Pull her head up like this," he demonstrated pulling on the reins. "You've got to let her know who's boss. That's the way, Kitten," he said encouragingly. "Now, dig the stirrups into her side. Use the crop if you must." I followed his instructions and to my surprise the horse began to move forward.

Our escapade took us along some of the most breathtaking trails on the island. When I dismounted upon returning, I could hardly walk. My legs and bottom were aching, and Allan was in the same condition. It was plain to all that Audrey got a big thrill and pleasure out of our discomfort.

For the remainder of the day Allan and I relaxed in the garden, enjoying conversation with Derek.

That night I undressed in a patch of evening light

filtering through the bedroom window. I stepped over and looked out. Evergreens were silhouetted against the twilight sky. What an awesome picture it was. It reminded me of a beautiful oil painting. I wearily slipped into my nightgown, and like an injured animal, crawled into bed and pulled the soft quilt around my neck. Soon I fell fast asleep.

John and Norma had planned a family picnic, to take place after church the next Sunday. No one in Tobermory ever did anything on the Sabbath, let alone go on a picnic. There was no doubt we were considered heathens.

Baskets, overflowing with all kinds of food, were loaded into the buggies and off we went. We were in a joyous mood, singing old Scottish songs at the top of our voices as we were carted off through the fields to the banks overlooking the sea.

We chose a spot beside a rambling brook. The sun glinted on the boulders as the water rippled over them. One couldn't have found a more peaceful place in the world.

It was a higgledy-piggledy kind of a picnic. But everyone had dropped their inhibitions and had a wonderful time. Even Audrey, who'd been such a madam, surprised me by attending in casual clothes. She wore no make up, and what lovely natural beauty she had.

We played rounders, football, three-legged races and anything else that took our fancy. The beauty at the end of that day, when the sun sat low in the sky, will be with me until the day I die.

Allan and I left the island to return to Tayport the following Tuesday. The rest of his family were to stay until the end of the month.

CHAPTER
26

Allan Leaves

O n the evening of July twenty eighth, Allan left on the six o'clock train from Tayport to Dundee to catch the half past seven train to London. In silence, we sat on the riverbank overlooking the Tay where we had spent many happy hours together in the past. No words were spoken between us, there was no need.

At the station, Allan's parting words, before he kissed me good-bye were, "I'll love you forever, Roselyn. Now keep your chin up. I'll be back before you know it."

A sharp pang of pain jabbed my heart. The overwhelming feeling that I'd never see him again engulfed me, so much so, that I wanted to shout out, "Please, don't go Allan!" But that would have been childish.

One last embrace and he stepped onto the train. Leaning out the carriage window, he threw me a kiss as the train shoogled out of the station.

My look concentrated on the train until it was out of sight, my eyes full of tears. I hurried along the deserted path to West Lights, memories of time spent with Allan flashing through my mind. It seemed like only yesterday that we had been children, running about barefoot in the sand, and now he was gone.

I went straight to my bedroom, sat at my little table and cried my heart out. I had the feeling that Allan had gone out of my life forever, an overwhelming feeling that someone was going to lure him away from me. I had no reason to believe this, nothing he had ever said or done could have led me to be suspicious of his honour. I had to be silly. Snuggling into my pillow, I cried myself to sleep.

A week later I had the first letter from Allan.

My Darling Roselyn,

It was six o'clock when the Flying Scotsman pulled into a smoke-filled Kings Cross Station. It had been a tedious and most uncomfortable journey. I hadn't slept a wink all night, preoccupied with loving thoughts of you. Oh, how I'm going to miss you.

The hustle and bustle in the station soon brought me back to reality. The huffing and puffing of engines shunting back and forth was deafening. People were dashing about every which way; many had young children by the hand, others were carrying sleepy-headed babies. But all looked lost. Just as I felt. Everything was moving so quickly, I felt like a country bumpkin.

I couldn't wait to get to 53 Maryvale Road, Brooms Grove. Brooms Grove is a quiet residential suburb in the west end of the city, a good half-hour's hoof-clopping ride from Kings Cross Station. I was totally enthralled with the activity on the streets of London at such an early hour. Milkmen were delivering milk, leaving the little pint bottles on the doorsteps. Young boys, newspaper bags slung over shoulders, slipped papers through letter-boxes. Baker boys were delivering morning rolls and bread.

My landlady is a tall rather buxom woman, her streaky grey hair pulled back in a bun and a beaming smile of welcome on her round face.

She welcomed me with, "Good morning, Mister Robertson," her spirited voice rang out, "My name is Anne. Let me help you with your things." She lifted the smallest bag and led me into the spacious entrance hall.

"You must be exhausted after such a long journey from the north," she prattled away happily as we climbed the red carpeted staircase to the top floor.

She drew me a nice hot bath. I think she's going to spoil me. I told her that I thought I'd be happy in this room until you joined me. I told her all about you. While the bath was filling I looked out the window. The mani-cured garden below was alive with all kinds of beautiful flowers and in the centre of the lawn was a huge goldfish pond. A grapevine covered the trellis framing the back porch. I knew from the first moment I saw her, that we were going to be friends. I know you will like her.

In the morning the loud chiming of Big Ben awakened me with a start. Totally disoriented, I tossed and turned, yawning and stretching. It took a while for me to realize where I was.

As soon as I had breakfast I decided to take a walk into London, exploring everything on the way. You will be thrilled with the delights of this magnificent city. Buckingham Palace! St. Paul's Cathedral! Piccadilly Circus! The Tower! St. James's Park! I can't wait to share all these wonderful places with you.

My room is nice but I won't be able to call it home until you're with me.

Monday morning, August the sixth, I started my new job. My boss is Michael Young. He is really nice. I think we should be friends.

My love, I'll write weekly to keep you in touch. I can't wait to be together.

Your loving, Allan.

Nothing was the same without Allan. My heart was empty for a long time. I went through the day automatically, not thinking.

At night I'd dream about him, think of him in the arms of someone else. I'd imagine him falling madly in love with some glamorous London belle. Dreams? Doubts? So many.

But as the weeks went by, it was as if his face and memory dimmed. Some days I hardly thought of him at all. Sometimes a week would go by and I'd not dream about him.

I had deliberately been avoiding Ralph and tried to push him out of my mind. But it was impossible. Deep down in my heart I knew that the moment I'd see him, I wouldn't be able to control myself.

Feelings of bitterness still bothered me when I thought about Annie and Terren dying so young and, for the first time since their deaths, I was really looking forward to returning to the infirmary in September. I was excited about starting my midwifery course.

My parents had been fully occupied taking care of Catherine. She was such a joy for them. It was as if she was their child. Having her certainly gave them a whole new outlook on life.

Long summer days, which had always passed so slowly when I was a child, were galloping by and summer was rapidly coming to a close. School holidays were almost over and Catherine was tickled pink with the idea of attending her big sister's school.

In late August, when the evenings were drawing in again, Mother took on a worried look. One day she was standing at the kitchen sink when I entered the room. Staring out the window, she was turning a tea towel in her hands.

I stepped over, put my hands on her shoulders and gave her a little squeeze. "You're upset at the thought of me going back to work in Dundee, aren't you, Mother?" She and her silliness about the train!

"Yes, yes, of course, I am," she said in a hurt manner looking me in the eye. She continued to turn the towel in her hands. "I have nightmares about that train. That bridge was never meant to be. Never."

"Come and sit down, Mother. We really have to talk about this." I took the towel from her and directed her to a fireside chair.

The moment she sat she buried her face in her hands and burst out crying, "You promised," she protested. "You promised me you'd find a job in Fife. Now I've to start worrying about you all over again. I can't stand the idea of that wicked train. That bridge makes me shiver."

"Oh Mother, Mother, I wish you wouldn't worry like this, it'll only be for another year. Then I'll find a job on this side of the river." I raised my right hand saying, "I swear on my life, Mother. You are the one who says I'm silly with all my imaginings and that. And here you are with the train on your mind all the time." I handed her a handkerchief to wipe the tears away.

She returned to wiping the dishes, seeming a bit more contented because of my words – if not entirely satisfied.

I kept my promise to Catherine and took her to Lammas Fair in St. Andrews. I can still see her chubby, freckled face, beaming with delight when we entered Market Street. The fair was in full swing! Music, crowds, colour. Her eyes sparkled with delight as we moved from stall to stall. The juice of the sticky candy apple she was eating trickled down her chin and my own mouth watered. When her teeth crunched through the toffee into the fresh crisp fruit, pieces of toffee clung to the edges of her lips.

She was so excited, pulling me this way and that. Her high-pitched voice bellowed out, "Oh Roselyn, look at that," or, "come, look at this, Roselyn." Suddenly, wide-eyed, she gasped, "Let's go on that! Please, Roselyn, let's!" She was pointing to the ferris wheel. I'm nervous of such things and was trying to pluck up courage to do so, when a familiar voice broke out:

"Yes, why not? It certainly does look like fun, Catherine."

I was face to face with Ralph. "Why, Ralph!" I gasped in surprise, my heart doing somersaults, "you're the last person I expected to see here. I didn't think ministers would be interested in such places."

"And why not? We're human, aren't we? I'm glad to see you having such a wonderful time," he beamed, changing the subject.

I could tell he was anxious to join us, but it was obvious he didn't know how to deal with the situation. "Catherine has been pestering me to go on the ferris wheel. Would you like to join us, Ralph?" I suddenly mustered up courage.

"I would love to, Roselyn," he beamed.

We had a marvellous time. After the ferris wheel it was the carousel, then the shoogie boat. We even tried our luck at the sideshows. Ralph was lucky enough to win a huge plush dog, which he immediately gave to Catherine. She was delighted and jumped up and down in delight.

When we alighted from the train in Tayport, Ralph offered to walk us home. I accepted his offer without giving it a second thought.

"I had a wonderful day Roselyn," he whispered, holding my hands under a brilliant sky at my front door. "I hope you enjoyed yourself as much as I did."

"Yes, I did, Ralph, I most certainly did," I answered, giving his hands a squeeze. Standing on my tiptoes I kissed him on the cheek, and bid him goodnight.

It seemed so natural for Ralph and I to be together. Earlier, he had invited me out the following day for tea. I was eagerly looking forward to that.

Catherine ran indoors ahead of me and when I entered the room she was excitedly telling my parents all about her adventures at the fair.

"Reverend Valente gave me this," she bubbled, hugging the plush dog.

Mother's eyes darted straight to mine. I had to think of an excuse, a reason, fast. "We met him at the fair and he spent the day with us. We had a marvellous time!" She accepted my explanation without question.

"I think it's to bed for a tired little girl," she said, taking Catherine by the hand and leading her upstairs to her bedroom.

"Ah, poor wee mite," she remarked as she resumed her seat. "She's exhausted from all that excitement and running about."

I couldn't get to sleep that night. I churned every detail of the day's events over and over in my mind. I pictured Ralph's face on the ferris wheel. Poor Ralph, he was trying desperately to be brave. But I could tell he was as nervous as could be. He looked like a scared rabbit. Being with him had certainly taken my mind off Allan. I tried to justify what I was doing by telling myself that he'd be having a good time in London. I couldn't believe that all my misgivings could have been wrong.

It was almost midnight when I tiptoed into the kitchen, looking for something to eat. As I stepped through the threshold of the kitchen door, I heard my parents' voices coming from their bedroom above. They sounded at loggerheads and they hardly ever speak to each other in raised voices.

I would've died if they'd suspected I was eavesdropping. As I listened, I realized their argument was about Mother's ongoing concern about me having to cross the Tay Bridge. She had such a fear that somehow or other the bridge was going to collapse and take me with it. Poor Mother.

"I only see disaster. She should not be doing this."

"Oh, woman, you are full of silly ideas. The bridge is quite safe. It's been built by one of the best engineers in the world, hasn't it? Safe as walking on the ground. So it is."

"Dear God," I prayed from the bottom of my heart, "please don't let my mother be so worried." I made up my mind there and then that I wouldn't come home as often and then only if the weather was fine.

I couldn't wait to go for tea with Ralph next day. I dressed in a pretty blue cotton print dress with white, lacy collar and draped a white shawl over my shoulders. Full of excitement, I rushed to the manse. My heart beat rapidly against my chest as I waited for Ralph to open the door.

"Roselyn!" he gasped, with a beaming smile as he took my hands in his. He kissed my brow and led me by the hand to the living-room and taking my shawl invited me to take a seat. "I've booked a cab for four o'clock." He glanced at his pocket watch, saying, "It should be here any minute." Smiling softly he bent and kissed my lips. "You look lovely, Roselyn!" he whispered.

I was so excited. My heart was beating rapidly and my whole being was saturated in love for him.

The cab arrived promptly at four o'clock. Ralph instructed the cabby to take us to the Old Mill, a secluded little inn, nestled in whispering pines, just off the Cupar Road.

In the cab he encircled me in his arms and began to kiss me on the lips and on the cheeks. He nibbled my ears and returned to my mouth with deep passion. I melted in his arms, returning his kisses with profound enthusiasm. We just couldn't seem to get enough of one another. By the time we reached our destination, my lips were as tender as could be. But I must admit I had enjoyed every minute. I felt as if I was on a cloud as we emerged from the coach to enter the inn.

I thought about the last day I had spent with Allan. Ralph had been right, Allan was my friend, my companion, and I couldn't begin to compare the feelings I had for him, with the strong passionate feelings I had for Ralph.

We had a delicious tea of battered haddock, mashed potatoes and peas and, of course, scrumptious cream cakes. Ralph's eyes were dancing and his face flushed as he watched me eat a wedge of cream sponge, the cream oozing out. He commented that he'd never seen anyone enjoying cream cakes so much, that he loved the way I licked the cream off my lips. We laughed so easily at each other's jokes, and I was so comfortable in his company.

"Patty's out of town," he whispered, "she's gone to visit a friend in Anstruther for a few days. We'll have the house to ourselves." He smiled and waited for my reaction. Now, what did he expect me to say?

"While the cat's away, the mice will play!" My glance went up to his and I smiled. This was something dangerous. "I'm afraid to be alone with you, Ralph. I don't think it would be wise."

"Why? Don't you trust me, Roselyn?"

"Oh yes indeed I do, it's myself I don't trust."

"Nonsense!"

That evening I talked about everything under the sun, avoiding the inevitable question that I suspected Ralph was going to ask.

"Roselyn!" he spoke softly. "Would you please give me the opportunity to get to know you better? I strongly believe if things don't work out, there'll be no harm done. I know you have strong feelings for me by your response to my kisses. What do you say?"

"To tell the truth, Ralph, you're absolutely right. I have very strong feelings for you. I can't control myself when I'm around you. Perhaps you noticed that too?"

"Oh yes, yes, I most certainly have! Then let's see what transpires, shall we?"

I smiled approvingly. My heart was bursting with joy. I knew deep down that this was the man for me and I was ecstatically happy. I will have to find a way to tell Allan of my change of heart.

CHAPTER

27

Parent's Aghast

I returned to my studies in the infirmary in September, but didn't come home as frequently as before. This seemed to put my mother's mind at ease. My mother was only happy when she knew I would not be on the train. Ralph came to take me out once a week on my day off. We would take long walks together in the country, and even climbed the Sidlaws a couple of times. What a spectacular view from the summit in every direction. Our favourite walk was along the Esplanade, up Roseangle, along Tay Street and up Constitution Road to my residence. We attended theatre plays and visited art galleries and museums. It seemed as if we both loved exactly the same things. It wasn't long before we realised we had fallen deeply in love. What a wonderful, wonderful feeling it was.

I rented a lovely room over looking the Tay in a large mansion house on Dudhope Terrace. The owner, Mistress Sword, a widow, had turned her home into a residence for nurses after her husband died – more for the company than anything else. She certainly didn't need the money. Her late husband was in banking and he had left her extremely wealthy.

I was really enjoying the midwifery course. The challenge of being sent out to the district, to assist doctors with deliveries was especially stimulating for me. Every time a baby was born, I felt I had witnessed a miracle. Because of my involvement in the district, I'd become accustomed to the Dundee people and their ways. I found that underneath the hard core they were full of love and generosity. Their warmth circled me and drew me into their lives.

Often the women were the breadwinners of the family, they toiled long hard hours in the mills, working from six o'clock in the morning till six at night, six days a week. The mill owners didn't employ men. They would have had to pay them more money than they paid women. Husbands stayed at home to care for the children. They were called the 'kettle boilers'. This made the women of Dundee very independent.

Many of the patients befriended me, and on occasion when I'd be in town, I could hardly take two steps without someone recognising me. They would even call my name from the other side of the street and wave. It made me feel somewhat important.

Allan continued to write to me once a week, giving me details of all his latest adventures. From the sound of things, he was highly regarded by Michael Young, the editor. He had originally planned to come home for a visit in October, but circumstances at work were so demanding, he couldn't spare the time.

However, he assured me he'd be home on December thirtieth to celebrate the New Year.

I believe I was a coward. I just couldn't bring myself to tell Allan that I was in love with Ralph. I planned to tell him face to face when he came home, I felt I owed him that. At least that's what I told myself.

Things between Ralph and me were developing rapidly and we were now talking marriage. I have to admit I had never felt for Allan what I felt for Ralph. I was engulfed with love for him.

I forced myself to get down to read Allan's latest letter. Every time a letter came I was drowned in guilt. I settled myself in the armchair in my room and opened the letter.

My Lovely Roselyn,

Things in England are very different to those in Scotland. It has taken much longer than I had anticipated to feel settled. I can't believe I've been with International Times for eight weeks now, and I still don't feel at ease.

Michael Young (Mike) invited me for tea to meet his wife and family. I know that he has grown to respect me and treats me very fairly. I was looking forward with great anticipation to meeting Mike's family. Dressed in my best attire, I took a cab to Hampton Court via a florist, to buy a bouquet of flowers for Gail, Mike's wife.

The Young's residence is a huge two-storey Elizabethan house set back from the road, surrounded by a beautiful garden with lots of mature elm trees. I happily ascended the marble steps and pulled the pull bell. Almost immediately the door flew open, and there, standing before me was a woman with blond ringlets resting gently on her shoulders. A pair of beautiful ice blue eyes was looking into mine.

She introduced herself as Pamela, and said that her friends call her Pam. She said that she hoped that we'd be friends. She brushed by me, to lead me into the living-room. She was wildly flirting with me and I felt like an idiot, standing in the middle of the room holding a bunch of flowers. I had come to see Mike and his wife and had no idea who this strange woman was.

"Allan," Mike gasped arising from his chair the moment I entered and welcomed me with a hearty handshake. "Come, I'd like you to meet my beautiful wife." He put his arm on my shoulder and led me to where Gale was seated. "Gale, this is Allan. Allan, Gale." He then introduced me to his daughter, Pam. In a funny sort of way she reminded me of you. She made me miss you all the more.

Oh, how I miss you. What a strange meeting.
Your loving, Allan.

I had to wonder why he needed all the details of this Pam. Was he doing this to justify himself in some way? Or to keep me anticipating our meeting? To keep me faithful? I wondered why he imagined I'd be at all interested in her. She sounded far too pretty and exciting for me to want to know her. It sounded as if she had made quite an impression on him. Was I jealous? Of course I was. Just a bit. But why? I didn't know.

Two weeks before Christmas I spent the weekend at home. Ralph and I had made plans to get married on the twenty-seventh of February. I had managed to keep our courtship a secret from my parents, but had planned to tell them about Ralph that weekend.

After Mother had tucked Catherine into bed that night, we all had tea. As we sat around a roaring fire, I nervously opened up the conversation. "I have something very important to tell you."

Their eyes looked at each other then to me, waiting to hear what I had to say.

"Since the middle of August, Ralph Valente and I have been seeing each other."

"What!" they gasped simultaneously.

"I know what you must be thinking - I'm engaged to Allan Robertson. Yes, that's true, but I intend to confess my feelings for Ralph to Allan when he comes home at the New Year. I'd rather do that than write it in a letter. Ralph and I are deeply in love with each other. Ecstatically happy. We plan to get married in February, next year."

There was silence. I was uncomfortable and began to fidget. Father was first to speak up. "Well, Roselyn" he gasped, "this is a shock as well as a surprise. I'd no idea you were seeing Ralph Valente. But your happiness is my concern. And you know, I think you'll make a perfect minister's wife." He smiled as he came over and kissed my brow. "I wish you all the happiness in the world, Cuddle!"

Mother arose from her chair, and putting her arms around me, kissed my cheek. "I've been thinking there was something in the wind. You haven't mentioned Allan Robertson's name for ages. I'm delighted for you, Roselyn. Ralph is so devout, I'm sure you have found your soul mate. Congratulations!"

I breathed a sigh of relief.

Catherine was excited about Christmas. She spent hours making pretty decorations for the living room and Catherine being Catherine, just had to have her bedroom decorated as well.

She was bubbling with excitement at the whole idea of Christmas; asking all kind of questions about Father Christmas and how he could possibly squeeze down our small chimney.

"Why can't you be home for Christmas, Roselyn?" her squeaky voice asked full of disappointment.

"I've already told you, I have to work Christmas

Day. We can't all be living the life of leisure, you know," I teased.

"But I want you to be here. Aunt Liz and I have made something very special for you."

"Oh! Catherine, Catherine!" I lifted her up on my lap, hugging her. "I'd love to be home for Christmas, but you know, sweet child, we cannot always have what we want in this life, can we?" Her head dropped and she sulked.

"I'll tell you what, I'll come home for the New Year," I giggled, tickling her tummy. "How does that sound? Just think, it'll be like having two Christmases. We can give presents all over again. Won't that be fun?" She forced a smile, slithering off my lap and continuing to tie up her parcels.

I went to my room and brought back Ralph's Christmas present, intending to wrap it. I had bought him a music box that played Claire De Lune and the book about the development of the earth in time and space. The minute I entered the living-room Catherine, eyes wide as saucers, went straight to the presents. She immediately spluttered out, "Who's that for?" She was such a curious child and missed nothing.

"Well, if you must know, it's for Mister Valente," I smiled, giving her a wink.

"For the Minister? What is it, Roselyn? Please tell me."

"No. You'll have to wait till New Year to find out."

"Do you have something for Allan as well?"

"Of course!"

Carrying the scuttle full of coal Father entered the room. He was in a joyous mood, humming away as he knelt in front of the fire to stoke it. "I hope this lasts all night, it's bitter cold out," he said, giving a shiver.

He had left the door open and Pat sneaked in,

making a beeline for the parcels. "Get that dog out of here before he wrecks everything," Father shouted. But it was too late, Pat had already ripped the paper off one parcel and was chewing the string of another. I lifted him up and took him to the kitchen. Scolding him, I put him in his basket.

Mother went about her happy preparations, singing Christmas carols at the top of her voice. My brother Tom with Ella and their little daughter Sarah were coming for Christmas dinner. That made her doubly happy. She had also invited Jim to come and enjoy Christmas day with his little granddaughter.

In the short time Catherine had been with us she had managed to ruffle a few feathers, but having her to bring up had given Mother a whole new interest. Catherine had helped bake all kinds of biscuits and cakes for the festive season. At least, she was led to believe so.

When I was leaving to return to the hospital that Sunday, Father reminded me I'd promised Tom I would baby-sit Sarah to let him take Ella to the Mason's Ball.

"I'm so glad you mentioned it, Father, I had completely forgotten about it."

They all accompanied me to the railway station, Mother, Father, Catherine, and of course Pat. It was the last time we'd be together until New Year.

It was pitch black with a light sprinkle of snow in the air. My parents just couldn't bear the idea of me walking to the station alone. It was bitterly cold, typical of December, but our high spirits kept us in a happy, joyous mood. We sang Christmas carols at the pitch of our voices as we hurried along the winding path to Tayport.

The train was already waiting at the platform when we arrived, so there wasn't much time for good-byes. I glanced about hoping Ralph would be there. But he wasn't. My heart dropped to my feet, I was so disappointed.

Mother had packed a basket full of food, including two bottles of elderberry wine. The wine was for my friends and me, to help us celebrate Christmas.

"Now, have a wonderful Christmas, Roselyn! Our thoughts and prayers will be with you," they told me as I slipped through the gate, a bit hampered by the basket.

Father reached over the fence and kissed me on the cheek. "See you at the New Year, Roselyn," Mother sighed. And Catherine waved limply as she turned, and trotted off hand in hand with Mother and Father.

To my surprise, as well as my delight, Ralph was sitting on the train waiting for me to join him. In the compartment we hugged and kissed and talked and laughed all the way to Dundee.

"This is for you, my darling," Ralph said, and opening a ring box, showed me an exquisite diamond and blue sapphire ring. He removed the ring from the box and, slipping it onto my finger, kissed the ring. Enclosing my hands in his he said, "This is forever, sweetheart!"

"Oh Ralph, Ralph, I love you so very much, more than you'll ever know!"

He took me in his arms saying, "I know you do. And I love you more than you'll ever know."

"But my dearest Ralph, I cannot accept this ring now. I'm still betrothed to Allan and I owe it to him to tell him of my change of heart, but I've decided to tell him about us when he comes home. I'd rather tell him face to face than write it in a letter. I know he'll understand!"

"How do you know? How can you possibly know?"

"Women's intuition, perhaps," I smiled, "I know

Allan like the back of my hand. Besides, if the tables were turned, I'd understand."

I returned the ring to him. He put it back into the box and sadly put the box back into his pocket. "Then - you'll get it on the first of January. Your New Year's gift!"

Ralph didn't get off the train in Dundee. The train we had arrived on was the last return train to Tayport and it left immediately. I waved goodbye to him from the platform as the train pulled away. My heart was bursting with joy. I imagined I was wearing Ralph's ring and I felt so proud that I would soon be the minister's wife.

In Dundee, the night air was crisp, and the moon was shining so brightly it was almost like daylight. I decided to walk to the residence. As I crossed from Reform Street to Meadowside, a young choir was filing into place beside the Christmas tree outside the Albert Institute. The boys and girls were from the Dundee High School, well groomed and neat as pins, red and white robes on for the special occasion.

The choir mistress raised her baton, demanding full attention. "One, two, three and .... 'Away in a Manger' poured from the high-pitched voices, rising in full blast up to heaven.

Prince Albert had introduced Christmas trees to Britain after he'd married Queen Victoria. This tree was a sight to behold, its branches decorated with candles and the star of Bethlehem on the top.

I lost all track of time as I listened to the sweet voices of the choir. My thoughts were torn between Allan, my lifelong companion whom I loved as a friend and Ralph, dear, sweet, loveable Ralph, the love of my life.

My thoughts were invaded by an old woman in a moth-eaten fur coat. She was wearing high-heeled boots, and a wide brimmed hat tied underneath the chin with a bright orange coloured chiffon scarf. She waltzed across the road moving to a tune that only she could hear. Perhaps she was fantasizing about a long lost love!

Somewhere a clock struck the hour reminding me I should make tracks. Leaving the Christmas tree made me sad. I paused for a moment as I crossed the street, looking back over my shoulder. The tree was such a beautiful sight, surrounded by the carol singers praising the Lord.

CHAPTER

28

Baby Sitting Sarah

I was scheduled to work nights for the remainder of December, but had previously arranged with my friend Jessie Hampton to work one of my shifts. This would enable me to take care of Sarah. It was such a busy time of year for everyone. Jessie was an exceptionally kind-hearted person and was happy to do me the favour.

The Saturday I was to look after Sarah dawned bright and sunny. I caught the six o'clock train from Dundee to Cupar that evening, just making it by the skin of my teeth. As the train was passing through Wormit station, I was hit by an unearthly feeling. My body was saturated with fear, my arms covered with goose bumps. For some unknown reason I was convinced that I would never see Ralph again. I began to shiver and perspire at the same time and I felt sick in my stomach. "For heavens sake Roselyn, give yourself a shake," I whispered under my breath, "You'll see him at the New Year."
It cheered me up to see Tom waiting to greet me when the train arrived in Cupar. I was proud of my brother; so dependable.

The moment I stepped off the train he hurried

along the platform and, taking my hand in his, kissed me on the cheek. We prattled all the way home bringing each other up to date with all our latest news. When we reached 'Holly Bank' on the outskirts of town, Sarah was standing at the window, waiting for us to arrive. She was already dressed for bed and hugging her favourite doll. No doubt she had been looking forward to having me read bedtime stories to her.

She was so excited and spluttering out a dozen things at once the moment we entered the house. "Calm down, Sarah, calm down!" I said lifting her up. "We'll have lots of fun when your ma and da leave, so we will?" I laughed tickling her in the ribs.

"Yes, and you'll tell me a story won't you, Roselyn?" she squeaked out.

"Certainly!"

Ella's auburn hair was artistically done up in a French Roll. This was decorated with tiny yellow flowers complimenting her green eyes. I helped her into her soft velvet dress especially made for this occasion. She looked lovely in green.

Tom was bursting with pride as he escorted her to the cab. He looked so much like my father, all dressed up in his formal highland outfit. Mother used to tease him when he was a boy, saying, "My goodness Thomas, you've got a rare leg for a kilt, so you have."

The moment Tom and Ella left, Sarah and I went directly to the kitchen to have tea. She sat opposite me at the table chatting away non-stop as we ate. As soon as we'd finished, she insisted on a game of Hide the Thimble, then I-Spy, and lastly Hide and Seek. She was a tired little girl by the time I tucked her up in bed. Her eyes closed halfway through the story of The Magic Mouse.

I sat on an easy chair in front of a roaring fire

with my legs tucked up under me, reading a letter I'd received from Allan the previous day. My heart was full of uneasiness. I really loved to read his letters yet they filled me with guilt. I was nervous of opening the correspondence, wondering what was in it.

"Darling Roselyn,

Only a few more days now and we'll be together again. Words cannot convey how much I have missed you. I've told you many times how extremely busy I've been. The newspaper industry is a very competitive business. Nevertheless, I'm enjoying the never-ending challenges of the job.

It has been very difficult for me, what with the new job and being here without you. However, Pamela has been a great help in making me feel at home. She is very kind and compassionate, as are her parents.

My world is empty without you, Roselyn! I've made up my mind that no matter what, I will not return to London without you. Perhaps I'm being a sentimental fool, but all the money in the world isn't worth the sacrifice of this separation. I love you with all my heart, my dearest. I'll never leave you again as long as I live.

Yours forever,

Allan."

On a piece of parchment he had written a poem, something he used to do when we were children.

You are my life my hopes and my dreams
You are my morning my day and my night
You are my sun my moon and my stars
You are my love.

You are the cold wind that blows

You are the frost that nips my toes
You are the seasons of the year
You are my love.

All of my love I give to you
All of my love my whole life through
Always I will remember you
You are my love.

Here he is sending me a love poem, and again mentioning Pamela. Why? And why am I so very jealous? Is the poem to soften his own guilt? I can't help feeling he is involved with this Pamela. I know it!
I read the poem again and again before tucking it into my pocket. I was totally distraught. I knelt on the floor to pray.

"Dear Lord, help me. I'm in a desperate situation. I have devoted feelings of love and friendship for Allan, but my heart is overflowing with love for Ralph. I wish with all my heart that Allan would meet someone whom he could love while in London, someone who would love him more than I do. Dear Lord give me the strength to explain my feelings honestly to him.

I have suspicions about Allan. Are they justified? Am I doing the right thing? Give me some indication as to what action I should take."

Amen.

The warmth radiating from the blazing coals made me drowsy. I curled up on the couch with Fluffy, the family cat, and with loving thoughts of Ralph fell sound asleep.

But it wasn't Ralph I dreamed about it was Allan. This was my dream—
Someone was leading me by the hand to Allan. I could see him clearly walking along Regent Street with his arm

around a beautiful woman. The light was sparkling as if frost was dropping in the air.

Little children with round faces, red noses and snowflakes on their eyelashes, were standing on a street corner, bellowing out Christmas carols. Father along the street a Salvation Army band blasted out 'Deck the Halls', clanging symbols high above their heads. What a jolly, joyous sound they were making. I wished I could have been there to join in the merrymaking. I felt completely shut out and excluded.

The young woman had her arm around Allan's waist as if she had the right to do so. Allan didn't seem to mind. In fact he looked rather proud to have this beautiful woman at his side. He stood tall and straight, smiling at the world. It was as if he was aglow and looked so happy.

They were being swept along the street in a sea of moving people, all singing along with the children. Now they were sitting in a charming little café on the south bank of the Thames, eating oysters and sipping Champagne. I have never tasted oysters but I imagine a slightly salty, bitter taste.

An older man appeared from nowhere. He was elegantly dressed in a top hat, long black coat with a fur collar and a dazzling white scarf draped around his neck. I sensed this was Mike. He bent and asked Allan if he would accompany Pamela to the opera.

I saw her clearly, in all her finery. She was in a lovely gown of crimson crape. The dress clung to her shapely body, she was a magnificent sight. Allan held her mink coat while she slipped into it. She had diamonds around her neck and wrist and long diamond earrings brushed her shoulders.

I convinced myself that Allan was feeling guilty for having such a good time; that he would much rather have been with me. However, it was plain to see he was full of joy in this woman.

They were at the opera; yawning their heads off. She whispered in his ear. I couldn't hear what she said. They left mid-act.

Now they were in her home, embracing in the spacious hall. There was music. I didn't know where it was coming from.

"Oh God, you're beautiful Pam! Absolutely, beautiful!" Allan declared. "The most beautiful woman I've ever seen."

The moment they entered the opulent living room Pam went over to the liquor cabinet and poured a whisky for Allan and a gin with lime for her-self. She moved across the room, handed him the glass and sat down on the music stool. Allan sank into a large leather armchair by the fireside.

She began to play, 'I Dream of Jeanie with the Light Brown Hair.'

Allan couldn't take her eyes off her. He sat upright as if he didn't want to miss a moment of her performance.

She began to sing, 'I love you Dearly'.

He stood up abruptly. "Stop it, Pam, stop it at once!" He demanded and walked deliberately over to the liquor cabinet and poured himself another drink.
Pam got up and waltzed over to him holding out her hands, "Come Allan, let's dance!" She began to hum a tune I didn't know.

He swallowed the whisky in one gulp and took her in his arms. They waltzed about the room to her humming. It was as if he imagined a full orchestra backing her gentle melody.

He bent his head into her breasts and kissed them. "You smell of mountain dew and angels." He whispered. "Simply divine!"

She gazed into his eyes. "I love you Allan! Oh Allan I love you! I've loved you since the first moment we met." He bent and kissed her neck, nibbled her ears and finally, made his way to her mouth, kissing her passionately.

"Oh Pamela, Pamela," he gasped. "If only things were different. If only..."

She covered his mouth with her fingertips. "Shh, shh, darling, don't say any more."

"Oh God, you're beautiful, Pam."

They clung together for a long time, long after she had stopped humming. It was like a tableau. A still life! "Come Allan my dearest! Come, I'll take you to paradise!" She led him upstairs to her bedroom and, standing in front of him, slowly undressed.

He kissed her all over, again and again. She was moaning in absolute ecstasy.

They lay on the silk covered bed, recuperating in each other's arms beautiful bodies twined round each other.

"What are we going to do Allan?" she whispered urgently. "I've got to have you, oh my God, Allan I've got to have you!"

He drew her close. "I know darling. Don't worry, we'll work something out."

"What will you tell Roselyn?"

"I don't know, I really don't know. I didn't mean this to happen, but it did, and I'm glad. But I don't know what I'll tell Roselyn."

Tom gave me a gentle shake. "Roselyn. Roselyn." He whispered.

Half opening my eyes, I reached for my wrap, and slipping it over my shudders, burst out crying. "Oh Tom," I sobbed, "I just had the most vivid dream about

Allan. I'm so overwhelmed! Oh God, it was so real. He was with another woman. I could feel his love for her. It was all so real. Too real to be a dream."

"Some dreams are like that, hard to tell the difference between dreams and reality sometimes," he smiled reassuringly. "You'd be far more comfortable in bed Tibby." he said as he poked at the smouldering embers. "It gets very cold in here when the fire dies down."

"I don't know what to think about the dream. Earlier this evening I asked God to give me some sign as to what I should do. I wonder if this was the sign? What do you think?"

He shook his head and putting his arm around me, said, "I think you're the one that has to define the dream. God gives us choices, but we have make the desition!"

I wiped the tears with my handkerchief and gave a big yawn. I bid Tom goodnight and staggered off to the bedroom. Quickly changed into my nightgown and jumped into bed. I took Tom's advice and began to decipher my dream. I realised I shouldn't have been so upset. Perhaps this was the sign I had prayed for? Although I had been sickened by it, I was relieved that Allan was capable of loving someone else. It gave me permission to love Ralph. Was the dream my imagination? Or was it a shadow of the truth?

Next morning I woke up with a deep sense of inner peace. I decided to use the dream as a comfort. Yes! That's it! God sent the dream to comfort me. It was as if I had been freed from Allan. As if he had given me permission to love Ralph. In church the next morning my thoughts of course were with Ralph. I pictured him in his formal dark suit, his hair shining in the sun from the stained glass windows, conducting the service with the utmost serenity. Oh how I loved him! Now I felt that my life could be spent at his side.

We arrived home from church around one o'clock. Ella insisted on cooking a traditional Scottish breakfast. We started with porridge, followed by sausages, bacon and fried eggs. Lovely home-baked bread too. It's always far too much food for me, but I eat it so as not to hurt Ella's feelings.

We sat around a roaring fire in the living room after breakfast, singing our favourite Christmas Carols, something we always did at this time of year. What a jolly, happy time we had!

"It looks as if we're in for a storm," Ella commented, pulling the curtains back and looking up at the angry sky.

"It certainly does! What a strong wind that is. I hope I make it to the train before the rain starts.

"Ach, it'll maybe blow over." Tom suggested, as he helped me into my cloak.

He and Ella thanked me profoundly for taking care of Sarah, and after lots of hugs and kisses I took my leave.

"Don't forget to bring Allan over at the New Year," Ella called as Tom closed the door.

"We'll have to see about that," I called over shoulder, knowing fine it would be Ralph I'd be bringing, not Allan.

It was a fair hike from Tom's house to the station; close to a mile I'd say. With the blustery wind trying to blow us off our feet, it took longer than anticipated to reach the station. I was a little worried about missing the train but we made it in time.

When we reached the station, the train was at the platform ready to leave. Hurry up Roselyn, or you'll miss the train," Tom said, handing me my bag and giving me a quick peck on the cheek.

The storm that had been brewing all afternoon broke loose with a fury that I'd never seen before. The wind kept blowing my cloak over my head and I had difficulty keeping my balance.

A porter was leaning his entire weight against the carriage door to hold it open for me. "Hurry up, lass, hurry up! The train's about to leave," he shouted.

Glancing back over my shoulder I waved to Tom as I climbed into the compartment. "See you at the New Year, Tibby," he shouted. The words were whipped from his mouth and carried off with the wind.

CHAPTER

29

Train Journey

As I settled myself in a seat by the window, I sighed with relief. How good it was to be out of the wind. Sitting on the opposite side of the compartment was a handsome young man. He smiled and acknowledged me with a nod the moment I got on the train. A healthy crop of blond hair framed his oval-shaped face and bright blue eyes. Bristly sideburns reached down to his chin. A lonesome curl drooped over his high forehead and a pair of spectacles teetered on the end of an aristocratic nose.

He was gripping the stag-horn handle of his cane so tightly his knuckles seemed to be bursting through the skin of his hands. A black bag identical to my own lay on the seat beside him and a large leather bag sat up on the luggage rack.

As the train was about to leave a young woman came running fighting against the wind. She was clutching a baby in her arms underneath her cloak.

The guard flung the door open and leaning his weight against the door he shouted. "Hurry up, lass, hurry up!" Gasping for breath, the woman clambered into the com-

286

partment. The guard slammed the door closed, blew his whistle and waved a green flag. The train moved slowly forward puffing out of the station.

"Thanks be to God I made it!" She gasped, when safely on the train. "What a relief it is, to be out of that nasty weather!" She settled herself down on a seat in the far corner and curled a fussing baby against her shoulder.

Swinging her legs up on the seat, she lent her head against the headrest unbuttoned her cloak and sat the baby on her lap. It was a red headed little boy. He was screaming his head off.

"Wheesht, wheesht," she whispered, coddling him and patting his back. But try as she may, she couldn't quiet him. Turning her back to us, she cradled the baby in her arms and nursed him. It was magic! He greedily sucked on his source of food and soon fell asleep.

As the train pulled away from the platform the fury of the storm worsened. Driven rain lashed against the windows of the carriage making it impossible to see out. I glanced at the young man sitting opposite me. He was as stiff as a poker, his eyes full of anguish.

"I beg your pardon, Miss!" He coughed, clearing his throat. "Allow me to introduce myself. My name is Matthew. Matthew Scott." He offered me a shaky hand. I hesitated momentarily remembering my mother's brainwashing when I was a child. Never, ever speak to strangers! But I could tell the young man was terrified. He wouldn't be a threat to any woman. So without further ado, I reached over and shook his hand.

"Roselyn Carey!"

With a gentle smile, he commented, "What a pretty name! Would you mind terribly if I call you Roselyn, Miss Carey?"

"Of course not!"

"You may call me Matthew if you wish!"

"Tell me Roselyn, have you ever crossed the Tay Bridge before?"

"Heavens, yes, all the time!" I answered confidently. Much more confidently than I had felt at that moment.

"You'll have to forgive me for being so nervous but I have heard conflicting stories about the structure of the bridge. Horror stories, to be precise. Apparently, it will not withstand the worst of storms that thunder down the firth. Not enough sway or something. Some say it'll collapse one day!"

"Well, Matthew, you can relax. I travel back and forth to Dundee all the time. Rain, hail, or shine and the bridge it still standing."

"I wish I had made the journey yesterday," he went on to say. "Unfortunately, circumstances didn't permit me to do so. But your assurance has helped me a lot." I could tell he was anxious to talk. Talking seemed to be taking his mind off the upsetting situation in which he found himself.

"Do you live in Cupar, Roselyn?"

"Heavens no! I live on the outskirts of Tayport, in the little hamlet of West Lights."

"I have an uncle in Tayport." he went on to say, "he has a medical practice there. Scott's his name. Kenneth Scott."

"Well, well, isn't it a small world? Doctor Scott's my family doctor."

"Then you must know him well?"

"Yes, as a matter of fact I do. I've known him all my life; he brought me into the world. I don't know him socially though, only as my Doctor.

"He's a good man, my uncle," Matthew commented, bursting with pride. "He put my brother and me through university. My brother was an outstanding student; he studied law. He was made an advocate last year and has a practice in Edinburgh. I followed in my Uncle Ken's footsteps. I chose the medical profession." He pondered, fingering his chin. "My Uncle Ken is my father's brother. He has taken care of us ever since my father died ten years ago."

I noticed that both mother and baby were dozing. The train slowed down and came to a stop outside Leuchars station. A violent flash of lightening showed a distorted impression of crofts dotted here and there against the rugged countryside. Mathew stiffened but we continued our conversation.

"And where is your practice, Matthew?" I asked out of curiosity and politeness. Anything to take my mind off the weather and the train.

"I don't have one. I just finished my house year in the Edinburgh Royal and have accepted a junior post in the Dundee Royal.

"Well – what a coincidence. I'm on the nursing staff there. We can accompany each other all the way if you wish." His face lit up and a smile curled the corner of his lips. He uncrossed his legs and crossed them on the opposite side. He looked totally relaxed. I was glad that our chatting had helped him.

The mother snored gently and the baby, cradled in her arms, was as still as a doll. Watching them gave me comfort. Everything was so normal, so ordinary. My breath took on the rhythm of the baby's breath, gentle, quiet. I had forgotten about my worries. The world outside didn't matter. We were warm and comfortable, in a cocoon of safety.

Sleep that's all that mattered now, sleep— sleep—sleep.

The train shuddered as if it would break in two. The young woman jumped to her feet. "In the name of some big house!" She burst out. "What's going on?" Her yelling wakened the baby and he began to cry. "Wheesht, wheesht!" she snuggled him in gently patting his back. Moments later he was fast asleep. "I hope to hell they know what they're doing!" She declared peering out into the darkness.

"Me too!" Matthew agreed.

The rain continued to beat full force against the windows. Violent flashes of lightning filled an evil-looking sky. The sound of the labouring engine was muffled by the wind.

The journey worsened as the train hurried down the track towards the coast. The storm had the river to itself. It rushed down the Tay Valley and out to the German Sea like a roaring lion. Black clouds hurried across the sky like wild jaws of death. Another flash and I clearly saw the bridge and for a split second I could just make out the outline of the Dundee Law.

No one spoke as the train crawled into Wormit station at a snail's pace. I glanced at my watch. It was ten minutes past seven.

"Good God almighty, Roselyn!" Matthew burst out jumping to his feet, retrieving his bag from the luggage rack. "I am getting off this train right now! I can't stand it another minute! I'm not crossing that bridge tonight!" He bellowed, shaking like a leaf."

"Don't be silly Mathew," I calmly reached for his hand. "If the authorities thought there was the slightest danger, they wouldn't allow the train to cross the bridge. — Now would they?"

"I suppose not," he agreed, and reluctantly resumed his seat. "I apologise for my outburst Roselyn.

But I'm extremely nervous. You must think I'm a big baby?"

"No— Oh no Matthew, I don't. I'm nervous too!"

A porter fighting against the wind was running along the platform shouting something to the engineer. He handed him what looked like a baton. Holding onto his cloak he stood back and watched the train puff slowly out of the station.

We were all pale faced looking from one to the other. A surge of sparks flared up against the darkness as the train gathered speed.

I was shaking, but mustered up enough courage to blurt out, "We'll be in Dundee in fifteen minutes!" There was a gigantic thrust. I was lifted out of my seat and thrown forward, banging my head on the opposite wall of the compartment.

When I came to, everything was quiet; so deathly quiet. It was as black as pitch. I couldn't remember where I was. A shaft of light streaming from above made Matthew's face clearly visible. "Ah, – now I remember where I am. I'm on the train!" I crawled over and peered out the window. All I could see was water all around. To my horror the train was on the riverbed.

I glanced about the compartment looking for the woman and her baby. They were gone. They must have been thrown out the window when the train went down.

Matthew was lying in a crumpled heap in the far corner. I inched over to him and gave him a shake. "Matthew, Matthew. Waken up, Matthew!" He slowly opened his eyes. For a moment he was dazed.

"What happened, Roselyn? Where are we?" He stuttered out.

"Well—you'll never believe it Matthew. We're still on the train—but the train is on the river bed."

"What?" he gasped. "You're mad!"

He reached for my hand, "Oh my God, Roselyn." he shouted in panic, staggering to his feet. "We'll have to get out of here. Quickly! Quickly! The compartment's filling with water!"

We crawled over to the window, removed the pieces of broken glass and squeezed out. Hand in hand we soared to the surface.

Dozens of people were floundering in the icy water, trying desperately to swim ashore. "Help! Help me! I can't swim!" Their weak voices were muffled by the wind.

I had no qualms about helping people. Both Matthew and I worked all night helping them. When everyone was safely ashore, I staggered up the embankment and threw myself down on the grass. My hair was streaming down my face like a wet rag. My sodden clothes clinging to my body.

How long I lay there I had no idea. 'Could have been hours, or even days. I had lost all track of time. Finally I found the strength to pull myself up. I dragged myself on my hands and knees to a high spot and sat on a rock.

"Matthew, Matthew!" I shouted at the top of my voice, cupping my mouth in my hands. Desperately my eyes searched the beach but I couldn't see hide or hair of him. "Where could he have gone?"

I looked over at the bridge. "Oh, my God almighty!" I gasped, covering my mouth with my fingertips. What a bleeding mess! Mother will be going mad; she'll think I've been killed.

The Sidlaws were standing out in brilliant clarity against a cloudless sky. The river was calm making no sound. "Must be the calm after the storm," I mumbled as I gathered my cloak around me. I gave one last look at the bridge. "Good God!"

I fled along the shore at great speed, absolutely devastated. My feet wouldn't stay on the ground. It was as if I was floating. "'Must have been in the water too long!" I muttered to myself. What a wonderful feeling it was.

I glided onward covering the two-mile journey home in no time. When I reached our garden gate, I hesitated. Nobody was about, not even the dog. I hurried up the path and burst into the house, calling "Mother, Father. Anybody here?" Pat was curled up in his basket on the hearth, sound asleep. He didn't even waken up to greet me. There was no one home.

I ran outside and leaped over the fence to the Burkes' house. They weren't home either. By this time I was hysterical. My heart was pounding like a hammer. I rushed over to the Lighthouse and battering on the door called, "Bob! Bob! It's me! Roselyn." He wasn't home either. "Perhaps they've all gone to take a look at the bridge. Of course! How stupid of me, that's where they'll all have gone. They'll have gone to look at the mangled bridge!"

My mind turned to Ralph. "Ralph! Ralph!" I gasped. "I must let Ralph know I'm alright." I hurried along the path to Tayport, all kinds of imaginings whirling in my mind. The moment I turned onto Tay Street there, standing with a group of people, were my parents. Thank be to God! I sighed.

As I approached, I noticed everyone dressed in black. How strange. And there's Allan. What's he doing? He's not supposed to be home till New Years eve. What do you know, he's also in black!"

"Well, well! What's going on?" I bellowed, full of beans. "Looks like you've all been to a funeral?"

Everyone ignored me. They acted as if I wasn't there.

"Allan! Mother! Father! In the name of heaven, somebody, answer me," I ran from one to the other. Allan turned and looked at me and immediately drew his eyes away. I was furious! I grabbed his arm. "For goodness sake Allan, what are you playing at? Don't you recognize me? It's me, Roselyn! I know I'm a mess but you have no idea what I've been through – –"

"Allan, son," his mother rudely interrupted, "what is it?" Her voice was full of empathy.

"Did you hear that, Mother? – Did you? – I could've sworn I heard Roselyn."

"You did— Oh Allan, you did!"—I blurted excitedly grabbing his hand.

Caressing his face with her fingertips, his mother whispered, "Allan you're imagining things."

"Oh no he's not!" I snapped pushing past her. "It is me Allan! For the love of God speak to me. I'm sorry for betraying you but I thought it would be better to tell you about my feelings for Ralph face to face. Please forgive me." He turned away not saying a word. I was livid! I couldn't believe that Allan would treat me this way. I thought, he of all people would understand.

Mother was holding Catherine's hand, and as usual Catherine was fidgeting. She was trying to persuade Mother to give her the book she was clutching to her heart.

"Aunt Liz, please let me have it. Pleeeaaase."

With tears in her eyes, Mother replied, "I've already told you, you can't have it. This belonged to my Roselyn. Now behave yourself."

My eyes went straight to the book. It was my little white prayer book. The one my grandmother gave me when I was five years old. Despair engulfed me. It was at that precise moment, I realised I was no longer of the flesh.

"Oh Ralph -- dearest Ralph." I breathed. "What am I going to do?" I left my parents in their hour of grief and drifted along the Cupar road to the manse. With trembling hand, I rang the doorbell. Not waiting for an answer I flung the door wide open and entered the house. I went from room to room looking for Ralph. He was in his bedroom, kneeling in prayer.

The moment I entered the room he seemed to sense my presence. "I know you're here Roselyn," he sobbed. "I feel you all around me."

"Dearest Ralph," I sighed, and reaching over encircled him in my arms. "I love you with my whole heart." I stroked his face with my fingertips, kissed his brow and left. I couldn't believe the situation in which I found myself. I was devastated.

Instinctively I knew I had to return to West Lights. Sitting down on the riverbank I buried my head in my hands and burst into tears. I cried for my parents; my dearly beloved parents whom I could no longer communicate with. I cried for Allan. Dear sweet Allan, my lifelong companion. But most of all, I cried for Ralph, the love of my life.

"God help me! Please God help me!" I called from the depths of my soul.

A rich voice spoke. "Do not weep my child. Come, give me your hand."

I raised my head and was blinded by the brilliance of the light shining from above. I covered my face with my hands. My eyes soon became accustomed to the brightness.

Rays of gold, reaching down from heaven surrounded me. There were no more painful emotions. My soul was filled with the glory of God.

I stretched my arms upward and was drawn back from whence I came.

***

There were seventy-five passengers and crew on that
train. There were no survivors.

Rescue team in search of the wreck.

Boats assisting in the search.

Pieces of wreck washed up on Broughty Ferry beach.